THE MOON TREE

A SHIMMERING TALE of a spirited young girl torn between her love for the raw Australian Outback and for the untamed suitor who shares it, and the lure of the big city and of a sophisticated, scandalous artist.

At seventeen, Clemency Cameron, as wild and sensual as the Outback from which she comes, has known no world other than her father's expansive sheep ranch in New South Wales and the company of the Brennan boys. But just as Clemency's father has sworn to drive the squatter Brennans from his land, so is he determined to give his daughter a proper education. Against her will, Clemency is packed off to the Misses Maybright's Academy for Young Presbyterian Ladies, in Sydney, leaving Matt Brennan, her secret sweetheart, and all that is familiar, behind. Town life with a disapproving aunt, schoolroom drudgery and the promise of marriage to a dull young man of proper background leave Clemency cold—until an artist of questionable repute sets her senses on fire as no man before him ever has.

When her mother's death and her father's precipitous marriage call Clemency home, she is trapped between her father's opposition to her childhood suitor, who he feels is inappropriate, and her passion for the man from Sydney she cannot forget. She is drawn to Matt by a timeless intimacy, that feeling of unity with the land they share, though the forbidden Sydney artist arouses emotions in Clemency she has never before

(Continued on back flap)

By Maud Lang

SUMMER STATION
THE MOON TREE

(Continued from front flap)

experienced. Caught between two worlds, Clemency stands on the brink of the most crucial choice of her young life in this compelling novel of a primitive land and an unconquerable love.

THE MOON TREE

MAUD LANG

COWARD, McCANN & GEOGHEGAN, INC.
NEW YORK

SBN: 698-10861-2

Library of Congress Cataloging in Publication Data

Lang, Maud.
  The moon tree.

  I. Title.
PZ4.L2682Mo   1977 [PR9619.3.L353] 823 77-10071

Printed in the United States of America

For Harriet, Jessica and Kirstin.

Chapter One

A gray parrot with a bright pink breast flew across the track, and Magpie shied, breaking into a gallop which she could not stop until they came upon the boulders at the edge of the creek.

The piebald pony drank the muddy water while she searched the branches of the ironbarks for parrot nests. Some of the trees were ring-barked. She urged Magpie past the cruel bands chopped deep into the red wood. He picked his way through the large boulders, flat pieces of sandstone washed smooth and holed in the middle; like crooked cottage loaves, thought Clem.

Narrowing her eyes against the glare, she looked up at the top of the gully. The Brennans' place was just a few yards away. This time she had a genuine excuse for calling—to tell them about her father's broken boundary fence. Until this year she'd never needed an excuse, but now they always asked her why she'd come.

The house stood on the crest of a slight ridge, a small brown rectangle beneath the huge haze of blue sky. As they approached it the smell of pink boronia became suffocatingly sweet in the still air. Clem listened for voices. The boys must have been in the fields for she could hear nothing but the soft rustling of the native willows, which followed the meandering creek toward the house.

She watched the willows moving gently as a woman shouldered her way slowly through the hanging silver tendrils. It was Mrs. Brennan, a water butt in each hand, wearing her usual drab dress, her hair pulled tightly back from her brown forehead.

The Brennan family, like most selectors in that part of the country, had not done well. They'd cleared forty acres of forest, cutting down the trees and grubbing up the stumps, but managed to grow only two or three acres of wheat each year, rarely producing a surplus. Mr. Brennan had lost heart many years ago, leaving all the work on the selection to his three sons. They had to work for the neighboring squatters too, or the family would have starved.

Mrs. Brennan maneuvered her way through the forest of stumps in front of the house. It's really just a shack, thought Clem as she jumped off the pony and ran to meet her. "Here, let me take me take one of those!" She pulled one of the butts from Mrs. Brennan's grasp, spilling water down her skirt.

"You don't want to grow muscles." Mrs. Brennan looked her up and down. "My, but you're burned! Doesn't do for a Sydney lady to be too brown!"

"I'm not a Sydney lady. My father says I was supposed to be a boy—John Joseph Cameron." She noticed the large, wet patches under Mrs. Brennan's arms as she lifted the heavy butt onto the veranda. Her arms were too thin, the skin shriveled and shiny, like a lizard's.

The hard earth of the kitchen floor was cool beneath Clem's bare feet. She lifted the water onto the stove. "I've got to hurry home. Can I have some water?"

Mrs. Brennan nodded. "You've got to go back to that school— Pat was tellin' me. You won't be runnin' away again, will you?"

"No. I've promised my mother I'll stay. I suppose I ought to be accomplished at something."

"Reading and writing's all your kind needs. The Maclean lad— Angus—he'll be back home soon and lookin' after someone like yourself, to be sure."

Clem shrugged as she took a thick china mug from the old wooden drainer. "May I help myself to milk?" Flies buzzed about her face and invaded the meat-safe as she carefully opened the door. "Would you like some?"

"Not now. The cow has just enough for those big lads of mine. Wish we could afford another, but . . . . "

Next time she called, decided Clem, she'd bring them some cheese or brandy or something. Their poverty, which she had taken for granted all her life, was starting to make her uncomfortable. The milk was warm and sour. She took one biscuit, the smallest, and offered the plate to her hostess.

Mrs. Brennan shook her head. She was pouring oatmeal into a large black pot. Her shoulder blades stuck out from her narrow back like a bird's wings.

Clem sat at the long, scrubbed table. Every stick of furniture had been made by the family themselves. The dresser, the cupboards, the six straight-backed chairs and three armchairs; all had been nailed together from planks of native wood by Mr. Brennan and his three sons.

Two of the walls were lined with calico; the others were of thick planks hung with watercolors of Irish scenes in rough wood frames.

Clem knew them all. The Brennans' place was as familiar to her as her own home, the modest watercolors as deeply embedded in her consciousness as the large oil paintings of Scottish lochs and glens in her father's drawing room.

She wandered into Mary's room. Her favorite painting, a blue lake with a background of low purple hills and gray clouds, was on the far wall. Mary was the youngest Brennan, the only girl. Her bed, covered with a thin patchwork quilt sloped slightly to one side. A crucifix hung at its head, and two dolls lay on the flat pillow, naked. Again Clem was uneasy. She had no dolls, but her sister might be persuaded to make some clothes for Mary.

She crossed to the small window and stared out at the first line of stumps in front of the house. These seemed to be standing in regular formation. Behind them, the tall, gray ironbarks hid half the sky. Suddenly Mary's room grew quite dark. She went back into the kitchen.

"I must dash now. There's a quarter mile of fence broken down by the quartz ridge. Father'll be furious!"

Mrs. Brennan turned from the stove, her wooden spoon dripping oatmeal onto the floor. "Mother of God! It's my Dan! Your father's tickin' off the other day made him wild. Now he's gone and done it! Quick and tell the boys!"

"Mr. Brennan? Do you mean Mr. Brennan broke the fence?"

"Yes. The rum does it. I'm past apologizin' for that man's stupidity. The boys'll get the fence up."

Clem moved toward the door. "I thought it was a swaggy." She was frightened by the look on Mrs. Brennan's face. "I promise I won't tell my father." She rushed out the door and through the stumps to Magpie.

She kicked him hard as they passed Mrs. Brennan standing on the veranda. She was crying. Clem was helpless in the face of adult tears. She remembered how Mrs. Maclean had cried when Angus had gone *home* to the university.

Clem galloped Magpie along the edge of the furrowed field, slowing up as Mary, a small, fair girl, ran to meet her. Pat stopped the heavy work horse, leaning against the animal's enormous shoulder. "Afternoon, Clem. What's all the dust for?"

Clem stayed on Magpie trying to avoid Pat's eyes. "Your mother told me to tell you about the fence. It's broken. Your father did it."

"What did he do?" His brown eyes, exactly like his mother's, were already circled by a mesh of tiny lines.

"Broke Father's fence. A whole quarter mile of it, down by the quartz ridge."

"Move up." Pat jumped up behind her, grabbing the pony's reins. For a boy of seventeen he was very thin.

"Matt and me'll put it up. You can boil the billy for us."

"I'm quite capable of nailing up a few chocs and logs," Clem said, offended.

"I know." Pat slid off Magpie's rump as they drew near the door of a lean-to shack—the Brennans' stable. "Matt!"

Matt appeared at the doorway. He was much taller and broader than his brother, with a head of tangled sun-bleached curls. He held a large iron wheel against his leg and rolled it toward Clem.

"It's a long time since Miss Cameron has visited the peasantry."

Clem looked at the buggy wheel. "I wish you'd let me help with the fence. Father need never know."

Matt looked past her, his eyes narrowing. "It'll be the last job we do for your father. He's told the old man there's no more shearin' work for us—or anythin'."

"But there must be something—"

"If there was I wouldn't do it. This'll be the last job—my oath it will."

Clem had never heard Matt talk like that before. He was staring at her with contempt. She looked straight at him. "Don't look at me like that. I didn't break the fence!"

Matt turned his back and rolled the wheel back to the shed.

She called out, "Do you want me to help?"

"Yeah, why not." She heard him laughing to himself.

Forgetting to offer Pat a lift back to the field, Clem rode off in the direction of her father's land, anxious to leave Matt's anger and his mother's tears.

In the early twenties her father had chosen a hundred thousand acres of crown land to pasture his newly purchased German Merino flock and had squatted on another eight hundred thousand. So far his right to this land had not been challenged. He was merely liable for a grazier's yearly lease, and that only when the governor remembered to send somebody to collect it.

John Cameron did not take leases very seriously. He felt that as a pioneer breeder of Merino sheep, prepared to travel hundreds of miles into the hinterland of a wild and unexplored country, he had a divine right to the land. It was the colony's duty to leave him alone and let him get on with the job of growing wool. Clem had always taken this attitude for granted, wondering why everybody hadn't done the same thing until Matt had explained the new land laws to her. But she still didn't really understand them. If only school would teach her things like that instead of French, music, and sewing. She shuddered, remembering she would soon be back at the Misses Maybright's school.

The pony jogged on, reaching the water hole in the middle of the afternoon. Of all the water holes on her father's land, this was the largest. It was surrounded by sheep—hundreds of brown lumps of knotted wool lying in a wide perimeter around the shallow hole.

In the hot weather the exhausted sheep stayed close to the water, returning to the vast paddocks only when the heat wave abated, their dusty bodies merging with the brown landscape.

Two emu bushes, short slender trees with long, olive-green leaves, grew at the edge of the water hole. Clem knelt in the shade of the tallest one, splashing brown water all over her face and throat, letting it run down the front of her blouse. She took a mouthful and spat it out. Magpie drank the fouled water noisily while Clem lay under the tree, remembering the look on Matt's face. Everybody hated her father, and now she did, too. He was forcing her to go back to that silly school and for no reason at all.

She studied her broken and dirty fingernails, then her hands and arms, scratched and streaked with dust, and the fine linen of her blouse clinging to her chest like a corset. "If only I'd been born John Joseph Cameron, then everything would have been all right." She sat up and folded her arms about her knees, rubbing her wet face against the bunched-up material of her skirt. A few minutes later she led the pony out into the sun, and tucking her skirt firmly into her pantaloons, she climbed carefully into the saddle and pressed her bare feet into the hard belly.

The afternoon sky lay on the western horizon in a milky haze. She gazed at the treeless plain in front of her. There would be no more water until the home paddock and very few trees to break up the monotony of brown earth and white-blue sky. The enormous space diminished them to a tiny dot on the endless landscape. Yet she did not feel isolated. This was her territory; she and the pony were as much a part of the earth as the stones and dust beneath their feet.

The stock horses were gathered about the water hole on the border of the home paddock. They nuzzled her for food as she dismounted and threw handfuls of warm brown water over her face and neck. They were a handsome bunch. Clem's father rode a thoroughbred English stallion.

They jumped the horse paddock fence into the home paddock, an area of some hundred acres surrounding the homestead which from this distance looked like a small town. Buildings of all shapes and sizes stood around a small square two hundred yards from the main house, which was sheltered by a triangle of pines and wattle. The yellow fluff of the wattle was a glowing mass of reflected pink and gold from the setting sun.

Every evening she returned just before sundown and seeing the yellow wattle would race Magpie across the paddock until she could smell the mimosa. Then they would walk slowly home while she imagined the familiar cool rooms, her warm bath, and her mother's pale face as she stood by the long windows at the far wall of her bedroom.

Tonight she imagined only her father's eyes scanning the horizon for her. She was late. Magpie refused to respond to her nervous coaxing, too full of water to hurry.

Soon she began to hear the sounds of home—the cicadas just lowering their shrill song, the voices of the men in the cottages and then the short, sharp, smacking sounds coming from the house. That was her father, swatting mosquitoes on the hard flesh of his arms and face as he stood on the veranda waiting for her.

Light from the long, low house flickered out through the wattles, and the young pines sent narrow shadows across the dry lawns in front of the veranda. There he was, his features wizened and dried beyond his fifty years, his eyes still half closed against the glare of day.

"What the hell've you been up to? It's after sundown!"

Chapter Two

"I'm sorry, Father. I called in to see Mrs. Brennan . . . I mean I came by there for water."

"Those Brennan lads no longer work for me. Don't go near that place again. That man is a degenerate, an ex-convict. Do you hear me?"

"Yes, but the boys are my friends!"

"You're going back to school next week. By the time you come back, you'll have changed. You'll not want to see them again."

She stood at the foot of the veranda steps looking up at him, an expression of hurt amazement on her face.

"Leave that pony. Someone'll take care of him." He paused. "Well, how are the fences?"

"All standing." She lied without a qualm.

"Good. Inside now, quickly." His hand came down hard on her shoulder as he opened the screen door for her. She shook it off and stepped inside.

The hall was wide with a low ceiling. Its walls were paneled in dark native wood from which hung portraits of unremembered soldiers. In between two heavily framed oils was a sampler. The vivid blue silk letters proclaimed: "The Lord is my shepherd: therefore can I lack nothing."

As her father did not employ shepherds, relying on fences and itinerant boundary riders instead, she had always thought the text highly appropriate to the Cameron property.

The lamps in Clem's room threw a soft light on the blue wallpaper and rugs. She rang for some water, pulling off her wet clothes and dropping them in a pile next to the small iron tub in one corner. She unplaited her hair as she crossed the room to her dressing table. It fell to her waist in thick yellow strands. She studied her face in the looking glass. Freckles covered her nose and cheeks, hundreds of tiny spots which would fade away during the winter in Sydney.

Her mother's old crystal powder bowl sparkled in the lamplight. She took off the top and gazed at her most treasured possessions—small pieces of gold quartz, almost 100 percent pure yellow mineral, representing over ten years of careful fossicking.

She heard footsteps and absentmindedly threw a thin silk shawl round her shoulders as the servant girl, Lizzie Bell, a robust Liverpool woman, came into the room carrying buckets of warm water for the bath. Her red cheeks were wet with sweat and her red hair fell about her face in bright wet strands. She stared at Clem's near nakedness, at the small round breasts on the tall, thin girl. "If you'd eat a bit of mutton or somethin' you'd be fair plump and pretty, so you would." She set the buckets down by the tub. "Will I pour it?"

Clem nodded.

"Did you see that Matt Brennan on your way?" inquired Lizzie casually.

"Yes. I saw him. Do you know him?"

"In a manner of speakin'." Lizzie stood in the doorway staring at her. Her breathing was short and wheezy, her chest and arms pink and sweaty from work. "Have yersel' a good scrubbin', Miss Clem." She balanced the heavy buckets on her wide hips and shut the door with her toes.

Clem climbed into the bath. Lizzie must have met Matt during the shearing or perhaps at the store in Burrundi. She washed herself with a large sponge and a cake of fine soap with a spicy scent which Una Maclean had sent from Sydney. Una was Angus's sister. Clem had not seen Angus for four years, yet it was taken for granted by both families that she and Angus would marry. Her father often mentioned the match, trying to impress her with the importance of her inheritance and above all of marrying somebody *on the land*. In John Cameron's eyes, land was everything. Without land, a man was nobody. His daughter's wishes, even her happiness, were subordinate to the importance of "holding on to the land."

Clem remembered Angus's attitude to her when she was a foolish twelve-year-old girl and hoped his opinion of females had altered during his four years in Edinburgh.

She put on her white muslin with the pink rosebuds she detested around the hem and tied a matching ribbon in her hair—to please her mother.

She knocked at her mother's door. "It's only me, Clemency." She went into the room very slowly. It was long and wide, the tall windows at the end opening onto a small paved garden of imported bushes. A lamp hung outside the windows to illuminate the pink of the oleander and the bright dark red of the hibiscus, whose vulgarly prominent stamens pressed their thick heads against the glass.

The room itself was dark, the mahogany furniture forming large shadows against the pale blue papered walls. The borders of the Chinese rugs glowed softly blue and pink.

"Mother?"

The dim white figure standing by the end wall moved into the light of the one lamp in the center of the room. "I have such a headache. Your father will never understand my ailments."

"Won't you be coming to dinner?" Clem strained her eyes, trying to determine if she were pale or flushed.

"Yes. Unfortunately I have to as we have guests—the Merilees—an English couple. You can do all the talking. Clara Merilees has not been long in the colony; she will be interested in meeting a native."

"What shall I talk to her about?"

"Just the usual nonsense."

"But I don't know any! Perhaps she'll be interested in sheep."

Her mother smiled. "I hardly think so. She's just fresh from London and is not aware that the streets of Sydney are paved with Merino fleece."

"Oh." Clem fiddled with the bow in her hair.

"Pink is not your color. I do wish you'd wear a hat when you ride. Brown skin and freckles are so ordinary."

Clem frowned. "A hat would fall off when Magpie gallops."

"The way you ride I don't suppose anything stays on for long. Well, miss, you'll soon be at your Aunt Margaret's and ladies do not ride astride down the South Head Road."

Clem clenched her fists. "Mother—"

"And remember that Angus will expect you to be a lady. He has not been in Edinburgh these last four years for nothing."

"Oh, Mother—stop talking about Angus. He will hate me. I wanted to ask you something."

"Yes?" Her mother already looked bored by the question.

"Why has Father said there would be no more work for the Brennans? We have only a few ticket-of-leave men. Surely—"

"I'm sorry, that's your father's concern." Mrs. Cameron busied herself with puffing out Clem's wide sleeves.

"But Mother—"

"Not now, please. Go to your room. Remember the Merilees—and my headache."

"Damn the Merilees," said Clem under her breath as she hurried down the hall to her room, trying to hold back her tears. What on earth would she say to the woman? She looked at her nails; they were still dirty. She hoped Mrs. Merilees would not make too close an inspection of her person.

By the time Clem reached the dining room, the malicious and interfering character of Mrs. Merilees had assumed gigantic proportions. Edith, the housekeeper, was laying the table with the best china and silver.

"I'm glad to see you in your muslin." She was a large woman, tightly corseted, with fat shoulders bulging from the satin of her best gown. "Your father's guest is an important man—something to do with wool—from home."

"Have you seen them?" Clem picked up a tiny finger bowl covered in forget-me-not.

"I have. Give me that, you'll break the thing." She leaned over the table to rescue the delicate piece of porcelain, then straightened her broad back and watched Clem's movements critically. "Shoulders back!" she barked, as Clem turned to go.

She slumped deliberately. If she put her shoulders back Mrs. Merilees might comment on her posture, or worse, if she didn't, her father would tell her to in front of everyone. She managed a compromise without looking too hunchbacked.

Clem's father rose immediately, propelling her toward the two people at the far end of the drawing room.

Mr. Merilees was short, portly, and elaborately dressed. His collar turned down over his cravat and his coat lapels turned back all the way to his waist to show off his brightly patterned waistcoat. He bounced off his chair, and bowing, took both Clem's hands in his. "What a pretty child! Don't you think so, Clara?"

"How do you do, sir—and Mrs. Merilees." She curtsied awkwardly, Mr. Merilees still holding fast to her fingers. She could see he was only being polite in flattering her looks. His eyes were riveted to the freckles on her nose. She gently extricated her fingers and stood self-consciously in front of Mrs. Merilees.

The woman waved her husband to a seat and bade Clem sit beside her on the chaise longue. "Now tell me, my dear, what does such a charming young lady do to amuse herself out here in the *bush*?" She beamed at Clem's father. "Do I pronounce it correctly, Mr. Cameron?" She turned back to Clem, placing her fan in Clem's fingers. "Pray use my fan, my dear, you are a little flushed."

Clem carefully opened the fragile piece of stiffened lace and slowly fanned her face.

"Excellent!" Mrs. Merilees smiled, showing a row of slightly discolored teeth. She quickly closed her lips and kept smiling with her mouth shut. "Come now. Is there much entertaining hereabouts? Do you play—or sing perhaps?"

Clem stuttered. "No—that is—no, I do not play." She studied Mrs. Merilees's dress. It was a full crinoline made of stiff shiny silk, with vertical stripes in pinks and mauves and the whole trimmed with pink rosebuds. The sleeves were extremely plump and on top of everything was laid a long piece of lace; a cape perhaps, thought Clem.

Her hair was dull and lifeless and her features ordinary, yet with her clever use of rouge and her mass of expertly tonged curls, Mrs. Merilees was quite stunning.

She was about to ask Clem another question when Mrs. Cameron suddenly came through the door.

After the usual introductions, the usual polite conversation followed, Clem mercifully ignored by all until her mother caught her eyes fixed on the luminous turquoise of her dress.

"My daughter realizes how outré we are out here. My lack of horsehair, for instance." She fiddled with her flaccid skirt. "It is

dreadful, isn't it?" Mrs. Cameron's dress was absurdly old-fashioned, the shoulders too wide and the skirt too narrow. Clem noticed
how very pale her face was in contrast with her black curls. "Of
course your cape is unheard of—even in Sydney!" She smiled ruefully at Mrs. Merilees.

"You must let me make you a present of this one." Mrs. Merilees
pulled the flimsy piece of lace from her shoulders and held it out to
Clem's mother.

"Oh, no! I couldn't!"

"Of course you could—you must. You are so cut off from everything—I mean in the way of fashion and such—out here. Do take
it." She dropped it into the other woman's lap. Mrs. Cameron took
it with such a look of gratitude, Clem was embarrassed for her.

Mrs. Merilees turned to face the men. "Is your conversation too
learned for we women, or would you flatter us by allowing us to join
you?"

Mr. Merilees twinkled at everyone. "My wife pretends an interest
in worldly talk. She affects an understanding of law and government
as do many women nowadays, but like all of them she only partici-
pates when the topic directly concerns herself."

"George, you are unfair! I profess to know nothing at all! But I
must listen!"

Mr. Cameron grunted and stubbed out his strong cigar.

His wife pointed to the crystal decanter on the tea table beside
him. "Would you care for a little brandy? We find brandy keeps best
out here; we drink it with water."

The Merileeses sipped the weak, slightly raw spirit with little
grimaces of delight. "Sydney town still abounds in rum shops," Mr.
Merilees commented.

"Most of them run by felons or ex-felons," growled Mr. Cameron.

"Mrs. Cameron coughed. "Very undesirable types I'm afraid."
She frowned into her glass. "The trade appeals to the drunkard, of
course."

"Of course." Mrs. Merilees nodded wisely, looking at her husband for confirmation.

He cleared his throat. "Er, these ex-felons of yours, these convicts—some of these chaps do a good day's work." He waited for
someone to agree with him. Nobody said anything, so he continued.
"Convict labor, in my opinion, was the prime factor in getting this

colony to its feet. Oh, except for the pastoralist—Mr. Cameron and his ilk.''

"Yes . . . " Clem's father deliberated for a moment, then nodded enthusiastically. "I would prefer more of the convict and less of the free settler. These small holdings lead to a lot of trouble.''

"Indeed?" Mrs. Merilees sat upright on the hard chaise longue.

"Leads to all sorts of newfangled ideas, democracy and such. These people are not content to keep working for good masters; they must become their *own* masters.''

"Oh." Mrs. Merilees frowned, a little puzzled.

"In London," explained Mr. Merilees, smiling at the ladies, "there are other ideas afoot. Many members of Parliament believe the New South Wales economy would benefit from the immigration of small holders to diversify the agricultural products.''

John Cameron's face was bright pink. "Wool is enough to keep this colony wealthy!"

"Perhaps large wheat farms?" suggested Mrs. Merilees nervously.

"No doubt some simpleton will lose all his money trying to grow wheat somewhere. These idealist fools—utopian scoundrels!"

Clem looked at her mother; she was staring at her red-faced husband, her eyes wide with warning.

Mr. Merilees went on bravely. "Well, Mr. Cameron, that's why I'm here. I was sent, unofficially of course, to sound out men like yourself. I represent a small group of shipowners and financiers who have a great interest in your pastoral industry. They wish to perhaps invest and to lobby the Colonial Secretary on certain matters—the resumption of transportation or whatever.''

"The latter can only benefit the squatter. I would be very much in favor of it." Mr. Cameron sat back in his chair and searched his pockets for his cigar case.

"More convicts! But, Father—"

"Silence, miss, until you are spoken to.''

Clem squirmed in her seat, her cheeks burning.

Mr. Merilees coughed. "Mr. Gladstone, the Colonial Secretary, would not object to a new convict system for your colony, somewhat along the lines of the Van Diemen's Land Probationary Scheme, if the populace agreed.''

"Populace! What kind of word is that?" Clem's father blew out a great cloud of cigar smoke. "It smacks of democracy!"

"The free settlers—if they would not object—the Government would favor a resumption of transportation."

Clem drew in her breath.

Mrs. Merilees laid her hand gently on Clem's. "One must provide an assigned man with only his food and leather," she said." Otherwise one has a *free* and never-ending supply of labor—is that right, Mr. Cameron?"

"Yes. And those fellows, once they are pardoned take a deuced long time to save up enough for their own selections. They drink most of their wages away, so one can expect a long working life out of them. Better a few thieves and drunkards than these democrats, eh, Mrs. Merilees?"

Mrs. Merilees just laughed and finished her brandy.

"Shall we go in now?" Mrs. Cameron rang the bell for Edith as Clem hurried ahead to open the dining-room door.

Edith, Lizzie, and the kitchenmaid, Fanny Old, the illegitimate daughter of a convict woman, stood ready to wait on them.

The tightly gathered floor-length velvet curtains glowed bright blue in the light from the six-pronged candelabra sitting in the center of the dining table. The curtains were too thick to allow the night air to filter through the opened french windows, and the tiny flames from the thirty-six candles intensified the stuffy heat of the room. Clem noticed Mrs. Merilees about to increase the speed of her fan, then think better of it. To have done so would have been tantamount to a spoken comment upon the lack of fresh air.

Clem winked at Fanny who grinned at her from beneath her starched housemaid's cap. Fanny was a little touched and subject to fits. Her mother had run off with a shearer, abandoning Fanny on her eighth birthday. She giggled and grimaced and was continually responsible for breakages and the mysterious loss of household equipment. She shuffled from the table to the long silk-fronted chiffonier and back again under the eagle eye of Edith, while Lizzie went from place to place ladling the soup.

Clem stood in front of her place, waiting until all were seated. Suddenly Mr. Merilees was behind her, dragging out her chair.

"Thank you." She sat down as he pushed it in, and her hair, too loosely caught by the pink ribbon, threatened to fall into her soup.

Her mother restrained a remark, turning to smile at Mrs. Merilees instead. "We do not often have the pleasure of such company as yourself and Mr. Merilees at Querilderie. My daughter had not made the acquaintance of anybody from *home* until she spent a year at my sister's house in Sydney."

"Good gracious! I have found not a whit of difference between your colonial way of life and that of *home,* as you call it, even though you be ten thousand miles removed from us."

"You are being too generous. We do not have too much time for being civilized out here, or too many of the items with which to practice the art."

"Well, it's not for want of trying, and that's all that matters."

Mr. Merilees suddenly stared with immense interest at Clem. "I believe you help your papa look after his fences. How many miles do you ride each day?"

Clem glanced at her mother who nodded.

"I don't know exactly. Sometimes it could be thirty or forty miles a day, if the country is not too wooded, or it might be only ten or twenty."

"A mere stroll!" Mr. Merilees laughed. "Do you hunt?"

"We do not. There are some gatherings nearer Sydney, I believe," Clem's mother replied.

"The stockmen hunt kangaroos," said Clem, her eyes upon Lizzie's plump hands, as she served the small, white, boiled potatoes from a heavy silver dish. "Thank you."

Lizzie did not acknowledge her thanks, as they had not been called for. She moved silently around the table, her face a complete blank.

"You *do* manage a good cellar here, I see." Mr. Merilees studied the wine bottle.

"We have a little put down. It doesn't do well in the heat. We usually have to manage on the local brew."

"I've tasted a few of your colonial wines, Mrs. Cameron. They're not bad, not bad at all. They don't travel well, or so I'm told." Mr. Merilees tasted his claret.

"No," Mrs. Cameron agreed. "Like all colonials."

Everyone laughed politely.

"Well, Mrs. Cameron," said Mr. Merilees, raising his goblet, "you do us a great honor. May I propose a toast? To the pastoralist of New South Wales: Long may he reign!"

The others laughed again, but their host sipped the dark liquid without smiling.

Clem discovered half a goblet of wine to the right of her place and took a sip. It was really quite palatable, she decided.

"Clemency is too young to be drinking claret, Edwina!" Her father glowered at her mother and turned to Edith who was hovering at his side. "Bring some water!"

At that moment Clem hated her father. Her fingers tightened around her knife and fork. How dare he behave like that in front of strangers. She debated leaving the room but didn't have the courage. Her mother's glance implored her not to protest. She pushed the goblet away.

"I hope the mutton is to your taste? There is so little beef as yet or pork. Our neighbor, Daniel Brennan, did try some hogs, but the animals failed. Why did they fail, dear?" she asked, raising her eyebrows sweetly at her red-faced husband.

"Brennan's hogs? Of course they failed. Everything on that place fails including Brennan's capacity for raw spirits. Rum! Pity he did not feed the beasts on that stuff. They might have thrived!"

Edith brought the water, but Clem did not touch it. She watched her father's face becoming even redder as he laughed hoarsely. His napkin was tucked into his waistcoat whereas Mr. Merilees's was placed neatly upon his lap. Her father regarded the fact that a gentleman did not have to dress for dinner when dining alone with his family in the far bush country as one of the few blessings of life in New South Wales. All his outfits were ancient, undergoing numerous alterations over the years by the fond and capable Edith. His shirt was a leftover from the officer's mess and his cravat the same he had worn on his wedding day.

Fanny cleared the plates with a deafening clatter and placed a tall jelly, wobbling dangerously, in the middle of the table along with some tiny pink meringues—Clem's favorites.

The ladies discussed the jelly—a loquat—unheard of in London. Clem saw her mother glow with pride at her exotic offering and remembered bitterly all the dinner-table conversations she'd had to sit through at her aunt's house in Sydney. Silly, fussy people with funny accents, talking about silly things. The girls were pale and giggly and talked of nothing but boys and picnics. She dreaded her return to Sydney.

Clem started. Mr. Merilees was actually clicking his fingers at her!

"I beg your pardon?"

"Where is your sister?"

"In the nursery."

"She is to play and sing for us after dinner, George." Mrs. Merilees bit daintily at her meringue.

"Is she a beauty like her sister?" asked Mr. Merilees, about to spoon a great slab of jelly into his open mouth.

Clem blushed and took a meringue, regretting her action as everybody suddenly stopped chewing to stare at her. She looked down at her plate, letting the meringue melt on her tongue.

Mr. Merilees swallowed his last mouthful of jelly and took a sip of wine. "Clemency is a true daughter of the colonies. A new type of beauty will be born here, you mark my words, Mrs. Cameron."

Mrs. Merilees nodded. "I think Mr. M. means the Italianate type will emerge triumphant. The sun, you know, it builds a different texture altogether. You can see a fine example of it in your daughter ."

Clem was confused. Should she be flattered? Or were they just being kind about her freckles? Perhaps Mr. Merilees really didn't mind them at all. They were not like Fanny's—all big and blotched and spread unevenly over her face and chest, pale orange, like her hair. She watched the meringues, hoping to be offered more.

Mr. Merilees saw her looking at them. "When I was a child, Clemency, I was assured by my elders and betters that other delights would replace my infantile cravings for meringues and jellies. However, I have now come full circle. What they omitted to tell me was that all else is an illusion. When you have reached an age where meringues once more take pride of place in your day-to-day existence, then you have reached maturity!" Her urged Edith to Clem's place with the meringues. "After you, my dear."

She took three. Edith did not often come up with such delicacies.

The ladies departed for the drawing room. Clem heard the men's chairs being pushed back and their feet scraping the polished wood floor in expectation of cigars and port. Drink eventually turned one's nose a bright red and gave one the gout. If that were true, what on earth would become of Mr. Brennan? Her mother drank a great deal, too, but that was to chase away her awful headaches.

Katharine was fetched from the nursery to play some simple songs for Mrs. Merilees. Clem's voice was too deep for her sister's high pitch, but the ladies clapped energetically and requested an encore.

Clem declined, but Katharine played away happily while the ladies whispered to each other from opposite ends of the room. Clem saw her mother gradually becoming more flushed, her eyes growing too bright, even beneath the brilliant chandeliers. She gazed at the vivid blue of the painted Scottish lochs and remembered the view of the harbor from her aunt's house. She would miss her summer swimming with the Brennan boys. When the creek flooded during the February rains they would all dive in fully clothed, letting the water bounce them off the boulders and drag them back into the middle as it tried to pull them under.

"A penny for your thoughts, Clemency." Mrs. Merilees smiled at her.

"Nothing—I wasn't thinking of anything."

Her mother's eyes were faraway, her mouth fixed into a half smile. She sipped brandy all the time, occasionally offering a glass to her guest who would refuse it with a tiny shake of her curls, a little limp now, suffering from the humidity, which one never mentioned at Querilderie. Any mention of the weather, especially by visitors from *home* was regarded by the inhabitants of the New South Wales bush country as an unwelcome reflection upon their constant struggle to keep their houses cool. One had to sit in all kinds of temperatures and bear them without so much as a sigh.

Clem noticed that Mrs. Merilees was perspiring heavily. Her forehead and chest were pimpled with tiny drops of moisture. Still, she did not increase the speed of her fan.

"Are you looking forward to school?"

"Clem hates school and all those picnics and things. She hates Sydney." Katharine whirled round on the piano stool, planted her feet firmly on the carpet, and stared at Mrs. Merilees's dress. "She just *hates* school." She returned to her music.

"I'm sorry to hear that," said Mrs. Merilees, quite perturbed. "One must perservere however. Is it just school, or being in Sydney, or both that you—"

"Both!"

"Oh."

"I wish I could just stay here and have Miss Owen for my governess. Kathy is having Miss Owen."

"Who—"

Mrs. Merilees's question was interrupted by Mrs. Cameron pouring herself another brandy from the heavy decanter. The stopper dropped from her fingers and rolled along the carpet. Mrs. Merilees knelt to retrieve it. "It's not broken." She put it back into the neck of the crystal decanter with a tight squeak. "There."

Mrs. Cameron leaned both elbows on one arm of her chair. "*Who* is the accomplished Miss Owen, the *beautiful* Marianne?" She took a large sip of brandy. "She is the governess at Glen Ross, that oasis of culture, the next-door property, belonging to our friends the Macleans."

"Why can't she tutor Clemency, too?" asked Mrs. Merilees.

Mrs. Cameron shouted above a noisy passage of Katharine's gavotte. "That is impossible. My husband has decided to send my little girl away from me, to Miss Thorne of Sydney, no less. He blames the convicts. The convicts!" She made an inelegant pouting noise, then resumed her fixed smile.

"The convicts!" Both Mrs. Merilees and Clem expostulated.

"Yes. My little girl is getting too grown up, or *mature*, as he puts it, to stay here. I am apparently quite safe and Kathy, but my eldest must be shipped off. She sees too much."

"Mother—please!" Clem stood up in consternation. "You're mistaken. The ticket-of-leave men aren't criminals. What harm can they possibly be?"

Her mother giggled. Her face was too pink. She picked up her fan, waving it clumsily. "Ask your papa. Here he is." She lay over the side of her chair, still fanning awkwardly.

Mrs. Merilees left her chair to stand next to Mrs. Cameron, the expression on her startled face warning Mr. Merilees not to interfere.

Katharine stopped playing and was putting her books away with a great deal of fuss as her father strode over to her. "Good night, Katharine. Wish our guests a good night, and kiss your mother; you too, Clemency."

Mrs. Cameron leaned forward and returned Clem's kiss with a smacking kiss on the lips, leaving Clem with the strange taste of brandy in her mouth. Her father bowed his head for his customary kiss on the forehead. Her lips just brushed his skin.

They waited at the end of the hall, hearing their father's loud laughter and Mrs. Merilees's gentler tones, then suddenly a shrill scream of mirth. They heard their mother shouting something, then more of her hysterical laughter as the door opened. "Good night, John. Will you not see me to my room? Then I must go by myself!"

Mr. Cameron stepped into the hall and grabbed her by the shoulders. "Quiet! Go to bed!" He pushed her toward the two girls who were flattened behind the thick frame of a painting. They tried not to breathe as their mother stumbled past, sobbing. She opened her bedroom door and shouted, "Don't forget to tell them all about Marianne!"

Clem sat on her bed, trembling. She reached for her favorite book, a volume of finely illustrated British birds. She studied the drawings, trying to forget the look on her mother's face, her wild eyes and distorted mouth. She wished she could draw. Miss Owen could; she could paint, too. That was why her mother had been so upset. It had been something to do with her father hiring Miss Owen for Kathy and not for her.

She undressed and climbed into bed, listening for further voices, but she heard only the incessant buzzing of the mosquitoes searching for holes in her net. Relentlessly they circled the bed, their fruitless dives into the taut cheesecloth becoming less frequent as one by one they drifted out of the half-open door in search of a more accessible prey.

Chapter Three

The next morning, pushing open the screen door to the yard, Clem stopped to dig her bare toes into the cool earth, then climbed up onto the balustrade to reach the grapevine covering the lower part of the roof. The grapes were overripe, their black skins shriveled. She ate them one by one, spitting out the pips along the path to the kitchen.

Fanny Old was cooking breakfast, kneading the dough with her large knuckled fingers. "Mornin', Miss Clem. Up early?" Her spotty gray eyes looked crookedly at Clem's bare feet. She grinned. "You look tousled, like. Where're you goin'?"

Clem shrugged. "Nowhere in particular. Where's the bread? I'm going to camp overnight."

Fanny wiped her fingers on her gray pinafore. "There's them wild natives about this time of year. Boss'll be angry. Bread's here." She dragged the big-bellied earthenware crock from beneath the long table.

"I'd like some salt beef or pickled pork and flour. Oh, and salt, of course."

Fanny handed her the salt box. "It's damp—almost wet," said Clem, digging her fingers into the box.

"Always is this time of year." Fanny's lopsided figure disap-

30

peared into the pantry. "I've found some beef. Brennan lads'll like that," she called out through the wire window.

"What do you mean—Brennan lads?"

"I knows what I know." She reappeared carrying a small square of pressed meat and a bag of flour. "And so does Lizzie Bell. That Matt—"

"What about Matt?"

"Lizzie ain't half soft on that Matt."

Clem stuffed the food into her saddle bag, scratching her hand on the buckles in her haste.

"Yes. That Matt and our Lizzie be right friendly."

Clem's stomach felt suddenly empty. "Really? Whatever can you mean, Fanny?" She laughed. She went to the sink to fill her water bags and remembered the brandy for Mrs. Brennan. "Is there some—" she paused, recalling Mr. Brennan's drinking habits and thought perhaps cheese would be healthier—"cheese?"

"Reckon so. I'll get it. And you'll be needin' lucifers."

"Matt'll have those. And, Fanny, don't you tell a soul where I am, not even my father. Promise?"

"Yes, miss." Fanny winked.

As she walked to the stables she tried to smile at Fanny's silly talk of Matt and Lizzie. What nonsense. Her stomach still felt empty; perhaps she was thirsty. She stopped to watch the sun come over the horizon. There was a red streak behind the line of gums at the end of the horse paddock which sent long pick shadows across the ground for half a mile.

They rode off into the blinding sky, taking the home paddock fence at a gallop. Then Magpie kept up an even pace to the water hole and again as far as the Brennans' woods where he trotted through the black-trunked trees, frightening the sunning lizards back into the earth. A carpet snake slithered along the track, glistening blue and green, and disappearing so quickly into the undergrowth, it might have been a mirage. She thought of her pet blue-tongue lizards who lived in the sandstone wall of the kitchen garden. She'd forgotten to take them their cabbage leaves this morning. She would miss them in Sydney.

Clem sighed, searching the horizon for her first sight of the native box—or Christmas tree, as the Brennans called it—which grew up against the side wall of their house. It flowered at Christmas, the flimsy white blossoms exhaling a pure sweet scent. As she came out

of the thicker part of the forest she saw it, shading her eyes to watch
the white patch above the gray plain. It was moving toward her, its
shape clean and sharp against the glare of the sky. Beneath it she
could see the bark shingles of the Brennans' roof glinting copper in
the morning sun.

She rode up to the house, hoping the boys had not left without
her. She jumped off Magpie and ran to the front door. They were all
home; she could hear their voices.

Pat's face appeared at the door. "Can Clem come in?"

"Let 'er in. Let 'er in!" Mr. Brennan's voice was slurred and
abrasive.

Pat opened the door and put a finger to his lips. "The old man's
wild again. Watch what you say."

She walked hesitantly into the room. The family sat around the table drinking mugs of tea. Mr. Brennan was slumped into his chair by
the stove. His beard was matted and his cheeks and nose raw with
cuts and grazes. "Been out and about for a coupla days, m'dear—
out and about." He laughed and banged a fist against the side of the
chair, wincing with the pain. "A bit of boundary riding and that."

"No need to boast, Father." Mrs. Brennan had been crying again.
She didn't smile at Clem, just pointed to a vacant chair. "You'll be
needin' a cup likely. Here, lass." She poured the black tea into a
chipped and stained cup.

Clem drank it down without looking at anyone.

"You come to help mend the fence?" asked Con, his perky sun-
spotted face grinning as always.

"Yes," she whispered, glancing over at Mr. Brennan.

"None of you'll get paid for that neither!" He laughed again.
"Gorn, you lazy lot, get goin'!"

Matt got half off his seat. His mother's arm shot out across the table to restrain him. "No, don't do nothin'. He doesn't mean it—he's
..." She looked at Clem. "He's ill."

Matt reached for his tobacco pouch. "I'll fill this. You go and get
the horses, Pat."

Con and Mary ran out of the house, leaving the door wide open
behind them.

Clem watched Mary running through the stumps, lifting her skirts
with chubby brown fingers. "Your Mary is growing up!" She forced
a smile from Mrs. Brennan. Then she remembered the cheese and
hurried out to Magpie to fetch it.

"This is for you, Mrs. Brennan."

"Is that cheese? You're a good girl, Clemency." She took the packet, unraveling the the cloth gently. "It's beautiful. I do appreciate it." Her face reminded Clem of her mother's as she had fingered Mrs. Merilees's lace mantelet.

Mrs. Brennan put the cheese away in the meat-safe, swatting the flies with a dishcloth.

Pat called out to them. He was leading a tall bay with two white flashes on his forehead.

"He's mine," said Matt. "Bought him off a bloke in Willawarrha. D'you like him?"

Clem nodded, studying the horse. He was a splendid animal. "I'll swap you Magpie and all my gold quartz and my blue tongues for him."

Matt laughed. "He's not for sale." He opened his saddle bags. "These all the nails you could find?" he asked Con, who was riding a thick-legged cob.

"Yep." Con shrugged. "Them's all."

Clem rode beside Matt. "I didn't tell Father I was coming here. Fanny knows though."

"Does Lizzie?"

"Why?" She resented the question. "Why should *she* know?"

"I dunno." The track narrowed as they reached some low outcrops of red sandstone, and Matt urged his horse ahead of hers.

What was the word Fanny had used about Matt? *Soft*—that was it. Surely he was not soft on that fat pink woman. She was always so sticky. Ugh.

They rode past the final outcrop of sandstone, the streaks of dazzling white quartz hurting Clem's eyes. She gazed at Matt's thick yellow hair. It flew out around his head in long damp twists. She remembered how it used to shine after their swimming expeditions, and how he had resented their teasing. He used to rub it with mud and let it dry in the sun, becoming a strange blue-eyed aborigine. She never seemed to see him nowadays. He never came swimming with them, or horse racing, or anything. . . .

The horses walked in a straight line toward the northern horizon, the sun immediately overhead. A flock of pink galahs appeared, high in the sky, then suddenly swooped down to fly among the outcrops, their raucous cries echoing through the smoothed towers of weathered stone. Clem watched the lizards scuttle into their tiny holes, all but a large frill neck. It stared at them from behind its prehistoric ruff. Nothing would ever frighten it; its ancestors had lived in this land for too long. Clem turned her head slowly and watched it, still alert, its eyes blinking at her across the flat red rocks.

They reached the open plain and cantered over the short-cropped dry grass. Clem kept remembering her mother's awful behavior in front of the English couple, and all because of her education. She supposed the Macleans would be pleased to let Miss Owen go. She was apparently quite expensive. Some people employed convict women as governesses—the respectable type, of course—as they were much cheaper, but her father wouldn't think of it. It was funny to think that Matt's father had been a convict, and Lizzie—Lizzie Bell was a convict woman. No wonder Matt and Lizzie were friends, they would understand all kinds of things that she . . .

Matt's voice interrupted her thoughts. "Come on up!"

She caught up with him. His horse was so tall she had to tilt her head back to see his face.

"It'll all be a bit different at that school in Sydney. No dampers for tea there."

She giggled. "Yes, Miss Maybright senior wouldn't approve of dampers or billy tea. She's the daughter of a Presbyterian minister who came to the colony to convert the natives and didn't succeed."

"Well, here's another native he wouldn't have converted. Me mother's Catholic, but I suppose I'm nothin'."

"What religion is Lizzie?"

"Dunno, why?"

"Well if you do get married you'll want your children to be brought up in *some* faith."

"Married! Lizzie and me! God Almighty, girl, you'd have me married off pretty quick, wouldn't you? I hardly know the woman!"

"That's good," Clem sighed happily. "She's too old for you, anyway."

Matt burst out laughing, throwing his head back, his reins held high in the air. "I'm never gettin' married to any woman! Can't stand them! That is, to be married to one—"

"Oh."

"I want to go away—once Pat and Con can look after my mother—to Moreton Bay, or across to the unexplored parts of the Northwest. There's millions of acres there, just waiting' for cattle. I'll find some land and squat on it, just like your old man did." He stopped his horse and took hold of Magpie's reins. "I'm not going to let anything stop me."

"Money will—the lack of it, I mean." He would need money to buy stock and equipment. Even squatting was only possible with a lot of money.

"Yep. Well, I'll get some money, my oath I will. And I know where from, too. Your father has no more claim to that gold in the quartz ridge than I have. He didn't pay for that land where the gold is. Before I leave this place I'll strip that ridge." He grabbed hold of her arm. "And don't you go telling anyone about it. Let them think it's fool's gold. It bloody well isn't, but I'm the only one who's goin' to know."

"You know I wouldn't tell anyone what you were doing!" She wrenched her arm from his grasp, her face white with anger. "You seem to think I'm your enemy!"

"You can never be anything else. People like you are always the enemies of people like me."

"I am *not* your enemy! I *love* you!" What had she said? She felt dizzy. She wanted to take it back, but it was too late—anyway it was true. She dropped her head, her body weak with humiliation.

His arm was around her shoulders. "I'm sorry. I suppose I love you, too, in a way. But you're too young to understand these things. We could never really be—well, you know—love each other. I shouldn't have laughed off Lizzie. She's the same as me."

Clem raised her eyes to his.   1893376

"We both have nothing, see," he said.

"Yes. But I'd give up all that—my father, his money, all the sheep, all that—just to stay with you out here." She started to cry. "I don't want to go to school or have beautiful dresses or marry Angus Maclean!" She sobbed bitterly. The tears flowed down her cheeks stinging her chin. "Oh God! How stupid you must think me!" She wiped away the tears viciously with her sleeve, hiding her face.

Matt was patting her on the head, like a puppy, thought Clem, which only added to her anguish. "I just want to stay friends with you. With your mother, too. My father said—"

"Never mind him—we'll be mates for as long as you want."

She started to protest but he stopped her. "No, don't argue. We'll be mates—all right?"

She nodded, still rubbing her face with her sleeve. "The boys'll see me like this."

"Doesn't matter. You're a girl after all." He grinned, pushing her plaits away from her face. "I can never see your eyes when they're like that."

They were almost at the fence. The long line of horizontal logs suddenly gave way to the remaining upright ones of the broken part, standing squat and black against the dense blue sky.

"A lot of it's down." Matt pulled up his horse. "But it shouldn't take us long." His eyes still focused on the fence, he said, "I suppose you think takin' that gold's stealin'."

"No. Gold belongs to whoever finds it first. My father didn't pay for that land; it wasn't a part of his original grant."

"That's what I thought. I've often considered goin' bush-rangin'—it's easy enough."

"But that *is* stealing! Clem's tears had dried. She stared at him wide-eyed. "You don't really mean that?"

"Not really. Those drays of wool that're disappearin', now that's too easy. Unless you're a convict on the run, then you'd do anythin'."

"Not murder troopers!"

"If you've got away from the bastards you've got to support yourself somehow, and if they're out to murder you, you've got to defend yourself, haven't you?"

She thought about it for a minute. "I would prefer to live off the land."

"That *is* livin' off the land! Unless you're prepared to go and live with the natives."

"Rather that than steal for a living."

Matt smiled condescendingly. "Your father stole this land from the Euragalla tribe." He pulled up his horse and pointed to the four points of the compass. "Lock, stock, and barrel. Don't you think *they* think he's a ruddy bushranger? We all are, as far as they're concerned."

Clem mulled it over, but she could not refute his argument.

"If I'd been deported like my old man for stealin' a coupla yards of shoe leather, I'd have gone bush and shot hell out of anyone who'd try to get me back. People like your father don't know what it's like to be without boots and expected to work stony fields for a livin'. They don't care either."

"I see." She could see his point of view, but still wasn't sure about shooting troopers. "Please don't ever murder anyone."

"Not if you think it's a bad idea." He pushed the plaits out of her face again. "You'd be better off with the natives, I reckon. You look like one most of the time."

"I don't mind. I'd rather look like that than—" she was about to say Lizzie Bell—"than Una Maclean or Miss Owen."

"Funny woman, that Miss Owen."

"When have you seen *her*?"

"Saw her over at Glen Ross—at the last shearin' there. Not a bad-lookin' woman, but scared of comin' out of the house or something—doesn't like talkin' to anyone."

"She leaves the house only to paint. She's very clever."

"Too clever for the likes of me. Is that what you mean?"

"I don't know. Do you like clever women?"

"Not if they *know* they are." Matt spurred his horse and galloped to the broken fence, pulling up abruptly at the fallen logs.

Clem studied the thick, upright chocs sunk deep into the earth. They were difficult to uproot and usually stayed put for years, whereas the long, slim logs nailed two deep across were easily brought down by wind or a herd of kangaroos, or a swagman who hadn't been given enough to eat at the homestead.

"Logs aren't broken," said Matt, as the others dismounted. "The old coot didn't have the strength for that."

They worked until late afternoon, stopping for Clem's black billy tea, so bitter and hot their foreheads formed great beads of sweat which ran down into their eyes and mouths. The nearest shade was a solitary tea tree. The horses stood beneath it, their heads bowed, occasionally nibbling at the short, white-brown grass.

Clem's back was aching. She rested against one of the chocs, then decided the shade of the tea tree would be cooler.

The black tree was short and bushy with dark green leaves. It stood starkly on the flat plain. During high summer it was covered with fluffy white blossoms. Clem had often camped beneath the thick, dark leaves and white flowers, as it marked the northeast corner of Querilderie and was a convenient halfway mark on her boundary treks.

She watched the boys working. Their backs were deep brown and running with sweat, their hair sopping wet and falling about their burned shoulders. They were such good workers; her father must be mad not to want to keep them on. Perhaps both her parents were slightly touched. She would be pleased to be away from them for a while, but not from home.

The gardens in Sydney were all too formal, and the houses so close together. Even the picnic spots had been trampled on by hundreds of people. There were places about here where no one—perhaps not even an aborigine—had walked since the landscape was formed.

She envied Matt his freedom. If only he would take her with him into the interior. She shut her eyes tightly, banishing such unreal notions with harsh thoughts of Sydney and Aunt Margaret's house. If she had been a man—a *real* mate—she would have gone with him.

She looked up into the branches of the tree. Matt said the aborigines called it a *moonah* tree. She called it the moon tree. At night, when it was a full bloom, it looked like the moon. She would be happy to stay beneath her tree forever. The few remaining flowers were slightly scented and covered with bees, their loud buzzing drowning the sound of the boys' hammering. . . .

The boys woke her at teatime. The mugs had been left unwashed from the last tea break, and the long leaves inside them had dried and shriveled like dead sugar ants. She scraped them out with a twig.

They sipped the tea gratefully, the soft slurping sounds magnified a thousand times on the silent plain. The sun had started its long descent into the west, elongating the shadow of the moon tree. The solid shapes of the horses were as motionless as painted figures against the watery, late-afternoon sky.

Matt stood up, scattering his tea leaves on the ground. "That might help fatten your father's sheep."

"I wish it would; then he might be better tempered."

"He's pretty rough, is he?"

She hung her head. "He's not a fair man. He's done this to you and now he's making me go to school. Why can't Miss Owen tutor me?"

"You're too old for that. It's time you were made into a lady. That's the reason." Matt spoke in a kind voice, turning away to knock his pipe on the heel of his boot.

"Clem'll never be one of those!" Con pulled her hair and punched her playfully in the arm.

Matt stood with his back to them, looking into the sun, chewing the end of his pipe. His dark silhouette against the sun suddenly appeared strange to her. He looked just like one of the men at the homestead. His back was full and his shoulders broad. He was a fully grown man—like her father.

She shut her eyes. She understood about Lizzie Bell now. It didn't matter that she was a few years older than he. Clem squatted by the fire, shovelling handfuls of dirt onto the embers. Her fingers were shaking.

When Matt turned to go back to the fence, she saw him with Lizzie Bell's eyes. He had suddenly stopped being Matt, the Brennans' oldest. He was now someone entirely new.

She spent the hours before sundown nailing split logs, working a few yards away from the boys, feeling increasingly uncomfortable in their company. She would have ridden home if it hadn't been so late. Her father wouldn't let her ride at night, as that was when stray aborigines attacked settlers.

Pat and Con rode off to the quartz ridge for firewood and Matt went on working until after dark, only putting down his hammer when he saw the firelight under the tea tree.

"Boys'll be back soon. They're gettin' a snake for supper. You'll like snake."

"Ugh." She crawled around the fire, meticulously turning each doughboy on its twig. "Do you skin it first?"

"Yeah. Then just stick it under the fire—like them." He pointed at the sizzling doughboys.

She kept turning them until they were crisp, then laid them on a tuft of grass to cool. "I suppose you'll have gone away by the time I get back from school."

Matt didn't stir. Clem stared at his face; he seemed fast asleep. There was no moon, just the stars very bright in the clear black sky. She sat still, listening for the horses.

Soon she heard the vibration of hoofbeats like a faint earth tremor under the flat plain, and the horses came into view. Pat was swinging a rope around his head—the snake. He picked it up by the tail and broke its back by twirling it in the air and cracking it like a stock whip.

This one was a prize specimen, very long and very fat. Con hobbled the horses while Pat cut off its head with one slash of his knife. He rapidly slit the skin from top to bottom and ripped it off in one piece, foot by foot, until the body lay naked, and dark pink in the firelight. He threw it on the fire.

They ate the crisp doughboys while the snake cooked. The muffled hisses and tiny sighs from the corpse seemed to come from every direction in the still night. Once they heard parrots screeching far off to the south, but after that nothing except the fire.

Slowly rising to his feet, Matt pulled the snake from the fire with two twigs, like chopsticks, then held it up in the air. "There y'are, blokes—roast snake!" He cut it into eight pieces. Clem took hers reluctantly. The others bit into theirs immediately, spitting out gristle and urging her to start.

She took one small piece and bit into it gingerly. She bit harder. It was incredibly tough! She chewed and chewed. If felt like eel but without the delicate salty flavor. She took one more bite and offered the rest to Con who had already consumed his.

The four sat silently round the dead fire, sipping the bitter tea from the blackened billy, then made their beds with their horse blankets and the hard bark of the moon tree. They didn't bother to light another fire, as Matt said spiders and snakes did not attack sleeping bodies.

She watched the boys moving about the fire as the sun came up. Then she stood up and shook the bark from her hair and skirt, folding her blanket. "I'll go home now. Father will be angry enough already."

"Sure." Con nodded. "We wouldn't like you to get into trouble because of us."

"Pity you have to go, Clem. You're not bad at fencin', for a girl," Pat complimented her, smiling.

She grunted, and kneeling down extricated a twig and some bark shavings from Con's hair, wondering if he ever brushed it. He was still smooth skinned as a boy.

The horses, seeing signs of life, hobbled over to the fire for water. Matt emptied his water bag into his hat. "This'll have to do them till tonight." With his blanket still around his shoulders he strode barefoot to the horses.

Refusing Con's blackened damper, Clem ran over to Magpie, passing Matt on his way back to the fire.

"Where are you goin'?"

"Home."

"Why?" He held his arm across her chest.

"My father will be angry." She stood perfectly still; his face was only two inches from her own.

"Because you've been with us?"

His breath filtered through her hair like a warm breeze. She dared not look up. "Yes—no. Not just because of that." The pressure of his hand increased on her shoulder and his lips seemed to be touching her forehead. "I *want* to go!"

His arms dropped to his sides, and he moved back. "Be seein' you then."

She took the hobbles off Magpie and saddled him. Too confused to say good-bye properly, she rode off with a perfunctory wave. They saluted her, three black figures against the pink horizon. There was a lump in her throat. She had wanted to tell them how much she would miss them, but had not known how to say it.

Chapter Four

Clem arrived home by midmorning, and Edith chased her to her room, scolding her and pulling at her clothes and hair. "And you stayed out without your father's permission!"

Clem slammed her bedroom door and rang the bell for Lizzie. She started to take off her clothes, then stopped. She didn't want Lizzie Bell to see her naked.

She couldn't picture Matt and the fat Liverpool woman together at all. Each belonged to a totally different compartment of her mind. She would keep them like that. All that business of Fanny's was imbecilic anyway.

Lizzie came into the room. "Yes?" Her red hair was neater, caught at the back with some thick tortoiseshell combs.

Clem eyed her warily. She seemed bigger today. She was large rather than fat, Clem decided. "Water please, Lizzie." She didn't rise from the bed but watched every movement of the other woman.

"Yes, Miss Clem. Your father's right angry with you havin' been with Pat and Con—and him too! All night!"

"Him? Who do you mean—*him*?" She waited for the woman to use the name as familiarly as she had used the other two.

"Matt, of course. Likely he'll be tannin' your hide, so he will."
Her wide hips swayed arrogantly as she went out the door.

Clem's whole body was burning with anger. Her father had never
touched her—and he never would! What did that woman know
about Matt—with her ham-pink arms and sweaty bosoms? He
wouldn't be interested in a creature like that. She couldn't mend a
fence or make doughboys. She wouldn't eat a snake—stupid female!

Clem took the lid off her crystal bowl. The quartz glinted dully in
the dim light from the half-drawn curtains. Well, he could have her.
She would never see him again anyway. He would be gone for good
in less than two years.

Her father did not arrive back until after dinner. He pushed open
the drawing-room door and stood just inside the room, still in riding
clothes, his eyes blinking at the bright chandeliers.

"You!" He shouted. "Clemency! Come here!"

Clem, who had been vainly struggling with her tapestry, dropped
it on the floor and tiptoed across the room .

"I didn't grant you permission to spend the night with those—
those Irish tinks! You didn't even ask me!" He looked at her for
some kind of explanation, his face dark with rage.

Clem stood, said, her hands folded in front of her in repentant
pose, "I'm sorry, Father. I did ask Fanny to tell you where I was going. You see, you were still asleep, and when the Merilees were
here, I couldn't ask you then."

"That has nothing to do with it! You should have woken me! Are
you afraid of me?"

"I dared not wake you—I . . ."

"Balderdash! All this is balderdash! You have defied me—that's
what it boils down to!"

She started to say something, but he continued shouting at her
hysterically. "Go to your room! And don't come out until the carriage is ready for Sydney!"

Her ears were ringing as she fled the room. He was still harangu-
ing her mother and Katharine. She stuck her fingers in her ears and
leaned against the wall.

Kathy opened the door and she heard his last breathless sentence.
"I hope it kills you! It's killed better than you!"

Clem was mortified. What did he mean? Children's manners did
not kill their parents.

The next morning at breakfast there was complete silence. Clem had gone to the dining room automatically, assuming that staying in her room did not mean being starved, too. Her father nodded to his oatmeal as she sat down, and Katharine ate without looking up from her plate. Her mother, suffering yet another headache, did not appear at all.

Clem gulped down her porridge, and refusing a plate of strong-smelling kedgeree, excused herself and ran to her mother's room.

Her mother was not yet dressed. In her white dressing gown and nightcap she looked more helpless than usual amid the heavy sun-bleached mahogany furniture. "Your papa is so angry with you— and me. He accuses me of being a bad mother and a wicked woman. He's right." She sank down on the green satin daybed at the foot of her four-poster. "He's always right."

She was so utterly dejected, so feeble, so unsuited to the role of motherhood, Clem thought. "It's not so bad, Mother. I'll be very good at my aunt's house and I'll learn how to speak French at school and to embroider. I'll try to enjoy learning to be a lady, I promise."

Her mother raised her head slightly. She smelled strongly of lavender water. "Oh, school, yes. The worthy Misses Maybright will teach you everything you *ought* to know and nothing more. Indeed they will."

Clem knelt on one knee by the daybed. She was determined not to be impatient with her mother these last two days, no matter how vague her behavior. "Mother, do you think I'm too thin?"

Her mother sighed. "Don't make the mistake of dieting."

"But ought I to be plumper?"

Her mother pressed the flat of her hand against her forehead. "Whatever for?"

"Oh, nothing. Mother—do you think Father will mind me living here when I come back from school? He—"

"What? Of course. Just go to school and don't take any notice of anything your aunt might say about me, and when you return Angus will want to marry you."

"I wish you'd all stop talking about Angus."

"The merger of two mighty Merino empires! Don't you know that is how your father sees it?" She giggled, stopping abruptly when she saw the expression on Clem's face.

"I will not marry Angus—or anyone—to please my father!" She stood up, her throat tight with frustration.

"Well, you'd better stay away from that poor little Brennan family until you go back to school. Your father will have no more of it. Your association with that man—Matt?—is out of the question."

"We do not *associate*, Mother. We are friends, we've been best friends since we were small children."

"That is a matter of opinion, not that I see much harm—" she paused. "Anyway, your father has taken a seat for you on the coach which the Merilees and some others have hired to take them to Sydney. You'll leave tomorrow."

"Why do you always take his side!"

"Because it's easier. Now run along."

Clem stared in exasperation at her mother's vacant face.

"Off you go, dear. It's been lovely having this little talk with you."

Clem left without a word. She wished her mother were more like Mrs. Brennan.

She wrote a good-bye note to Mrs. Brennan, hoping to leave it at the Burrundi store, remembering Mary's sad little dolls as she sealed the envelope. Now she wouldn't have time to persuade Kathy to make the clothes. How she hated her father!

Breakfast was a slight improvement over the previous day's mealtimes. With Clem's departure at hand, her father could afford to be cheerful, but her mother's face was strained beneath her appearance of gaiety.

Kathy chatted endlessly about Miss Owen, bringing a slight smile to her father's thin lips. He even seemed engrossed in a description of Kathy's latest tapestry—a subject which normally failed to interest him.

Playing the proud father, thought Clem bitterly.

"Mother," said Kathy, "when does Miss Owen arrive?"

"Dear Miss Owen comes to us on Monday, child. Is that not right, John?" She smiled too sweetly.

He nodded, then added gruffly, "The lady will be fine for Katharine, but Clemency needs a stronger hand."

"Never mind about Katharine, John. Will the lady be fine for you too?"

Edith dropped the silver sugar bowl. The contents spread all over the carpet in front of the chiffonier. In the confusion, Clem missed her father's muffled reply.

Her mother shook her head wonderingly at Fanny's clumsy efforts to clean up the sticky mess and left the room.

"May I leave the table, Father?" Clem asked, watching Edith and Fanny on their knees sweeping up the piles of damp brown sugar.

"Yes. The driver's waiting." He flicked a blowfly from the lace cover hanging over the milk jug and chased it off with his napkin. It buzzed up to the ceiling, awaiting its next opportunity.

The sweet tang of orange marmalade followed Clem to her room. She shut the crystal bowl and the bird book away in her bureau and, tucking Mrs. Brennan's letter into her purse, looked once more around her pretty blue room. "Farewell, room." She blew it a kiss as she shut the door. "Until two years."

Chapter Five

Clem looked back once, but she could not see her father or Kathy behind the thick cloud of dust in their wake. At least he'd kissed her good-bye; that is, she thought ruefully, he'd lowered his head so I could kiss him.

Her mother sat huddled in the opposite corner, dressed for town. Her traveling dress was a bright turquoise, quite extravagant for Burrundi, thought Clem, as she noticed the abundance of trimming on the small bonnet. "You look lovely, Mama," she lied. "But you do look a little tired; are you unwell?"

"I have been unwell for years."

"I'm surprised Father doesn't send you to a doctor in Sydney."

"He would begrudge the money. No, he would rather I rot in my room than set a foot in Snydey. Without him I would be a pauper. So you see I can't go there myself. Your Aunt Margaret could afford a surgeon, but she doesn't trust the sawbones for some reason."

"But surely you could just see a doctor. Couldn't Aunt Margaret have you to stay, too?"

"Next summer she'll have me, as I'm coming to see you ."

"Oh, I hope so!" Clem felt a little happier. Her mother was not deserting her altogether. "You *will* come?"

"I am determined to, in spite of your papa."

Her mother settled herself more comforably in the wide button-backed seat, staring out the window at the endless paddocks. Clem sat back, too. She could think of nothing to say as she saw her beloved Querilderie floating past. At least *it* would still be there on her return. Whatever happened to the people, the land would remain the same. Her mother breathed deeply, her eyes closed. She doesn't want to talk either, thought Clem. She tried to sleep but kept thinking of her aunt's house, and her aunt's unaffectionate face and manner.

Suddenly her mother opened her eyes and took Clem's hand. "I must tell you something."

"What?" Clem instinctively withdrew her hand from her mother's silk-gloved grasp. She hated intimate revelations.

"About your aunt—and me. You're old enough to know now." She drew in her breath. "Your father was supposed to marry *her*—Margaret—but he married me instead. I had no money, but he thought he loved me more than he did her. Goodness, how romantic that sounds! It wasn't. The whole thing was—is—dreadful. Your aunt should have been your mama and it is all a terrible mistake."

"Mother! I am *your* daughter!"

"Yes. Although your father would have had it otherwise."

"Rubbish, Mother. I don't understand." She felt as though she might burst into tears. "You and Father are just the same as all couples—quite happy—I—"

"Yes, yes, of course. But you see she was engaged to John before Edmund, my brother—God rest his soul—passed away. You see, Edmund and your papa were brother officers. When he died John sent for *both* of us, as Margaret was entrusted with all the money and was virtually my guardian. So I came out here from England, and I married him instead." She pouted at Clem like a conspiratorial schoolgirl. Then she shrugged. "She'll tell it all differently. Never mind. Don't argue with her." She took Clem's face between her hands. "No, never argue with your Aunt Margaret. She may be your only salvation!"

"Please, Mother! What can you mean!" Clem was suddenly numb with shock. Her mother's face was deathly white, her eyes terrified.

"Your *inheritance*. Your whole *future*—God knows what will become of you—if—" She searched frantically inside her purse, dragged out her smelling salts. "If that woman—"

"Aunt Margaret?"

"No!" Her mother sniffed at the bottle and let it fall into her lap. "No. It doesn't matter. Try to sleep, the journey to Sydney is awful." She dismissed Clem with a feeble gesture and sank back into the seat again, closing her eyes.

Clem was amazed at her outbrust. She was afraid of asking for a further explanation. Perhaps her mother was a bit touched by the sun. She was too frail to travel in such heat.

The brown plains and solitary gums slipped by behind a curtain of dust which lasted to Burrundi. Clem watched the movement of her mother's eyes. Every few seconds her eyelids would twitch nervously.

Clem spotted Burrundi from six or seven miles away across the flat land—a small settlement, stuck on top of the plain like a dark brown wart. One good dust storm and it would be flattened in an instant.

There was only one street in Burrundi, Darling Street, named after Governor Darling, and not, as she had once imagined, so called because the two rows of dusty, verandaed buildings were particularly beloved by their inhabitants.

The carriage stopped in front of O'Brien's store, while Jock, the driver, went in to buy a box of groceries for Mrs. Cameron's friend, Mrs. Oxley.

Two old men, their faces relaxed from a surfeit of rum, slept side by side under the veranda. At their feet lay two mangy red dogs. Their rib cages moved in and out rhythmically, the skin so taut across the thick bones it threatened to split.

Her father's sheep dogs were kept almost as thin as those two. They were fed only after a long day's hard work, then briefly petted, never at any other time. Her father said they preferred rank meat. "Treat them like dogs, they'll work like dogs!" His maxims were usually sound. He treated his men like men, too, not like servants. The trouble was, thought Clem, he didn't know how to treat children—women either. She didn't envy Miss Owen her time with the Cameron family.

Mrs. Oxley was Mrs. Cameron's dearest friend, her only friend mused Clem as the carriage pulled up at her modest residence. She was a poor widow whom Mrs. Cameron had taken under her wing when her husband, an emancipist doctor transported for mercy killing, had died some years ago. The cottage was nearly all verandas enclosed by wire screens, and the small plot of land was planted with close rows of orange trees, Dr. Oxley having been a great believer in the nutritious value of the orange. The property was surrounded by a dirty white picket fence.

Mrs. Cameron almost ran up the front path, helping Jock carry the box of groceries. Mrs. Oxley, a tall, thin woman with graying hair, met them at the front door. She told Clem to fetch herself some milk from the pantry and drew Mrs. Cameron into the tiny front room.

Clem's father had never approved of the friendship. One might employ members of a convict's family or even transact business with them, but anything more intimate was out of the question.

When Clem returned to the front room, the two ladies were seated together on the frayed, maroon velvet sofa, sipping brandy and talking in subdued tones. The room was dark and stuffy. Heavy curtains were drawn against the sun, and tiny rays of light just penetrated the tops of the folds, turning the dark red material to scarlet and the rough ceiling moldings to a translucent pink. The women's faces were hardly visible in the dark room. They seemed to talk in a cryptic language all their own.

"Here is your beautiful daughter." Mrs. Oxley gazed up at Clem, her face relaxed and suggestive of a former youthful beauty. "Run into the garden, dear, and pick some oranges for your journey."

Clem's mother jumped up from the sofa and ushered her briskly from the room, chatting gaily of her daughter's new wardrobe for Sydney and making jokes at the expense of Edith's old-fashioned ideas of dressmaking.

Mother enjoys the role of fairy godmother to Mrs. Oxley, thought Clem as she walked through the first grove of orange trees. She was quite a different character in that house, even her voice was lighter, and her step energetic.

She chose a dozen oranges, large, thin-skinned ones with blood-red patches, and started to peel one as she stood by the front gate staring at the deserted street. Having removed the tight skin and all the pith, she ate it, segment by segment, carefully licking the juice from each fingertip while still gazing at the wide expanse of Darling Street and the dust-covered shop fronts, mesmerized by the stillness of the town.

As she turned to go into the house, she heard soft footsteps coming from the other end of the street.

A man was approaching the picket fence. For a moment his face was directly above hers, blotting out the sun, and she couldn't see who it was, then she widened her eyes.

"Have you come all this way to say good-bye to me?"

"It'll be a long time before I see you again. I might be gone or you might never—" Matt's eyes, dark blue away from the sun, searched her face.

"I wish—" she stopped in confusion. She'd been going to say she wished she wasn't going and then had suddenly realized it was Matt she would miss more than anyone or anything, more perhaps than Querilderie itself.

He moved closer, one foot between two of the fence slats. "What?"

"Just that I'll miss you—I have a letter . . ." Her hand gripped one of the sharply pointed slats.

"You'll cut your hand." He lifted it from the fence. "I'll miss you, too." He lifted her hand and kissed it, rubbing it against his cheek and mouth. "I wish you'd—no—that's impossible."

She wanted to lean over the fence and hold him. His mouth was twisted with sadness. "I'll come back soon. Please don't go away."

"I'll come back for you if you want me to."

"What about Lizzie Bell?"

"She's nothing to me. I like her, that's all." He kissed her hand again, turning it over and kissing her palm and wrist.

Clem gave him the letter. She was flooded by a delicious feeling of relief. "Lizzie Bell doesn't love you like I do." She leaned forward.

Matt pressed his body against the fence and pulled her to him, kissing her hard on the mouth. Then he took the letter and stepped back from the fence.

Clem tried to tell him to give the letter to his mother, but the words wouldn't come.

"Good-bye." He turned and walked off down the street, his steps quickening as he reached the row of shops.

The picture of his anguished face remained vivid as a great lump welled in her chest and her eyes began to sting. She rubbed them, the orange juice only making them worse.

"Come inside, Clemency!"

Her mother was at the front door. "Jock will be back in a minute. Kiss your poor old mama."

"Oh, Mother." She bent to kiss her, and her mother returned the embrace, clinging to her and kissing her on each cheek. Clem could smell the brandy on her breath.

"Take care, my darling, and never forget your mama."

"I'll write every week. Will you come and wave?" Her mother's hands were on her cheeks. They were soft and damp, yet she could feel the slim bones pressing into her flesh. "Take care, Mama. You're so thin and pale."

"You mustn't worry about me. *Your* life is just starting."

Mrs. Oxley's shadowy form loomed behind her in the narrow hall.

"Please look after my mother." Clem knew no one else cared for her mother except poor Mrs. Oxley. The two women were happy only when sitting together in that tiny dark room, divorced from the vast uncaring plain which surrounded them, nourishing each other with affection and brandy.

Mrs. Oxley offered her hand. "I will, dear."

Clem took the long moist hand briefly in hers and then backed out the door. The whole house had begun to take on the smell of over-ripe grapes.

When the carriage reached the end of Darling Street, Clem thought she could still see her mother's figure behind the green of the orange trees, but it was only a glimpse of turquoise sky.

Chapter Six

Despite the oranges Clem was biting into compulsively, there was a hollowness in her stomach, and her throat was dry. Her father had rejected her, and her mother—already rejected by him long ago—had been too weak to take her part. Her father had been even more uncomfortable in her presence lately. Was she being sent away just because he still resented her for not being John Joseph Cameron? She started to peel another orange, angrily pulling off the pieces of red, bruised skin.

Her only comfort was the memory of Matt's face. He hadn't wanted her to leave. He and Querilderie were all that mattered—and her mother, but she was so faded and dejected it seemed a solid person made of flesh and blood by the name of Edwina Cameron hardly existed any more. If she really were ill, ill enough to waste away and die, her spirit would remain in Mrs. Oxley's small house, the only place where Clem had seen her truly alive.

She went over the events of the past week until her head throbbed. The idea that her mother's headaches were more serious than she'd ever imagined kept nagging at her until the last stretch of drab paddock and gray-leafed tree swam past the window and the town of Willawarrha appeared like a quivering mirage on the flat plain.

The carriage drove in through the stockyards—acres of runs in which tightly bunched flocks of sheep, pink with dust, bleated pathetically. Other runs held small herds of steer, continually jostling each other against the loose fence poles.

Outside the hotel, an imposing three-story building made top heavy by a protruding first-floor balcony, stood a tall thoroughbred, on which sat a young man, dozing beneath a wide hat.

Clem looked again. His face was vaguely familiar.

Jock silently opened the door, let down the steps, and followed her into the hotel where he signed the register and left her with the manager. Clem peeped through the door at the young man on the horse. She hoped he wouldn't recognize her, whoever he was, as she couldn't tolerate dandies like that.

The manager bowed obsequiously. It was in his interest to make the local squatters and their families particularly welcome. Their patronage raised the tone of any establishment from that of a grog shop with rooms on top to a good-class hotel. The owner of this one had discouraged rough trade by opening two rum shops at the other end of town. Unfortunately, some of the older hands still preferred their original haunt, and the barman was at that moment trying to shove a particularly stubborn and unruly character out the side door.

Clem watched, giggling, as the man was finally persuaded by a kick in the posterior to make his way to O'Halloran's Rum Palace at the other end of town. In the meantime, the manager had summoned the porter and she was taken to her room, a dark, frowsy little room with wooden walls and a door opening out onto the front balcony.

"Thank you." Clem watched the porter set down her trunks at the foot of the bed. He had the broad face and curly auburn hair of an aborigine. He stood by the door and stared at her from dark limpid eyes.

"What time is dinner?"

"Seven, miss." He backed out of the room slowly, still staring.

I suppose, thought Clem, as she studied her blurred reflection in the fly-spotted glass, we must appear stranger to them than they do to us. What must they think of our towns? They probably regard a place like Querilderie as I regard Sydney. She decided to do her hair and to wash properly in case there were any of her parents' acquaintances in the dining room.

The foyer was empty, the dining room also. The large square tables were laid with starched white cloths and a great deal of cutlery—heavy silver spoons, knives, and forks—softly glimmering in the faint light from the thick curtains.

She imagined that a promenade before dinner was the thing to do, so she stepped out the front door, and finding herself walking in the direction of those dens of vice, the rum shops, crossed the road and walked along one of the newer streets of the town. All the cottages were exactly alike, built of large gray stone blocks with small windows and corrugated iron roofs. Each had a brownish front lawn with a white pebbled path bordered by vivid pink and red geraniums. Their luminous petals seemed to have sapped every bit of moisture from the surrounding earth, the houses, too. They were slowly baking to dry dust beneath their white-hot iron roofs.

The nearest plant had started to glow with a strange intensity, suggesting the approach of twilight. Clem looked up at the sky which shone with the blue that heralded the gold time—that unearthly moment when everything and everyone turned to gold.

She walked back along the little road and onto the main street just as the sun went down. She peered up the side alleys for signs of life, but the town was quiet except for the distant bleeting of the sheep.

As she reached the hotel, an anxious manager met her at the door. "Where have you been? You were not supposed to go out unchaperoned, Miss Cameron. Your father's letter gave me strict instructions—"

"I'm sorry. I felt like walking."

The manager mumbled something under his breath and brushed a speck of dust from his tight trousers with a white lawn handkerchief. "Even I do not venture out after dark in this town. There are all sorts about—bushrangers, felons—up to no good." He sniffed and opened the dining-room door, ushering her in.

She remembered to put her shoulders back and walked stiffly to her place. The first person to draw her attention was the young man who'd been on the thoroughbred outside the hotel. She remembered him now. He was an acquaintance of Una Maclean's—a wild young man whom she'd met at a picnic in Camden. He didn't appear to recognize her, a fact for which she was grateful.

Three other people sat at a far table—a middle-aged woman, a man, and a younger woman. The man glanced up briefly. He was very dark, and his hair was extremely long and curly. Clem lowered her eyes. She ought not to stare so.

"Clemency!" Clem raised her eyes from the tablecloth to see Mr. Merilees standing beside her. "Such a lovely surprise! You must dine with Clara and myself!" He pulled out her chair and led her to where Clara Merilees was sitting, her face still flushed from the heat, her small eyes sparkling with pleasure at Clem's approach.

The usual polite dinner table talk ensued, Mr. Merilees chiding his wife whenever her gossip became too frightful. But she ignored him, telling Clem that men, when left to themselves, were far worse scandalmongers than women. After one particularly colorful story, she said, "George is such a hypocrite. He loves scandal as much as I do—his job *is* scandal after all!"

Mr. Merilees was genuinely annoyed. "Enough, Clara! That is enough!"

While Mr. and Mrs. Merilees ate in silence, Clem ventured another glance around the room. The young man from Camden had funny gold-flecked eyes which flickered continually from one person to another.

"I believe your aunt has many friends in the wool trade!" Mr. Merilees inquired, starting to devour a huge marmalade pudding.

Clem nodded.

"My wife and I would enjoy making her acquaintance."

"Yes indeed," Mrs. Merilees agreed.

Mr. Merilees quizzed Clem at length about her aunt's friends and made her promise to beg her aunt to call on them. "We'll be at Petty's Hotel."

"Of course she will call." Clem was still wondering how Mr. Merilees's job could have anything to do with scandal, unless it was the scandal of transportation. She smiled politely at both of them; they were a jolly couple after all, and not too English, either.

After dinner the company retired to a small drawing room, the young man with the wandering eyes introducing himself to Clem as a Mr. Pike, recently from the county of Somerset. The other three people asked the footman for an extra chair so they could sit in a corner of the room, far enough away from the Merilees for privacy. Clem was quite fascinated by the dark man. He had fine bones and deep-set eyes. She glanced surreptitiously at him during each pause in the conversation. His suit was an unusual cut and seemed too loose, hanging awkwardly from his broad shoulders. He once saw her studying him, and she blushed in confusion.

Mr. Pike, on the other hand, seemed intrigued with Clem. She could feel his eyes following her out of the room as she accompanied Mrs. Merilees upstairs, the latter very concerned for her rest as the next day's journey was to be a tedious one.

The bed had been turned down, and a linen nightgown and bedcap which had belonged to her mother's trousseau lay unfolded on the worn, pink quilt.

Clem picked up the cap. She had never worn one and did not intend to now. She would probably resemble Fanny Old in such a creation! She opened the window and leaned out into the warm night air. She heard voices in the distance, from as far off as the rum shops. The drunken rabble, as her father called them, was enjoying itself while she was confined to her hot cell.

How she would love to be a fly on the wall in one of those places. They were apparently full of bushrangers and murderers and loose women, whatever they were. She sighed and leaned further out, waiting for the return of a pair of drunken men walking arm in arm up and down the main street, singing a soft Irish ballad. She watched them pass the alleyway one more time, then as she turned to wash in the earthenware bowl, she heard whistling coming from the balcony.

She opened her door to see Mr. Pike, astride the balustrade, smoking a large cigar. "Ah," he exclaimed, "the lovely Miss Cameron has decided to join me in taking the night air."

"No, that is, I didn't know it was you."

"Or you wouldn't have come?" He got down and bowed, holding his cigar behind his back.

"I enjoy the night air, too. Are you on your way to visit someone in the Willawarrha area?" asked Clem.

"No. I have already done all my visiting."

"Are you a wool merchant?"

"You are very curious, Miss Cameron. No, I am not one of those. I am an entrepreneur."

Clem looked puzzled. "I don't know what that is."

"Then do let me enlighten you."

She waited with bated breath. The man's eyes were extraordinary. They could not keep still for an instant. They would swivel round to look over the balcony, then back to her door, then move up and down her person with such rapidity they made her dizzy.

"An entrepreneur is someone who deals in buying and selling anything from animals to gold, from properties to—to other people's debts. Do you understand?"

"What have you bought in Willawarrha? There are only sheep here."

"And rum!" He smiled indulgently at her ignorance.

"Do you sell rum to Mr. O'Halloran?"

"I might do—and other things. But that's enough questioning. These hot nights lead to not just the exposure of too much flesh—" here he stared at her throat and the tiny half-circle of her brown chest above her dress— "but to far too much of everything."

"My sister's governess says that. She never talks about herself anyway, but she always says she . . ." Clem knew she was gabbling, but the man's eyes unnerved her. "She says on these hot nights it is better for one to remain a closed book."

"Governess, did you say?"

Clem nodded. His eyes were riveted to hers now.

"What's her name? Is she fair? Would you say she was pretty?"

"Her name is Miss Owen and she is fair and I suppose—pretty. Oh, and she paints beautifully."

Mr. Pike was about to ask another question but thought better of it. "Well, Miss Cameron, it has been most interesting talking to you, but now I must be off to the rum shops."

"The rum shops!"

"You look positively outraged, my dear. They are establishments created in the utmost spirit of magnanimity where one may drink away one's sorrows undisturbed."

"Of course, but aren't they full of bushrangers and ladies who—who—"

Mr. Pike pretended to cough. "Some of my most charming acquaintances come from the ranks of the bushranging fraternity."

"Is it safe to go into those places?"

"As safe as anywhere else in this colony. It's a jolly sight safer than being on the roads at night. Better to drink with the chaps than to fight it out on the road with your pistol."

"Oh, yes."

"I wish I could take *you* with me, but . . ."

"Good heavens! Could I—I mean—"

Mr. Pike's shifty eyes stopped admiring her and swiveled back to the street. "Not tonight. I have some business, er, that is, with a landlord or two, don't you know." He bowed and left her, the smell of his cigar still strong in the humid night air.

Chapter Seven

At breakfast Mr. Pike tried to attract Clem's attention, but she did not acknowledge him. His eyes worried her; like their owner, they were far too busy.

She was relieved to climb into the waiting coach, if only to escape Mr. Pike's glances. She was still wondering why an English gentleman from Somerset would want to go anywhere near a rum shop, let alone converse with bush rangers and "loose" women. She settled herself next to the two women from the dining room who both wore very elegant afternoon coats. Next to them was a trooper, his uniform rank and mud caked.

The Merileeses, with a great deal of fuss about where their luggage ought to go, finally sat quietly in the stiff-backed seats, and the coach trundled out of town onto the Sydney Road.

The passengers were silent for the first few miles, until Mr. Merilees coughed politely, then made a lengthy speech on the monotony of the scenery.

"I don't think it's monotonous at all," Clem said nervously. "Each tree is quite a different shape from the last, and there are hills and sometimes kangaroos."

She felt the blood rush to her cheeks as the dark, curly-haired young man looked her squarely in the eyes and said, "How right you are. Nothing about scenery can ever be *monotonous*. It changes constantly, even if it is only with the weather or the wind. And the driest, most windless desert is capable of producing mirages." He looked at Mr. Merilees with a half smile. "So you see, sir, that even the blankest landscape, like the blankest mind, is capable of the wildest fantasy to relieve the emptiness."

"You have convinced me, sir." Mr. Merilees winked at Clem.

Clem could not acknowledge his wink as her eyes were transfixed by the dark man's. "I see you are a native, Miss—"

"Cameron," whispered Clem, "Clemency Cameron." She managed to drag her eyes away and look past him.

The trooper asked Mr. Merilees if he were intending to settle in the colony, then wiped his brow with the back of his hand, leaving a large black smudge on his forehead.

Mr. Merilees explained his brief to the trooper who at the mention of wool sat bolt upright in his seat. "Wool! Now there's a subject close to my own heart!" he exclaimed. "I am in these parts also because of wool. Whole drays of the stuff are disappearing before our very eyes!"

"Good gracious—whatever do you mean?" Mrs. Merilees extracted a tiny ivory fan from her purse and fanned herself vigorously.

"There are one or two gangs of thieves—we call the bounders bushrangers—working these roads, and they have purloined so many dashed wool drays it's not funny. My horse was just shot from under me and two of my best men wounded. We still don't know where they hide the stuff or how they get it to Sydney or any bloody thing!" He coughed into a filthy handkerchief. "Pardon my language, ladies. I've been stranded out in this hellhole for too long. I'm a Northampton man myself. Captain Orville, at your service." He saluted each lady in turn.

"My dear Captain—how dreadful!" Mrs. Merilees leaned forward a little. Now that the man had established his rank as an officer, she was not afraid to breathe his air, no matter how soiled. "What do you propose to do about all of this?"

"We intend to catch the fellows red-handed on the roads and hope they'll tell us who's behind it. Someone must buy the wool—someone who has enough money to afford it."

"And there must be a go-between, someone who arranges the 'deals.' Is that how it works?" asked Mrs. Merilees.

"We believe so, ma'am. There are not a few wealthy Sydney wool merchants who wouldn't be above receiving a stolen clip or two, you know."

"Never, Captain! My husband and I have met such men, been entertained in their most gracious homes—never!"

"Ssh, Clara," Mr. Merilees frowned. "We ought not pursue this subject, Captain Orville. These matters are a little confidential to be discussed so openly."

The captain nodded and stretched his legs, preparing for sleep.

Clem, completely disregarding Mr. Merilees's warning, asked, "How can it be transported without anyone noticing it?"

The captain yawned pointedly. "We can't check every vehicle at the Sydney tollgate. Thousands of pounds' worth of stolen wool has been transported to Sydney by the Parramatta Road over the past few months." He stretched his legs again. His face was cruelly burned, and he reeked of stale sweat.

Mrs. Merilees whispered to her husband. "Surely it would not be worthwhile for those merchants to buy the wool. Don't they have enough already?"

"It's a criminal's market, dear. They would pay half the market value of the wool and gain vast profits. Now, please, let's drop the subject." Mr. Merilees stared out the window, pretending not to listen as the dark man questioned the captain further.

Clem tried not to look at him. He was very pale with a luxurious black beard. "Are these men escaped convicts or free men?" he asked.

"A few of both. Some are against the government for not granting them land as freeborn colonials while the Englishman with a bit of capital behind him is entitled to buy up acres and acres of it."

"And with their ill-gotten gains they will no doubt venture into the remoter areas to squat, just like so many others have done before them." The dark man, of indeterminate age, seemed pleased with his conclusion. "After all," he went on, "when the law finally reaches those areas, they will be too well established for the law to remove them."

Clem nodded. "Squatters like my father have appropriated crown lands and been allowed to keep them."

"Indeed, yes, and by means of the same laissez-faire policy."

Clem could understand why men turned outlaws in the face of such privilege enjoyed by the tiny minority of squatters. She had so often heard Matt complain of her father's thousands of acres and his own father's miserable three hundred, and that bought with his mother's money, earned while his father still served his time. It was unjust, decided Clem, that selector's sons—men who were born in New South Wales—had far less chance of owning enough land out of which to make a living than a "Johnny Grant" did, a man with a bit of inherited money from home. No wonder Matt had sometimes looked at her with contempt.

"Thank God, Port Philip is a free colony," said the older lady, a smooth-skinned, middle-aged woman with an English accent.

"But you have the *exiles*," said Clem.

"What are they?" asked Mrs. Merilees. She was beginning to succumb to the heat, her fanning hand weary and her hair falling about her cheeks in wet ringlets.

"That ridiculous probationary scheme of the Home Government's. They do not appear to know where else to abandon their undesirables," the Englishwoman answered, thoroughly disgusted.

The dark man grinned. "What about the undesirables who abandon themselves there, Mama?"

"It's all Mr. Gladstone's fault. *Exiles* indeed! They're just another form of criminal, probationary or not!"

"Mr. Gladstone needs cheap labor for his property, don't you know." The dark man laughed and, looking at Clem, asked, "Have you been south at all?"

She shook her head.

"It's so green—so like home," said his mother, sighing at the scene outside. "So green!"

"As green as Miss Cameron's eyes."

Good heavens, he'd actually said that in front of all those people! Clem stared at her tightly clasped hands in her lap.

"William!" His mother scolded, "Please don't be so forward! My dear," she touched Clem on the knee with her fan, "may we introduce ourselves? I am Mrs. Thomas Purley and this is my daughter, Hester, and my son, Mr. William Purley."

Clem then introduced the Merileeses, Mrs. Merilees inquiring immediately why the family was traveling the enormous distance from Port Philip to Sydney.

Mrs. Purley explained that her son was a painter and they were on their way to set up house in Sydney for him while he established himself there as a teacher.

Mrs. Merilees continued, "What do you paint, Mr. Purley?"

"Landscapes, my dear lady, landscapes."

"My brother had a commission from a Mr. Findlay MacLelland to paint his wife and daughter. Are you acquainted with the family, Miss Cameron?" Hester Purley turned to Clem.

"My parents are."

"Does your son obtain many commissions from the squatters' families?" Mrs. Merilees asked.

"Er, yes, quite a few, you know. Nearer to Port Philip, of course. My husband is a landowner there, you see."

"I see." Mrs. Merilees seemed quite breathless. Clem wished she would try to sleep. She always asked so many questions. "And was the MacLelland portrait a success?"

"There was no portrait!" Mr. Purley laughed ironically.

Mrs. Purley frowned at him. "William decided, after dragging his poor old mother and frail little sister all these hundreds of miles to the west, that he would not paint either Mrs. Findlay MacLelland or her daughter!"

"They insisted on hiring a coach for us so I felt obliged to come and tell them in person why I wouldn't paint his 'Gainsborough' portrait." Mr. Purley laughed.

"It was really too much of William." Hester Purley took off her little blue bonnet and shook her damp ringlets. "Really too much."

"Couldn't bear the sight of the fellow after a bit. He had already decided on the painting—colors, costumes, even the composition! Wanted fir trees and a loch—a loch!"

Clem giggled. "Do you prefer billabongs?"

"Why not? If I knew what the deuced things were. And gum trees and brown grass and wallabies and all the rest of it. I'd paint the natives, too, given half a chance. Blighters won't stand still for long enough."

Mrs. Merilees nudged her husband. "Mr. M. and I saw a native just outside Willawarrha, didn't we, dear? He stood still for a very long time—and on one leg! He curled one leg about the other and stood like that for ages. We stopped the carriage to look at him. He was like a statue."

"They don't like a fellow to paint them. They believe part of their soul, or whatever they call it, will be taken away from them."

"That's true in a way." Clem pondered this idea for a few seconds. "My friend Mathew Brennan says that certain members of the tribe are forbidden by law to look upon certain others. Perhaps it is just as dangerous to have one's image looked upon."

"Ah, yes." Mr. Purley regarded her thoughtfully, his eyes staring into hers disconcertingly. "I may have been born in England, Miss Cameron, but I am beginning to feel like a native now—about the countryside, I mean. I think you and I share a great deal in our appreciation of the bush country."

Clem agreed shyly. She wished she had a fan to hide her red cheeks. Now she understood why ladies used their fans so much.

"If I were to paint your portrait, I would regard it as more of a landscape. It would blend so naturally with its background. You are so *truly* a part of your landscape."

"I am flattered." Clem had never recieved a compliment from a gentleman before, apart from the jovial ones of Mr. Merilees. As she had no idea how to respond, she covered her cheeks with her hands and sought refuge by staring fixedly out the window, unfortunately so caked with dust that any pretense at sight-seeing was impossible.

The day grew too hot for comfort inside the airless coach. The upholstery, stuffed with horsehair, caused prickly rashes on the ladies' necks. Finally, it was agreed that the windows were to be opened wide, as suffocation by dust would be a preferable death to roasting alive.

Even Clem felt the heat. Her underwear was wet through. Miss Purley's face was a silvery mask of tiny droplets of perspiration. Her cheeks were no longer pale, unlike her brother's which were unhealthily white for someone who'd been in the colony for a number of years. Was that what his mother had said? Clem supposed that painters (a rare commodity in New South Wales) did not indulge in too much outdoor activity. She was strangely disturbed by the looks this phenomenal Mr. Purley gave her with his intense gray eyes.

The dust soon filled the coach, working its way into every fold of clothing and each tiny wrinkle of flesh. The passengers coughed and blew their noses. Finally, both gentlemen and ladies placed their handkerchiefs over their faces. Clem's tiny embroidered square hardly covered her nose and mouth.

Mr. Purley leaned toward her, speaking softly. "I'm glad your handkerchief is so inadequate, Miss Cameron, otherwise I would be denied the sight of those fine green eyes for the remainder of this hellish journey."

Her features were too suffused with heat to blush further. She knew she ought to say something witty, even scathing, to make a pretense at fending off the man's attentions, but she was at a complete loss.

Miss Purley came to her rescue. "William! Leave Miss Cameron be! You are annoying her!" She touched Clem's fingers with her fan. "Take no notice of him. He talks in this ridiculous manner to everyone."

"Rubbish, Hett. I usually don't talk to anyone at all. I want to paint Miss Cameron, therefore she and I must become thoroughly acquainted as soon as possible."

Miss Purley sat back, abashed.

"Me? Surely you don't wish to paint me. My mother says I am a tomboy and wild-looking. Why on earth should you want to paint me?" She waited for him to laugh at her.

"Why do I want to paint you? Probably because you have freckles." He gazed intently at her features.

"William!" His mother reprimanded. "Do not stare so! You are frightening poor Miss Cameron."

"Miss Cameron frightened? Not likely! Will you let me paint you? Freckles too?"

"I would—would be honored. But surely you have more important subjects—"

"No! You will do instead of a landscape. Is that settled?"

Everybody stared at her.

"Yes," she replied very faintly. She turned to the window again, this time holding her handkerchief tightly over her mouth. The dust made her eyes water until large brown drops ran down her cheeks.

The sun became even more relentless as it passed through the middle of the sky and bore down mercilessly upon the black roof of the coach.

By the time they reached Jebbo—a town, which to the inexperienced eye could have been Burrundi or a dozen others in that part of the world—Mrs. Merilees had to be revived by a smelling bottle, and Mrs. and Miss Purley both looked faintly green.

Jebbo was built on the banks of the Euragalla River, a wide, shallow waterway which was almost dry but would very quickly flood

the town as soon as the first rains came. The Jebbo townsfolk were
flooded every year. It never occurred to them to move their houses
further from the river. They looked forward to the annual flooding
with pride. Clem realized that their attitude was one of many ways
to keep up their tough pioneering tradition. To move the houses
away from the river would have been an act of downright effemina-
cy.

Their mosquitos were legend also. They boasted the biggest mosquitos in the Colony.

The passengers lunched at the Jebbo Inn upon dry mutton and
hard-boiled potatoes with a steam pudding for dessert. Poor Mrs.
Merilees was persuaded by her husband to stomach a little of the
mutton and immediately fled the dining-room to rid herself of it.
Clem followed, steering her toward a tiny vine-covered hut behind
the primitive inn.

Mrs. Merilees felt less feverish with an empty stomach and suggested they sit down on a wooden bench on the tide-marked veranda
of the inn.

"I'm afraid I'm not the pioneering type," she confessed, after listening with undisguised horror to Clem's stories of the Jebbo citizens' eccentricities. She'd shrunk from an attractive woman of fashion to a sopping wet rag doll with bright red cheeks. "What a fright I
must look!"

"Don't upset yourself. These journeys always have an unfortunate effect on newcomers to the colony. My sister's governess, Miss
Owen, is the same way. She cannot travel two miles in summer
without having a fainting fit."

"Why doesn't she take a position nearer the coast?"

"I don't know."

"I don't know why anyone who has been used to something better—of course I mean only in the way of *climate*—would voluntarily
bury themselves out here."

Clem wondered, too, especially about Miss Owen. She often said
she felt buried in the bush country, yet wouldn't even go into Willawarrha for ribbons without being bullied into going by Mrs. Maclean. She never went to Sydney for her holidays, preferring to
spend them painting all day at Glen Ross. Clem felt Mrs. Merilees's
forehead. It was cooler.

"Had you met that young man, Pike, before?" she asked Clem.

"Yes, at Camden."

"An interesting one that—and fancy riding such a great animal into town! He is a big-headed young man. What is his profession?"

"He said something about buying and selling things—rum, I think."

"Really?" Mrs. Merilees suddenly recovered her composure.

"He calls himself an entrepreneur." Clem shook out her wet skirts.

"Mmm . . ."

The two ladies rose to return to the coach when from around the corner of the building the tall figure of Mr. Purley suddenly materialized.

Mrs. Merilees smiled charmingly at him. "Ah, Mr. Purley. I'm sure you must know our friend, Mr. Pike, from the Willawarrha Arms Hotel?"

"The chap at the hotel? Never met him. Why?" He took Clem's arm. There was something pleasantly aromatic about him. He pressed her arm to his side and she felt absurdly excited.

"Like most young men in the colonies he is out to make a name for himself."

"Yes, probably," replied Mr. Purley, uninterested.

Mrs. Merilees was undeterred. "Is that how you would describe yourself, Mr. Purley?"

"I am concerned only with furthering my art, ma'am. If a name and fortune ensue, then so much the better."

"Many painters in London and Paris are forced to pursue their fortune by other means."

"With respect, ma'am, I have no doubt some reprobates indulge in all kinds of immoral activities, but I happen to have private means—my father's property, you know."

Clem was horrified. Older ladies might be allowed to question a gentleman so in *London*!

Mr. Purley squeezed her arm and laughed. "Don't be distressed, little bush maiden. Mrs. Merilees and I understand each other perfectly. She imagines that as you are the heiress to a few thousand mangy Merinos, I am after your innocent affections."

This made even Mrs. Merilees falter. "Goodness gracious, sir! You do me an injustice. I had no idea Miss Cameron was an heiress. No idea until this moment."

Mr. Purley, vastly amused, looked into Clem's eyes and said, "But I did."

He offered the ladies each an arm and escorted them back to the coach.

On the road once again, Clem pondered her newfound status and wondered who could have informed Mr. Purley of the extent of her fortune. She had never before thought of herself in the role of heiress. No wonder her mother was so intent upon her retaining her inheritance if it were universally presumed to be so large. She worked out on her fingers just how much the huge flock of Merinos was worth in gold coin and was agreeably surprised. Perhaps that Mr. Pike had known about her fortune and had tried to compromise her in some way. She suddenly felt very vulnerable.

They were to stay the night in the big town of Pringle. It was the junction of many roads and stock routes and the scene of a weekly cattle market and frequent sheep sales. It was also the favorite haunt of stockmen with a month's wages to squander, itinerant workers, and every traveler on his way west, south, southwest, or east.

Pringle represented to John Cameron everything that was wrong with the colony. It abounded in rum shops and unsavory females openly plying their trade upon the streets. Twenty-four hours a day the wide streets of Pringle were full of drunken, brawling men and women—the result, according to Clem's father, of excessive freedom. Ex-convicts were by nature incapable of helping themselves and, unless working for good masters, would spend all their money on liquor and less salubrious commodities. Until the governor built more jails and granted fewer pardons, Pringle would remain a hell on earth where all this freedom could be plainly seen for what it was!

Clem, given strict instructions to stay inside the hotel, did not accompany the others on the evening promenade to the Pringle River. She had to wait until they crossed by punt the next morning to view the wide mud flats and the yellow weed.

Mrs. Merilees had taken on the job of Clem's chaperone. She had written to Mrs. Cameron expressing her heartfelt desire to look after Clem's interests for as long as she and her husband were in Sydney. The letter had included a long list of impeccable referees and a section of her family tree, so that Mrs. Cameron would not be in the least alarmed. "You will be in good hands, my dear, if you let George and me escort you and present you to some of our Sydney friends. We know a lovely family of girls in Parramatta whom you would find most interesting." She enumerated countless good families who would be sure to accept Clem immediately.

Clem had no idea Sydney held such an enormous quantity of excellent, well-bred people. The Merileeses appeared to know everybody who was anybody in New South Wales. Those Parramatta girls sounded the most formidable of all! Highly accomplished and all engaged to the most eligible young men. The idea of actually having to enter their drawing room turned Clem's mind blank with terror. Perhaps she could feign illness or a sudden bereavement each time a visit was proposed.

That evening after dinner, when the sun and the claret had driven all the other passengers into a stupefied sleep, she sought the advice of a dozing Mr. Purley, whom she knew would be easily able to solve such social problems.

"You will have to establish a precedent. Make yourself known as an eccentric who abhors the company of more than one or two people at a time. In this way individuals may call occasionally, to eliminate a completely isolated existence, and you will be able to avoid invitations to those sickening formal gatherings to which I, too, am allergic."

"You, too? But why?"

"They just bore me. People have those wretched 'At Homes' so they can show off their newest piece of furniture from *home,* imported at great expense, or one of their relatives, also recently imported and dressed accordingly."

Clem laughed. "But I'm supposed to attend all these functions. You see, if Angus Maclean won't have me, and he won't, I'm sure, then someone else must, and whoever it is must have a fortune to match my own and must be *on the land,* otherwise my father will never speak to me again."

"Would that be a bad thing?" Mr. Purley asked.

Clem laughed again. "Perhaps not. But there must be someone to inherit Querilderie, that is, a man and his sons. I have a duty to Querilderie which overrides everything else."

"I see—so you are here for the marriage market."

"I suppose so," Clem said ruefully. "And it's all so silly, as I'm not yet seventeen."

Mr. Purley shook his head slowly. "That is sad. I had imagined you two or three years older. . . . "

Clem wondered how he could possibly have imagined that. She felt so ignorant and inadequate talking to this man. If only she had concentrated more on her lessons at the Misses Maybright's she might have been able to impress him somewhat. She would have to try to learn something as soon as possible, otherwise the kind of man whose company she so enjoyed would soon cease to enjoy hers.

Mr. Purley reached for her hand, then drew back. "Well, never mind. I'm sure you will remain unspoiled. I believe you have a natural instinct for seeing through sham—like me. We two are children of nature." He smiled.

Clem suddenly felt a warm glow of affection for this strange man. He was so understanding, he saw her problems so clearly, and he was so kind to her. She mentioned her proposed sittings, and he suggested he might give her drawing lessons in return for her modeling fee.

She was thrilled. If he saw her as a model rather than as a commission then he must really think of her as a good subject. She flushed with pleasure at his obvious interest in her. He was so completely different from anyone she'd ever met. She'd heard that artists were sometimes a bit extraordinary.

"I ought to pay you for my lessons."

"No, but you might try to drum up some students for me—I'll need some eventually, to be able to survive financially."

"You told Mrs. Merilees that you have money."

"Did I? Oh, the old fellow has some put away. Not much for me, I'm afraid. Nevertheless, I'll muddle through."

"You have a fond mother; she'll not see you starve." Clem regarded the sleeping Mrs. Purley. Her skin was not that of a country woman; it was too soft. There were no lines about the mouth and few about the eyes.

"Unfortunately it is I who must not see her—them—starve. While I'm in Sydney, I'm the breadwinner!" He seemed very amused by the whole idea and could barely contain his mirth.

Clem didn't know how to take these sudden revelations. She suspected that if they were not exactly lies they were somewhat exaggerated. "I wish you well then. I'm sure you'll find a studio and gather many students about you. There must be few painting teachers in Sydney."

"There was only one in Port Philip and that was I. I had few pupils, however, as the place is still pretty primitive in spite of their lack of a criminal class. Amazingly they regard themselves as highly civilized down there and Sydney as a kind of northern hell!"

Clem started to speak but he forestalled her. "That's enough polite conversation for one evening; I prefer the atmosphere of the grog shops to this stuffy little drawing room. Let's creep out of here while they're all sleeping and sample some of the Pringle rum."

"You mean I might accompany you?" She remembered Mr. Pike's half-hearted invitation and watched Mr. Purley's face for a sign that he was in earnest.

"Of course. I wouldn't go without you. However—" he paused— "you'll have to dress as a chap. Women—that is, nice ladies like yourself,—are not usually welcomed wholeheartedly in such places." He studied her build, then smiled. "My top hat and some old riding clothes, I think."

Clem jumped up from her seat and clasped her hands above her head. "A rum shop!" she breathed, as Mr. Purley laughed and pointed to her head. "And plait your hair or it'll fall out of the hat; it's bound to be too big."

Five minutes later, dressed in Mr. Purley's ill-fitting riding clothes, her hair plaited and concealed under a shiny top hat, Clem followed her companion to the foyer. Mercifully it was empty and the two gentlemen made their way down the middle of the starlit road to the rum shops.

"Will I have to drink the stuff?" asked Clem, as he took her arm, suddenly aware of the possible consequences of her folly.

"No, just pretend. Oh, and as you couldn't possibly pass as any kind of gentleman in that rigout, for God's sake keep up your delightful country accent."

Clem was cruelly abashed. Until that moment she'd no idea she possessed such a thing. She'd been striving to improve her vowel sounds each time she'd opened her mouth at the two inns, remembering her promise to her mother and not wanting to appear entirely uncultivated to all these refined city people. She shrugged. "Very well," she mumbled and tried to walk like Matt, her hands in her pockets.

Suddenly Mr. Purley started to roar with laughter until, alarmed at his raucous display, Clem shouted at him to stop. "Someone might discover us! And we might never get to the end of the road! And if my father ever found me out—he'd—"

"What?"

"He'd send me to jail!"

"Rubbish. Everything you do at your age is part of your education."

"Well, so far I know nothing at all. This will have to do instead. I can't even hem sheets!"

Mr. Purley pulled her round to face him. "I wager a girl like you can dance and ride magnificently!"

"The former no, the latter I have some proficiency in." Clem wondered if he had really imagined her to be eighteen. She *would* be seventeen quite soon. She tripped along by his side, suddenly feeling quite important.

O'Halloran's Rum Palace advertised its unwholesome presence by a large sign over what in another kind of establishment would have been a front door. This entrance was merely a gap in the stone wall which bore neither door nor frame. Two drunken men sat along either side of it, as inert as a pair of stone lions. Clem could hear low laughter and a tune, delicate and sad, from a high-pitched instrument.

"Swagger a bit, me fine fellow," urged Mr. Purley as he unceremoniously pushed her through the entrance. "There it is." He pointed to a row of barrels lined up against the opposite wall, lit by candles stuck to plates on the wall shelf above. Clem could see nothing but this dim scene, as all else was in darkness.

A bout of agonized coughing greeted them as they stepped over the pairs of feet to reach the rum. Gradually the feet became visible and she sensed staring eyes. Looking around for faces, she made out only vague shapes. The coughing stopped as a gobbet of spit was ejected loudly against a wall. Someone grunted, and the low chatter started up again, the music, too. It was a flute.

Mr. Purley banged his fist on top of one of the barrels.

A guttural voice called out, "Help yourself, Squire. Leave the pennies on top!"

"Thanks, friend." He reached up to take two small pewter mugs from the wall shelf and filled them to the top, polishing the rim of Clem's with his sleeve before he handed it to her. He threw some pennies onto the top of a barrel with a loud clatter.

The faces were now visible in the candlelight. They were strikingly similar, dark and heavily whiskered, with deeply furrowed foreheads. Most of the men wore wide-brimmed hats which hung from thick cords biting into the hard skin of their sunburned necks.

Clem drew in her breath and turned her head away. Any or all of them might have been her father's stockmen!

"Drink up!" Mr. Purley jogged her arm. He finished his in one gulp and poured another.

She lifted the mug to her lips and tasted the rum. It was like fire! She tried not to choke. "You'll have to drink it, I can't," she whispered.

The talking had increased in volume and Clem knew that no one would be looking at her now. She followed Mr. Purley as he pushed through the crowd to the far corner of the room.

They passed a table where two women sat, one with her feet up, the other sprawled across her chair like a bundle of washing. The former resembled Lizzie Bell, and the latter—Clem stared—the latter did not resemble anyone or anything Clem had ever seen or dreamed of in her brief, sheltered existence.

She almost tripped over her feet in astonishment. The woman had frizzy gold hair of a hue that was glaringly unnatural even in that dim light, and her face was painted so heavily it glowed! The bodice of her dress was low enough to expose three quarters of her bosom! Her skirt was pulled up over her fat knees, and her calves crossed upon each other with a lewd disregard for propriety.

Clem had stared too long.

"Fancy a bit of that, do you, me darlin'?" The woman's loud, nasal tones caused Clem to shrink back in alarm. Suddenly she grabbed Clem's knees and pushed herself up from her sprawling position to press her bare bosom into Clem's waist.

Clem screamed and freed herself from the woman's hold, falling back against Mr. Purley. Her rum flowed over the woman's head. The latter kicked at her and swore so vilely Clem was incapable of any response.

Mr. Purley was heaving with laughter, trying to drag Clem backward across the room while the woman continued to scream obscenities at them. In the confusion Clem heard a man say that the lad was too young to do the right thing by Yellow Mary anyhow, and the whole place erupted in abandoned mirth.

Having recovered her balance and extricated herself from Mr. Purley's arms, Clem ran into the middle of the road. "Will she follow us?" she cried, pushing one loose plait inside her hat. "What is she?"

Mr. Purley looked wonderingly at her. "For such a wild one you are amazingly naive. She is a lady of the streets, only in her case she does not go so far to ply her trade but does so only in the room above that stinking den."

"Oh, good heavens!" She started to brush her clothes frantically. She had been accosted by one of those women! They were diseased!

He took her arm kindly. "It's quite safe to touch them; they transmit their infections by other means."

She did not know whether or not to believe him, unsure of what other means they might possibly employ. The woman had spat at her. She inspected her clothes, finding them free of muck, thinking all the time of the woman's distorted face and the line of froth between her bright red lips. "I want to go back to the inn, please."

She reached her room without further incident and hurriedly shed her male attire, throwing it through the door to a highly amused Mr. Purley, who was, nevertheless, impatient to return to the rum barrels.

She wished him a subdued good night as he kissed her hand, then quickly retired to bed, putting on her mother's bedcap as a blow for gentility and remembering to pray for the soul of the ghastly wretch in the rum shop.

Clem had a nightmare that she would remember for the rest of her days. It was in vivid color: Lizzie Bell, painted and dressed like a porcelain doll, held Matt Brennan in her arms, while both of them laughed at her from the doorway of O'Halloran's Rum Palace.

The next morning it seemed that she had dreamed it again and again, yet it could have been only once, and then during the few seconds before she awoke, hot and sweating beneath the linen sheet and her mother's linen nightdress.

At first, in the coach, she could not bear to meet his eyes, being consumed with shame. She felt her absurd actions of the night before must have been the result of the colonial claret Mr. Merilees had insisted she drink with dinner. Perhaps she'd inherited her mother's derangement. Only a very flighty person would run off on a jape like that.

She'd scrubbed her body to get rid of any hideous disease the unclean harridan might have given her and washed her hair twice with soft soap, demanding extra hot water from the grumbling chambermaids. She could never wash away the shame of such an expedition, however, and again she wondered why gentlemen would wish to frequent places like that. Finally she did glance at Mr. Purley, and he looked back at her with such a light in his eyes and such a funny smile that she was forced to laugh at her old-maidishness.

"I'm sorry I spoiled your evening, Mr. Purley," she whispered beneath her fan.

"Don't mention it, my dear. It was a most delightful and, may I say, most amusing experience. You were the talk of the town er, that is, your alter ego. Such a rum chap! You might say!"

Mrs. Merilees perked up suddenly. "What was that?"

"Nothing, just a joke. Mr. Purley was making a joke at the expense of my thoughts upon Pringle morality."

Mrs. Merilees subsided thankfully into her seat, too exhausted by only three miles on the road, to attend to her chaperoning duties.

All the passengers were soon asleep; Mr. Purley, too. He had dropped his head on his sister's shoulder and his features, calm and white and so subtly molded, were quite lifeless, save for the gray shadows circling his eyes. She watched them contract and expand gently with each breath. She compared his face to his sister's. Miss Purley was one of those women who can at one moment be quite beautiful and at the next quite plain. Her skin was as soft as her mother's and completely unlined. Her features were slightly flat when she was asleep. She didn't look at all like her brother who had a much broader and finer bone structure and a paler skin. With her lips parted and a hot flush on each narrow cheek, Miss Purley's nostrils became suddenly obvious in their roundness, a roundness too marked against the rest of her appearance.

They stayed one more night at a hotel high in the Blue Mountain ranges, invigorated by the fresher air and wooded atmosphere, but when they reached the Parramatta Road on the afternoon of the next day they were exhausted and almost dehydrated. The sun had again transformed the coach into an oven.

The Parramatta Road was packed with bullock drays loaded with wool bales and some with delicately balanced mountains of thick logs from the forests of the North. Herds of cattle and tightly bunched flocks of sheep blocked the road at every mile. Public houses lined the route, their patrons overflowing into the road. The air was heavy with dust and the raucous voices of the draymen. Mr. Merilees closed the windows, sealing the passengers safely inside their burning box.

Clem saw a family of half-starved, vermin-ridden natives sitting dejectedly outside one of the rum shops, apparently waiting for some kind of salvation. None would be forthcoming now, she thought sadly. They were the pitiful remnant of the bygone lords of this continent—creatures whom history would conveniently forget.

Chapter Eight

In the stale heat of the late afternoon, her body glued to Mr. and Mrs. Merilees by damp clothes caked with dust and rank with sweat, Clem realized they were stopping at the tollgate. She mentioned this to the others, all of whom were semiconscious and did not so much as nod at her happy news. She tried to peer out the half-opened window at George Street, the main thoroughfare of Sydney town, but could only glimpse the post office and market place briefly as the coach trundled through the heavy traffic toward the docks.

She had already exchanged addresses with the Merileeses and Mr. Purley and was in the process of arranging her first sitting with him when she recognized her Aunt Margaret's carriage drawn up at about twenty-five yards from the stables. She made a hurried farewell and hastened toward Miss Thorne's groom who had been sent to collect her trunks.

Clem prayed that her aunt was not in one of her moods. She was such a well-organized, punctual woman that any delay or even the slightest disturbance of her daily routine would either produce tears or, when she was feeling particularly well, a very nasty temper.

Clem knew the coach was late and her aunt would be upset. She prayed for tears rather than anger, as the latter was sometimes frightening.

She could see her aunt's hard, white face staring at her from the window of her elaborate carriage.

"Aunt—"

"I have been waiting here, in this dreadful heat, by these dreadful docks for over two hours! No, don't interrupt. What possessed you to be so late? It's a disease with your family. Your mama was the same. She will be late for her own funeral!"

"But, Aunt—"

"Don't 'but' me, Clemency!"

"No, Aunt, you see it was the road's fault. Did you expect me to run all the way from Parramatta?"

"How I loathe unpunctuality—it is a vice!" Her pale blue eyes brightened with frustration.

"I'm so sorry about your long wait. Couldn't you have ordered tea?"

"Who from? The felons working on the docks? The sailors, perhaps?"

"The groom might have fetched it or—"

"They had to stay here to protect me. A lady must be protected on a Sydney street. We are still on the frontiers of civilization here." Her aunt leaned forward and planted a firm kiss on Clem's cheek and squeezed her hand, a gesture of forgiveness. "Why I haven't sailed for home years ago, I don't know. To look after *your* interests, my girl, that's why."

Clem sighed as she settled herself in the seat. "I hope we can reach your house without delay, then you can have your tea within a few minutes."

"Within a few hours more likely. The traffic in Sydney is atrocious! Too much recent money driving too many fancy vehicles. The place has deteriorated since you were last here. All that building by speculators for all kinds of jumped-up people. Goodness knows where it will all end—in purgatory, I'll be bound."

Clem wasn't listening. She remembered Mr. Purley's comments upon Sydney society and thought ruefully of the months ahead as she stared out the window at the Sydney streets. They were hot and dusty and too full of people. She knew she wasn't likely to meet anyone remotely like Mr. Purley among her aunt's acquaintances and hoped she might slip away unnoticed to visit him. She opened her purse and looked in her diary for his address. It was in a region called "The Rocks."

"Aunt," she inquired, as soon as Miss Thorne had paused for breath during her never-ending tirade against the Sydney new rich, "where is The Rocks?"

"The Rocks?" Her aunt paused and then made a sudden grab for Clem's bonnet. "What is *that*?" She removed it from her head and laid it on the seat. "The Rocks? Why it's an area down near the docks, a very rough place."

"But how far is it from the Point Piper Road?"

"Miles—but why are you so interested? Surely you—"

"I'm not interested at all really," lied Clem. "Someone mentioned it on the coach journey, that's all." She realized that any mention of an artist would horrify her aunt. Respectable people did not know artists; they only knew *of* them. She would find it difficult to walk all that way and back again without anyone finding out, so she would have to think of another more devious means of renewing their friendship. Perhaps if she were to behave extraordinarily well, to study hard and be extremely polite to her aunt's friends over the next few weeks, she might be allowed to sit for him.

For a moment she was tempted to tell Aunt Margaret all about him. She so needed to talk about him, but she stopped herself just in time. It would have only started an argument, and reasoned argument with her aunt was impossible.

Aunt Margaret was absolutely set in her ways and views. She made a virtue of being wilfully ignorant of any modern ideas upon manners or society, and for over twenty years her daily pattern of existence had not varied except by the rare accident or Act of God. Clem knew that she must fit into her aunt's household like a new, unobtrusive piece of furniture. She must be cut down, remodeled, and wedged firmly into Aunt Margaret's routine, now so sanctified by time it could not possibly be stretched to accomodate her.

"I have spoken to the Misses Maybright about you. They will take you on provided there is no further nonsense. Theirs is one of only two possible establishments in Sydney, so for heaven's sake behave."

"Of course I—"

"Good." Clem felt her aunt's thin body go tense. "How is your mama?"

"Not very well."

"The headaches again, is it?"

"Yes, and she seems a little, I don't know . . ."

"Vague? She has always been given to fancies and vagaries. She hasn't done her duty by you either. You are still a tomboy."

Clem was about to say how very grown up she was feeling but realized it would seem silly. She *had* aged over the last few days and wondered if it was Mr. Purley's attentions which had affected her. He had noticed her as a *person*. Mr. Merilees had done the same; he'd said she was a colonial beauty, and Mr. Purley had likened her to a landscape! Until then, she'd had no identity of her own, hardly even a family identity. Neither of her parents ever spoke of a family or a past. Other than the sampler in the hall and their one family portrait—her father's mother, a thin woman with severe hair and fanatical blue eyes—there was nothing to look back upon, no family continuity. But perhaps there was not much of that in many colonial families.

Both men had identified her with her country, had expanded her existence, which in Sydney might have become even more hazy and uncertain. It did not matter so much now, her father pushing her out of the way for reasons of his own. She *may* have been an exile—as much an exile as those poor people the Home Government was condemning to life in Port Philip Bay—but Mr. Purley had made her feel important, at least to herself.

"Thank goodness, we're here at last." Aunt Margaret brushed imaginary specks of dust from her coat and fidgeted with her gloves and curls. "Your mother was always a sickly little thing, drinks too much brandy, too. They all do out there; they tell you it's the heat! More like the boredom in your mother's case. She was always a terror for the gay life."

Clem remembered her mother's lithe figure flitting about Mrs. Oxley's tiny house. That was the only time she'd ever seen her exhibit any natural gaiety.

Aunt Margaret grunted as the coach stopped. "I really must have that drive rolled. Well, here we are. Just retribution—that's what I call it. Twenty years of boredom has no doubt cured her of a little of her flightiness."

"You sound very bitter."

"Bitter? Yes, I'm bitter. So is he. He'll not let her come to Sydney. He would rather his daughter travel unchaperoned than let her come."

"What do you mean?"

"It's his way of punishing her."

Clem felt her face color violently with shock, "What on earth has she— did she— do?"

"She deceived him into marrying her."

"Deceived him?" Clem's hand trembled as she leaned over to open the carriage door.

"Yes, she trapped him in a most disgraceful manner. I shall never forgive Edwina as long as I live." Her aunt squeezed past her as the groom let down the steps. "But that's enough of that."

"You seem fond of me, yet I'm her daughter. I—"

"I'm very fond of you. You are so like your papa."

"My poor mother is unhappy and ill. You should feel sorry for her. All that was twenty years ago." Her voice was quivering with anger.

"When one is forty-three years old, twenty years seems quite recent."

"Yes, Mother says you never change, that you've looked the same since you were first in Sydney."

"That is the ordered life, my dear. No husband, no children to worry me. No financial troubles and good wholesome food. But above all—order."

"Order?"

"A regular routine for one's social life, private life, and toilet."

"Oh." Clem nodded, remembering that it was no use being angry with her aunt, as she ignored all displays of emotion.

"So my poor mama deserves her headaches. You must *hate* her."

"And one must eat plenty of fruit. It is so good for the complexion, and—"

"Aunt!"

"Never leave your front door without bonnet and gloves. Remember the lines."

"Do you hate her?"

"Even if the face is unlined, the hands can give away the awful truth. Now, come along. The servants are waiting." Aunt Margaret elbowed Clem's bonnet into her grasp and stepped down onto the wide gravel area in front of the tall stone house.

It was built in the Regency townhouse style so popular with the wealthier citizens of Sydney and set fifty feet back from the road behind a high wall. The four Doric columns of the porch were her aunt's special pride. The garden was full of imported shrubs and flowers giving way to native shrubs and trees behind the house where the lawns were terraced down to a shallow creek. The creek meandered beneath heavy green foliage, then through a tunnel of tick bush where Aunt Margaret's garden met the next-door property. Clem remembered the creek as a place of refuge from her aunt's house, and she longed for its quiet banks before she had even reached the front door.

The staff was lined up to greet them. They stood silently on the wide sandstone steps. Nearly all were emancipists; some of the women still bore the marks of years of hard labor in the Female Factory. Clem shook the hand of each in turn just to show them she was not typical of her aunt's friends—a high and mighty lot left over from the early days who still believed it was imperative to keep one's distance from the criminal classes, freed or otherwise.

Her aunt bustled her off to her room on the first floor, leaving her to unpack with the help of a chambermaid, Biddy Wright, who had been dispatched during the last year of transportation for petty larceny. She'd stolen a cheap fairground brooch from her young mistress and had received seven years' transportation for her mischief.

Biddy kept her face averted, unwilling to talk. She merely nodded or shook her head at Clem's questions. She was a slim, fair-haired girl of about twenty-two or three, her skin hardened and lined from too much outdoor work, her mouth set into a straight embittered line.

To be deported from one's own country and family at the tender age of seventeen as a criminal, and for the kind of petty jape that every young girl commits sometime in her life, was surely a terrible injustice. Clem's anger at her own enforced exile was but a fraction of what poor Biddy must feel.

She noticed her wide pink ribbon lying on top of her trunk. She picked it up and carefully rolled it around her hand and offered it to Biddy, clumsily pressing it into her hand. "Would you like this? It doesn't suit me at all. It would go with your coloring, being so fair."

Biddy looked worried. "Oh, no, miss. You must keep it." She bent over the other trunk.

Clem touched her lightly on the shoulder. "But you must have it. Please, otherwise I'll throw it out."

"All right, I don't mind." She took it and put it in the pocket of her frilly apron. "Thank you."

Clem went on folding her starched underwear, packing it into the heavy walnut chest. Neither spoke until it was time for Biddy to help lay the table for dinner.

Tea had come and gone without Clem being sent for. She supposed the tidiness of her room was more important than the satisfaction of her appetite.

Biddy curtsied as she went out the door. "Dinner, miss."

"Will I see you tomorrow?"

Biddy just shrugged and hurried along the hall to the backstairs.

Clem wished now that she hadn't given her the ribbon. Biddy obviously regarded her action as some kind of insult, just the usual patronizing gesture of the mistress to the servant. It left her with a nervous feeling in the pit of her stomach. She hurriedly pulled off her clothes and did her hair, then searched for a suitable dress.

"Clemency, are you ready?" Her aunt's voice made her jump.

"Almost, come in."

"I am in. Now look, dear, I know you have a generous heart—like your father used to—but you must not go giving the servants things. I saw Biddy show that ribbon to Sybil, and proud of herself she was, too. They'll soon be after you for everything. It's just *bad training*."

"I wanted to give it to her as it didn't suit me."

"Don't make the mistake of being magnanimous to that lot. They just laugh at us behind our backs. Keep your distance or they'll exploit your kindness mercilessly."

Clem was speechless. Her aunt went on, lowering her voice. "Corrupt you, too. Oh, yes. Don't put it past them. The criminal type like nothing better than to corrupt the innocent."

"I'm sure your exaggerate Biddy's evil powers. She is a poor, wronged girl. I would be sulky, too, in those circumstances."

"You have fallen into the trap already. It happens to some degree to us all, but most of us soon get over it."

Clem managed to change the subject to her wardrobe, of which her aunt was highly critical. She expressed the opinion that Clem's dresses were as unfinished as she was, and she fussed about the room pulling out pantaloons and petticoats until the bed and floor were completely covered with piles of white cotton and linen.

"All this is very well for Menagerie but hardly the thing for Sydney!"

"Querilderie!" Clem stepped into a very stiff petticoat with some difficulty.

"You look as though you are mounting a horse," expostulated Aunt Margaret.

Clem sighed. "I wish I were."

"Angus Maclean will take you riding soon, when he returns from Edinburgh. He is due on the next clipper. You will make a good match, I'm sure."

"We will not!" Clem was flushed and hot and wished she might miss dinner. "Do I have to join you for dinner?"

"Of course. My friends, the Westons will be here. You will enjoy their company. You have exactly two minutes left in which to dress." Aunt Margaret's thin, straight-backed figure moved to the door without once altering its direction in spite of the heaps of clothes everywhere.

Clem clenched her fists and kicked the clothes out of her way as she sat at the dressing table. She looked at her muslin in the glass. It was not too hideous, although it looked a bit peculiar over that horsehair crinoline. Her face was pale and sulky, her hair dusty from the road. She prayed that this new couple who were being forced upon her would not be too old or too fashionable and had been warned in advance of her primitive state. Mr. Purley had expressed a delight in all things primitive, but she doubted her aunt's friends would share his preferences. She got up and slipped out of the stiff, uncomfortable petticoat.

She remembered nothing of the dinner apart from Mrs. Weston's concern for her mother's health. "I believe she's been ill these last three or four years. Do the doctors know what it is?"

Clem had just shaken her head.

"We can only hope it is not one of those dreadful wasting diseases," her aunt had said, inspiring a quick glance of shocked surprise between Mr. and Mrs. Weston.

Clem was excused early because of her fatigued state, and although she longed for sleep, she lay awake for what seemed like hours, wondering how much truth there was in the Weston's and her aunt's insinuations. Perhaps her poor mama was really very ill indeed.

She had to suffer many evenings alone with her aunt or her aunt's stuffy friends, with only brief walks in the forest and long hours of schoolwork—which had to be undertaken as her ignorance was so appalling—before she was allowed the privilege of seeing her friends the Merileeses again.

She persuaded her aunt to call, and as Petty's Hotel, although fairly new, was an agreeably respectable address, her aunt did so in quite a good humor and the Merileeses were invited to dine. They made a very favorable impression on Clem's aunt, so favorable they were not only invited again and again to Miss Thorne's house, but also to the houses of her friends and acquaintances which made Mr. Merilees particularly happy, as Mrs. Merilees never stopped reminding Clem, still regarding his amazing interest in wool as a huge joke.

"Mr. M. is still fascinated by wool, dear!" confided Mrs. Merilees one evening late in the month of August. "I do believe he would prefer me to be a woolly sheep rather than the human creature I am! It's all such a terrible bore!" She giggled, Clem, too, suddenly wondering just what her suitor Angus would like *her* to be. Not a sheep, but perhaps a young woman of far greater accomplishment and refinement than she now was, and prettier, too. If so, perhaps he might leave her be, which would be by far the best thing.

Clem smiled at Mrs. Merilees politely. Her behavior had been impeccable over the last few months, and she'd hoped by this time her aunt and Mrs. Merilees would think her responsible enough and sufficiently grown-up to be allowed to call on Mr. Purley. She had never ceased to think of him and hoped that by the time they were able to resume their friendship he wouldn't have forgotten her entirely. She would so enjoy his frank conversation for a change. She was usually quite unable to talk to most of her aunt's friends, especially the girls, none of whom had made any friendly overtures at all, unless pressed into them by anxious parents. They seemed to regard her with a kind of surprised resentment, as though she were a strange, exotic creature of whom they were a little afraid. Clem gradually gave up trying to talk to them and found efficient ways of ignoring them entirely without being too impolite.

At each of the Merileeses' visits she'd mentioned Mr. Purley's name, though so far she'd had no success. She sat staring at Mrs. Merilees, imagining her as a plump white sheep, then suddenly gasped, clapping her hand to her mouth. Her aunt must also be wondering what Angus would think of her—and what better way of impressing him than—"Aunt!" she cried, gripping the arms of her chair. "Do you think Angus would be more impressed with my charms if my portrait were to be painted? Isn't that the kind of thing one does to please one's fiancé?"

Her aunt, suffering from an effusive bout of kindness brought on by the burgundy at dinner, smiled at everyone in turn, then appealed to Mr. Merilees for his opinion.

"A capital idea! Indeed, yes! Capital! What about that chap—you know the fellow in the coach you women are always gossiping about—Purley? Would he accept the commission?"

The ladies remained silent, both pursing their lips, while Clem awaited Mr. Merilees's next idea.

"And I insist on paying the chap! If her fiancé won't have it, then I will! What a souvenir of the Antipodes, Clara—well—what do you say?"

Mrs. Merilees nodded. "I shall chaperone her, Margaret, you need have no worries. The fellow was quite respectable, that is, respectable enough for an *artist*, and his family appear quite well to do."

Aunt Margaret was forced to nod, and then when not one other artist could be thought of for the commission, she was good-naturedly badgered into loaning her carriage for the next afternoon.

Clem was overjoyed, and, miraculously, they *did* set out the next day and soon found themselves outside the small terraced house in Argyle Place which, ordinary though it was, proved on second reading to be the same address which Mr. Purley had written in the last page of Clem's diary.

Chapter Nine

"An interesting neighborhood," remarked Mrs. Merilees, not making the slightest move toward alighting from the carriage. She looked askance at the narrow houses, with their ornate cast-iron balconies and tiny attic windows.

"It looks perfectly respectable," said Clem. "And the gutters are clean." She leaned over to open the door, calling to the groom to let down the steps.

Mrs. Merilees still appeared reluctant to descend.

"You stay here while I knock at the door." Clem did not listen to her protestations, but jumped down from the carriage and ran up the two steps onto the veranda of the house. The cast iron was painted a bright yellow and there was a small date palm potted in a wooden barrel next to the yellow front door.

She knocked twice, feeling butterflies in her stomach and listening for signs of habitation.

The door was opened slowly by Miss Purley, neatly framed in the narrow strips of yellow wood. She was clad only in a peignoir, her face unpowdered and her hair hanging loose over her slim shoulders. "Oh, Miss Cameron! I, we had not expected you!"

"I am sorry if I've arrived at an inconvenient moment, Miss Purley. I was in the area and remembered your brother's kind invitation to—"

Miss Purley looked a little preoccupied but said, "Come in, come in." She disappeared down the dark narrow hall.

Clem beckoned to Mrs. Merilees who descended grandly from the carriage and carefully lifting her skirts climbed the small steps and stood just to the right of Clem, trying to peer over her shoulder.

Clem's butterflies were now dancing wildly. She walked slowly down the hall. "Miss Purley," she called, "are you there?"

Mrs. Merilees did not follow. She appeared to be waiting for a formal invitation to enter.

Miss Purley's white face glowed at them from the end of the hall, "Do come in!"

Clem went back to Mrs. Merilees and taking her silk-gloved hand pulled her along the hall and as far as the doorway of a room which might have been a kitchen.

The walls were hung with Arabian rugs and the windows curtained with cashmere shawls of an Indian or perhaps Persian design. Clem stayed in the doorway, studying the intricate blue-and-green pattern of a tall vase full of dried feathery grasses which stood beneath one of the windows. Her eyes moved slowly from the vase to the dresser lined with heavy pots of brushes and broken pieces of Chinese porcelain, then back to the walls again. The strange room possessed a faint scent of pomander, like her aunt's linen cupboard.

In front of the dresser was a long table piled high with books and papers and at one end sat Mrs. Purley. At the other, Mr. Purley, a faint smile starting to illumine his abstracted features.

When he saw her his expression changed to one of amazed delight. He jumped from his chair and came toward her, taking in every detail of her appearance with his light gray eyes. "You have come to let me paint you." He took her hand and kissed it, letting it fall reluctantly; and all the time his eyes appraised her face so intently she could feel every freckle, every tiny sun line.

She could not meet his eyes and stared at his clothes instead. They hung loosely from his lean frame, yet his shoulders were wide, and his hands—she resisted an impulse to touch them—strong and capable. He took her hand again and squeezed it until she felt a peculiar weakness overtaking her whole body.

"I—" she began.

"You do want me to paint you, don't you?"

"Yes." She lowered her eyes again. His had such a strange effect on her. He was even paler than she'd remembered, his beard longer and his eyes more deeply sunk into their dark gray sockets. She stayed in the doorway. He had mesmerized her into coming to him. She looked for Mrs. Merilees behind her, then saw that she was already seated at the table talking to Mrs. Purley.

Mr. Purley smiled at her again, this time so disarmingly she had to dispel her unaccountable notions of a moment before and found herself sitting next to him as Mrs. Merilees's eyes darted about the room, her fingers making fidgeting movements on the surface of the scrubbed pine table.

"How happy we are to see you again," said Mrs. Purley, regarding Mrs. Merilees's white silk fingers from the corner of her eye. "I do apologize for our circumstances, but we have not been able to, that is, I have been ill with a quinsy and my daughter—" she looked at her son, pleading with him to offer an explanation of their condition.

He patted his mother's hand and winked at Mrs. Merilees. "My dear mama exaggerates, as mothers will." Then he sat back in his chair and called to Miss Purley for tea.

"No! Do not trouble yourselves," begged Mrs. Merilees, looking about her for an uncluttered surface or any evidence of staff or even good housekeeping. "We're not staying." Her inspection stopped at a far corner of the room from where a naked, voluptuous female carved from yellow stone frowned at her with polished almond eyes.

"Do you imagine we are about to poison you, ma'am?" asked Mr. Purley.

"Not at all, sir. I merely suggested that—"

"I am now both a corrupter of child heiresses and a poisoner of innocent ladies!" He laughed, catching Clem's eye.

Clem giggled and Mrs. Merilees managed a pale smile as Miss Purley came through the scullery door with a tea tray. "Would you like tea?"

Her brother nodded, then as soon as she was gone from the doorway, he pushed back his chair and knelt at Clem's feet, kissing her hand with the greatest passion. "Ah, you magnificent creature of the wilds, you have not forgotten me, a humble artisan?" He grinned up at her, then after kissing her hand once more, he resumed his seat, waiting for Mrs. Merilees to speak.

Mrs. Merilees's mouth and eyes were round with shock. They

swiveled from the statue to Mr. Purley's face, then back to the statue.

Mr. Purley reached for Clem's hand and kissed it again, just as Hetty came in with the tea. "Tea!" she called rather ungraciously and set the tray on the table with a bump, knocking an ivory pipe out of the way. "Remove that object, Bill, it stinks!"

Mr. Purley shrugged and, picking up the pipe, stuffed it into his top pocket. "Hett, you're not dressed!" He frowned, waiting for her to rise, and when she did not, he repeated his remark, this time with a degree of menace which produced an embarrassed silence around the table.

Hetty got up and left the room, her heels clattering on the stone floor.

"Miss Cameron!" Mr. Purley rested his hands on the table and leaned toward her. "I have an attic at the top of this hovel which must do me as a studio until I can afford something better, and where I will start painting you tomorrow. Tomorrow?"

"Oh, yes."

"I hope I will be free, Clemency," warned Mrs. Merilees. "That is, I hope your aunt gives her blessing." She looked meaningfully at Clem who ignored her.

"In that case, you may expect me."

"I don't think your sister looks well." Mrs. Merilees tried to steer the conversation away from painting.

Mr. Purley continued looking at Clem. "You pour, little scrub maiden," he finally said.

Mrs. Merilees brushed Clem aside and placing the odd cups and saucers around the table poured the tea from the thick spout of the old teapot with admirable dexterity.

Clem glanced around the room admiring the colorful disarray, while Mrs. Merilees embarked upon a discussion of the various brands of kitchen tea available in Sydney. Mrs. Purley sipped her tea apprehensively, apologizing for the flavor, as she was well aware her guests were used to something more fragrant.

Clem wished Mrs. Merilees would stop talking. Mr. Purley was obviously concerned with things of a more noble nature than the cost of the latest shipment of Chinese tea. She hoped he didn't think that Mrs. Merilees's views reflected any part of *her* personality. "This tea is very good," she said, holding out her cup for more.

"But not as good as the eucalyptus brew, eh?" Mr. Purley

laughed and Clem shook her head, meeting his eyes quite naturally. How superior he was to all this pettiness.

Hetty hovered in the doorway, dressed in the same afternoon dress she'd been wearing on the coach, her face a mask of white powder.

Without turning round, Mr. Purley said, "Go to bed, Hett. You look ghastly."

When Hetty's steps had faded on the stairs, he said quite cheerfully, "I'm a bit off-color myself. Perhaps it's all the dust, or the weather or something. Whatever it is, I'm deuced absentminded lately."

"You perhaps suffer from a lack of nourishment, Mr. Purley? I have seen others exhibit such symptoms when in a state of near starvation. One becomes quite lightheaded."

"What a wise woman you are, Mrs. M. I have not eaten much these last few weeks. My dear papa has forgotten to send me my allowance. I believe he has lost the address. Hett will have to go out and find herself a position, and I must find some students. How about yourself, Mrs. M.? Surely you have always hankered after the drawing board?"

"I have as yet seen no evidence of your own draftmanship, Mr. Purley. May we be permitted to view your works?" Mrs. Merilees looked pointedly from wall to wall.

"My son's sketches and some of his pictures are hanging in the drawing room," Mrs. Purley hastened to explain.

Mrs. Merilees, obviously relieved to at last receive an invitation more fitting to her situation in life, gathered her skirts together.

But Mrs. Purley, quite distressed, added, "I must confess I am forced to remain in the kitchen," her eyes entreating Mrs. Merilees to understand. "Our drawing room here is so cold, and in the dining room the flues do not work properly, and we have not yet found a reliable sweep."

"Oh, if that is all the trouble I am sure Clemency's Aunt Thorne will be able—"

"My mama prefers the kitchen as she cannot *stand* my pictures!" remarked Mr. Purley good-naturedly. "Tell them what you think of my painting, Mama!"

Mrs. Purley cleared her throat. "I find my son's paintings most objectionable, Mrs. Merilees," she admitted slowly, then went on, "I am of the old school, you see."

"How unfortunate. Well, we must go now. Clemency's Aunt Margaret will be—"

Mr. Purley interrupted. "Not yet! You have only just arrived! Take no notice of my mother. She is not a reliable critic." He smiled endearingly at Mrs. Merilees. "Presently, my dear lady, I shall escort you both to my studio and there *you* may criticize my new set of sketches. I've been working upon Sydney Cove, pen-and-ink stuff. If you do not think too badly of them, perhaps you will consent to take a few lessons? At a reduced rate, of course."

"You cannot teach an old dog new tricks," said Mrs. Merilees, "even at reduced rates."

"I think you should let me be the judge of that." He stood up. "Let us go up to the attic now. I must get on with my work. I can't afford to sit all day gossiping with women." Mrs. Merilees flinched at the last word as he drew her chair back and ushered her out of the room and up a staircase hung with Eastern shawls and robes. Clem lagged behind, touching the soft cashmere and silk fringes lovingly with her fingertips.

His studio was roomy but not well lighted. Despite the inadequate lighting, the ladies viewed the dozen small sketches pinned up on the wall away from the window and made appreciative noises. Clem did not think the sketches too bad, although they appeared unfinished and a little smudged.

"They certainly have the look of the Cove about them. Yes, they could not be of anywhere else," Mrs. Merilees commented.

Her verdict was not appreciated by the artist. "If they are of the Cove, then they *are* of the Cove, ma'am," he snapped. "What do you think, Clemency?"

Clem was still irrationally excited about his easy use of her first name. She stuttered, "Indeed, yes. They are quite lovely. I admire the way you suggest the sky—I mean the weather—the wind."

"That is precisely what obsesses me. You have understood immediately what I am trying to do. I knew from the first moment I saw you that—your being so in harmony with nature—you would also possess the innocent eye."

She was not quite sure what he meant and waited with eager expectation of further enlightenment, but none came. He merely stood by the door and stared at her as she moved self-consciously from one sketch to another.

She came upon one which looked like an unraveled ball of black wool hanging over a blacker sea. "Is this the Cove at night?" she inquired, hoping she was not too far out.

"I think that was more a reflection of my mind at the time than of nature. Those still, clammy nights drive me insane. Do they drive you that way too, Clemency?"

Mrs. Merilees grabbed Clem's arm. "Goodness, it is so dark in here. How you can see to paint at all baffles me! We must go now. Miss Cameron's Aunt Margaret is expecting us."

"Must we? But I was—"

"Yes, we must." Mrs. Merilees propelled Clem toward the tiny door, pushing past Mr. Purley with a neat sidling motion which left him looking after them in some surprise.

"So soon? When am I to expect you tomorrow, Clemency?"

"Perhaps in the afternoon."

Mrs. Merilees stopped halfway down the stairs. "In that case, I suggest you bring soap and water with you, my dear, and clean that window. Otherwise you may very well turn out a blackamoor." She put her head around the door into the kitchen.

The two ladies looked up and started to rise.

"Do not trouble yourselves. We will see ourselves out." Mrs. Merilees pushed Clem down the hall in front of her and opened the front door.

Mr. Purley's voice could be heard from the attic stairs. "Good day! Until tomorrow—my beautiful model!"

Mrs. Merilees made some disparaging remark under her breath.

"What did you say?" Clem found herself being hurriedly bundled into the carriage and hardly had time to look once more at the yellow house before the horses were trotting off down the little street.

"I said, beautiful model indeed! That man is an ill-mannered oaf, and you must not return there under any pretext, and most definitely not as a model!"

"He is a little eccentric, that's all. I've heard that artists have a different temperament from ourselves. We must not judge them in the same way as ordinary people."

"Did he tell you that? My dear child, do not be taken in by all that *eccentricity*. It was just bad manners, not due to an artistic temperament, which hides a multitude of sins even when the individual *is* an artist."

"But he *is* an artist!"

"I doubt it—those sketches!"

"They were very interesting."

"Yes, and that is the best one can say of them, interesting. That is precisely the word one uses upon viewing commonplace work when one is at a loss for something more definite to say. The whole house is interesting to a degree!" Mrs. Merilees snorted, then laughed, fanning herself vigorously. "And that sister!"

"Miss Purley doesn't look well."

"No, she does not look well. She looks as though she might be on her deathbed. And no wonder with a brother like that! Going out to work! To work at what—one wonders!"

"Perhaps as a seamstress or something." It suddenly occurred to Clem that young ladies did not go out to work, even to support penniless artist brothers. "Perhaps he was just making fun of her."

"It is difficult to tell whether the fellow is jesting or serious or for that matter lying about anything or everything! Is that woman his mother? If so, he treats her with none of the respect due a member of his family—the sister either."

"He is right about one thing, Mrs. Merilees. You *have* got a suspicious nature. I have a great admiration for him and I *do* intend to return tomorrow for my portrait—black or white!" Clem sat forward and watched the Sydney streets go by. There were many narrow roads of small terraced houses, all with little front gardens—tiny patches of cultivated earth, keeping the thicker, prickly vegetation of the forest at bay.

It seemed to Clem that the whole of Sydney was there only by virtue of unending battle against the forest. The rocks had been cut away, but the virulent scrub remained, waiting for an opportunity to return—to smother the tiny gardens and climb over the sturdy houses, to push and pull at them until finally they would crumble back into sandstone and wood dust.

Aunt Margaret's house was perhaps too solid a building to succumb so easily, but it, too, would not last forever, thought Clem as she walked through the front door and up to her room, overhearing her aunt and Mrs. Merilees conferring in the hall. Her aunt's horrified exclamations followed her as far as the door of the bedroom. She knew she would forbid her to return to the Purley household, so she resolved to be devious.

She prepared herself for deception by putting on her aunt's favorite evening muslin, leaving her hair down and donning sweet, innocent expression as she entered the drawing room.

The two ladies were standing with their backs to the french windows, awaiting her.

"I gather that you've been telling Aunt Margaret all about the Purley residence, Mrs. Merilees. Well, I am—" She was about to say that having thought about it seriously she'd decided not to return, when her aunt silenced her with a frenziedly wagging forefinger.

"That is enough argument, Clemency!" She pulled Mrs. Merilees with her. "I shall write to your papa and see if he cannot make you see sense."

Aunt Margaret was employing her father's trick of standing with his back to the light which exposed every tiny change in Clem's expression, but left his invisible, thus completely demoralizing her.

"Aunt Mar—"

"Enough!" Her aunt gasped for breath. "And to be received in the *kitchen*! And Clara says there are Bedouin robes and scented things hanging all over the place!"

"Margaret, dear," remonstrated Mrs. Merilees, "let her speak."

"I do have some sense. I won't sit for Mr. Purley. He only wished to please me."

Mrs. Merilees sighed. "My dear, he says you are kindred spirits or some such rubbish, when you have only just been introduced— no, *thrown* together on a coach journey! You're so naive. That man has other motives for painting you."

"Oh, I know it's not because he really thinks I'm a good subject. He wants me eventually to take lessons and to attract other girls of the wealthier classes to his studio. I know that . . . ."

Mrs. Merilees took her hand, blushing. "But will it end there? I don't wish to hurt your feelings; however, it is my duty to warn you that you would be more than wise to avoid further contact with that man."

Clem nodded wisely, amazed at her ability to lie so blatantly.

After tea, she wandered into the garden with her French grammar and her embroidery.

Her suitor, Angus Maclean, was in town and due to call at any moment, a fact which had persuaded Aunt Margaret to implore Clem to persevere with her sewing. The sight of a young, freckled-faced girl with clumsy fingers, struggling over a bunch of English garden flowers upon a tiny piece of linen was, to Aunt Margaret's eyes, a picture which could not fail to win the heart of any man.

She found her favorite flat piece of sandstone by the creek and sat down clutching her embroidery and her book. Both had fallen into the undergrowth by the time it was time to go inside. The French irregular verbs remained unlearned as she sat—an inert, dreaming figure—upon the yellow stone.

She wondered whether Mrs. Brennan had ever received her note and tried to imagine what Matt would think of Mr. Purely. They were alike in some ways, both gruff and outspoken, although Matt preferred not to have to talk at all, believing anything worth saying was capable of being reduced to a few monosyllables. She had a sudden vision of his sun-bleached curl and squinting blue eyes, and she became suffused with a dreadful fear. It was quite possible she might never see him again!

She stood up and searched among the bushes for her needles and thread. She was terribly angry—angry with her father for sending her away and angry with her aunt for treating her like an infant.

"Aunt Margaret, you and my father would have made a good match. You are a pair of bullies—and worse than that—snobs!" She shouted her sentiments at a pair of slender eucalyptus trees and through tears of frustration saw the purple bark waver and dissolve into two strange blue figures.

The forest of ironbarks between the Brennans and the quartz ridge came back to her, engulfed her like a huge column of dark gray ghosts, as she clasped the nearest tree and pushed her cheek into its rough surface. "How I hate this house and school and everything! I *shall* go to see him. I *want* him to paint me. I would *love* him to paint me. I'll go tomorrow—walk if necessary." She wiped her eyes with the linen and made her way slowly back through the shrubs to the house.

She put the embroidery on her dressing table and lifted her mother's pearls from their box. Mrs. Cameron's beloved brother, Edmund, had given her these pearls, and she had presented them to Clem as an act of self-sacrifice, an atonement for her lack of motherliness. As she fingered the smooth little stones, she experienced an overwhelming nostalgia for her mother's face. She loved her mother—when she was three hundred miles away from her. Together, their feelings were so strained the love turned to irritation. Each time she had wished her mother good-bye, even on her short trips to Willawarrha, Clem had always regretted she'd not said or done something to show how much she really cared for her—any word or gesture. But at the last moment she'd always held back. Too much emotion was frowned upon in the New South Wales bush country. There was no time for such a luxury.

Biddy Wright came into the room, inquiring if there was anything she might do. Clem amazed her by begging her complicity in her plan to deceive her aunt. Sunday afternoon was Biddy's day off, and she planned to drive to the Rocks district to meet her young man. She promised to take Clem then, too, and also assured Clem she would persuade the groom who would drive the dogcart to "keep mum."

Clem sat through the Church of England service, trying not to imagine the afternoon's escapade in case she should lose her nerve. The sermon was long, all about God's love for the poor and the rich alike. Everyone was equal inside the church, thought Clem, but as soon as they stepped off the porch, everything changed. Divisions were strictly maintained, and there was little forgiveness of sins out there, especially the sin of being poor.

She looked at her aunt's face. It was relaxed, her eyelids half closed, her breathing too, even for somebody fully awake. Her housekeeper, Sybil, stared earnestly at the minister. The fact that Sybil, neither convict nor emancipist, should willingly take on a position of servitude always baffled Clem. Her father's housekeeper was the same. She could understand why convicts were servants—they *had* to be—but why anyone *chose* to be amazed her.

"What will you do with yourself this afternoon?" asked her aunt after luncheon.

"I intend to sketch in the hills."

"Why not have Biddy accompany you—better for her than gallivanting around the docks with her followers."

"Oh, no. She needs some time off, *some* freedom. Remember the minister."

"What? Oh, the sermon. It's the same every week. I've given up listening to it."

"Perhaps it has changed of late; otherwise I can't believe you've ever listened to it."

"I hope you are not about to be insolent!"

"No, I'm merely suggesting that although the minister—and presumably God—thinks that everyone is equal, you apparently do not."

"Everybody is equal once they are in heaven. They must *prove* it first. Biddy has proved no such thing to me. She *shall* accompany you."

"May we take the dogcart?"

"Yes, you're so like your papa, the way you argue." Aunt Margaret kissed her, "Get along with you. Don't let that sulky hussy Wright ruin your inspiration."

Clem now felt fully justified in her deception. A woman with as little humanity as her aunt did not deserve an honest niece.

Jim, the groom, and Biddy sat on the front seat of the dogcart and the three drove without speaking through the lonely Sunday streets. Biddy's dress was a fresh, bright pink, and she wore Clem's wide pink ribbon in her wispy curls.

Clem was dropped in Argyle Place, and it was arranged she should be collected at five o' clock. They left her standing nervously by the dusty date palm clutching her sketching easel with one hand, her bonnet, purse, and drawing case with the other.

Chapter Ten

The door was flung open by a black-haired, wild-looking young man who immediately stepped back into the hall and bowed. He took Clem's easel and drawing box.

"Are you moving in?" he asked. "No, I can see you are a pupil. Bill is a lucky fellow." He let her pass.

"I am expected today." Clem preceded the young man down the hall. She glanced back at him. His hair was long and neglected, his beard also, and his clothes of extraordinary materials of the most peculiar cut. "Are you an artist, too?"

"I sometimes tell myself I am. I am a sculptor."

"Do you carve in stone?" Clem did not think he looked hefty enough.

"I am a fancy stone carver so people call me a sculptor, but where they draw the line between the two I don't know. Here's Bill."

Mr. Purley was sitting at the kitchen table puffing his pipe and drinking a frothy substance from a tall mug. "Give my model a glass of ale, Hett. She looks flushed." He uncrossed his legs languidly and pushed his chair back with a loud scrape on the stone floor. He pointed to a vacant chair beside him. "Rupert, old chap, find another chair, will you?"

The young man followed Miss Purley into the scullery. Clem had not yet seen her clearly in the dim light but had sensed she was still angry with her brother.

The sculptor returned bearing a glass of ale and a wooden stool for Clem. "She's certainly a beauty, Bill. Where did you find her?"

Clem sat down carefully while the sculptor eyed her professionally.

"You always regard women so lasciviously, Rupert," said Hetty petulantly from the doorway.

"I regard beautiful women from the aesthetic viewpoint—*that* doesn't come into it at all." He placed Clem's ale on the table and took hold of her shoulders, pushing her gently around in a circle. "Magnificent bones and eyes."

"Yes," said Mr. Purley, regarding her with narrowed eyes. "She is magnificent." He paused, then, "Go upstairs, Hett."

Clem's hands felt suddenly cold as she reached for her glass of ale. Hetty's steps could be heard ascending the stairs and Mr. Purley laughed, banging his hand on the table.

"God Almighty, why did I bring these two women with me? Why, Rupert?" His angry eyes stared hard at Clem's.

"Your generous nature, old man. I would never do it. I must be alone. How about you, Mercy? Do you prefer to be solitary?"

"Oh, yes. When I'm at home I ride for days alone."

"Herding sheep?"

"Why not?" She managed to release her eyes from Mr. Purley's and sip her ale. It was very bitter.

"Stick to herding your sheep, Mercy. And don't end up like Hetty, here."

"Shut up, Rupert. For God's sake go back to Lady Whatsername."

"Who?" Clem asked, holding her mug with two hands and studying the froth. The two men had not taken their eyes from her face for a second.

"Just a commission. I'm supposed to make these old harridans beautiful, even in stone!" Rupert sighed. "The task usually defeats me. That's why I'm unpopular and impecunious."

"Poor Rupert." Clem smiled warmly as he saluted her on leaving the room. He was awkward and lanky and far too fragile-looking to be chiseling away at hard stone.

"That's something of his." Mr. Purley nodded in the direction of the almond-eyed woman in the corner. "It's not bad." Then he shouted after Rupert, "What we need are a few dukes and such out here—the traditional patrons of the arts! Too many bloody builders and wool merchants!"

Rupert called out something in reply, then the front door slammed.

"When will we start?" asked Clem.

He got up and held out his hand for hers. "Now. You will be my antipodean muse." She followed him out the door, her body overtaken by the same weakness she'd felt the day before.

The attic was not dark that day. A huge shaft of light fanned out from the small window, transforming the lumpy old daybed of the previous morning into an opulent sofa of rich blue velvet. Above it hung a piece of thickly embroidered Italian brocade in dark gold and translucent pale greens.

He helped her take off her coat, then set her on the sofa, gently pushing down her sleeves to expose her throat and shoulders. "Now drop your head a little." He knelt by her and twisted her head to one side, his hands pressing into her cheeks. When he rose, she could feel the imprint of his damp fingers.

He took a large piece of stretched canvas from the pile of wood and rolls of yellowing canvas in the middle of the room. "This one's primed." He placed it on an enormous easel which stood just to the right of the window.

Clem reached for the palette knife which she'd noticed wedged between the floorboards in front of her.

"Don't move!"

"It was only my arm. I—"

"And stop gabbling at me!"

"I wasn't. I only said—"

"Shut up!"

He began by covering the canvas with washes of diluted color, then chose a finer brush and started drawing with wild, circular strokes. He held the brush at his side like a sword and kept backing away from the canvas, then lunging forward into the attack, repeating these ferocious movements for the best part of an hour before Clem was brave enough to request a breathing space. She was dizzy with lack of air, not daring to breathe too deeply in case the muscles of her face and throat moved. Her voice was a tiny croak: "May I rest now—please?"

"Five more minutes."

She braced herself for another eternity of pain. The muscles inside her thighs were being wrung out in a mangle and her neck was a pillar of burning cords cruelly stretched to hold her heavy head in its awkward position. "It's torture!" She shook her head and legs and rolled off the sofa onto the floor, panting for air.

"I'm sorry—I got carried away. Let's stop now for tea. You're a good model."

"Can I see it?"

"No, not until it's finished. You wouldn't understand it now—unless you're acquainted with the works of Constable or Turner. I don't suppose you know the Barbizon School, do you?"

"Miss Maybright mentions them. They're very modern, aren't they? I don't think Miss Maybright approves of one of them. Too wishy-washy, she says."

"Corot, probably. Silly woman. Don't listen to these people. They know nothing."

"Miss Maybright has traveled widely. My aunt thinks her remarkably cultured."

"I suppose she thinks that having seen a couple of Corots in a museum she is qualified to cast aspersions upon his genius. These people read books by critics who have read other books. None of those writers have ever put brush to canvas, yet all are critics! I'd shoot the lot of them! Bloody parasites!"

"Miss Maybright is not a parasite. She earns her living by teaching girls like me."

"The spoiled daughters of the rich."

"I couldn't help being born into a wealthy family."

Mr. Purley grunted. "I wish I'd been born with money. I need it more than you do."

"Should I give my money to a charitable fund for poor artists?"

"No, just to me."

Clem laughed. "Mrs. Merilees suspected you were after my money!"

"She is damned right!"

"You're shameless!" Her eyes lit up with excitement. His brutal confession thoroughly delighted her.

"She ought to be glad it's only your money and not your body."

Her face turned a bright pink. "What's wrong with my body?"

"Nothing at all. I'd like to paint it some day." He touched the canvas lightly. "Some day, out in the forest . . . Do you swim?"

"Yes."

"Then I will paint you in one of those small lakes. What are they called?"

"Billabongs!" Clem stood up and brushed the dust from her arm, giggling.

"I'm serious. Whatever it is, you would enhance its beauty." His voice had a queer catch to it.

She walked to the back of the easel. He'd stopped painting and was staring at the far wall.

"You'd stand among those slim native willows . . . they're quite silver in the sun. Your hair would be silver too . . ."

Suddenly he bent down to pick up a piece of cloth and wiped his brush carefully, his back to her.

She waited for him to continue, but he started to whistle softly, then kicked the palette and rags to one side. As they were descending the narrow stairs, he said, "I'll be needing a model for the figure. My last one's gone all bones on me."

Hetty made the tea and the three drank in silence. Noticing the poor state of Hetty's complexion and her scurfy elbows, Clem wondered how she could have let herself degenerate so. "Have you found a position yet, Miss Purley?" she asked nervously.

Hetty shook her head slowly. "No—there's nothing for me. I'll have to be a ladies' companion, I've not the education for a governess." She rose wearily from the table and carried out the tray.

Mr. Purley pulled out Clem's chair and took her hand, leading her toward the stairs.

"I'm so sorry Hetty can find nothing."

"She's a model. It's a good profession really, but not one always understood by—"

"Colonial ignoramuses like me?"

He shrugged.

"Oh." Clem withdrew her hand. It was stained with blue paint.

Mr. Purley resumed painting, holding his brush high in the air now, like a spear thrower. Clem sat motionless for another hour, managing deep breaths only when he was squeezing the enormous tubes of paint and squirting great blobs of viscous color onto the palette.

He would often curse as volubly and loudly as the roughest shearer, his body continually moving backward and forward, up and down. He would bend toward the canvas at awkward angles and, grudging even the briefest glance away from the painting, would contort his body into amazing attitudes to pick up brushes, paint, and palette knives.

The whole performance reminded her of a wild ceremonial dance, the kind of abandoned, ferocious, ballet the aborigines indulged in during their religious festivals.

Finally he backed up against the wall, his body hunched, staring at the painting. "Can't do any more today. We'll go on tomorrow. Oh, and by the way, I have a name. It's William."

"Yes, I know." She watched his eyes as they moved swiftly from her to the painting. A peculiar sensation suddenly overcame her. She and William and the painting had all merged into one being. Then the room went black and she had to shake her head violently to become fully conscious again.

Clem stood on the veranda, wondering why she liked him so much. Everything Mrs. Merilees had said about him was true, apart from lack of talent, yet she was completely captivated by him—his atrocious manners, his ability to laugh at himself, but above all perhaps by the darker, more brutal side of him.

She fingered the dry, elegant foliage of the date palm. It was planted in a mess of dry dirt and rubble, its beauty enduring without any obvious nourishment. The floorboards gave way beneath her right foot. They were riddled with white ants.

Sensing a slight movement, her eyes followed the lines of rotten wood to the corner behind the date palm. It was a red ants' nest. As she watched, a long line of the transparent, wine-colored creatures, dragging their distended abdomens, hobbled to the nearest hole and disappeared into it in orderly formation. It was probably their tunnel to the Purley's larder. She watched them at their unceasing labors until Jim's dogcart drew up, and Biddy and a tall fair man climbed down.

Clem swayed toward the balustrade and leaned so far over she would have fallen head first onto the footpath if her easel had not lodged in the wooden rungs beside her. For a second she'd thought the man was Matt. She straightened her back and stood still, staring at Biddy's young man. His face was heavily tanned, his hair long, and his eyes dark.

Biddy nodded to her, whispered something to the man, then waved to him as he walked away. "Are we late, miss?"

Clem did not answer. She was gazing after the slow, effortless gait of the tall blond man, her eyes gradually focusing on the yellow curls clinging to the back of his neck.

Finally she said, "Will you help me with this blessed thing?"

The two girls stacked the easel at the back of the dogcart. As Clem was climbing in, Biddy said, "Harry says that's a bad house you've been in. He can't think why a young lady like you's in a place like that."

"Whatever do you mean?"

"It's that painter chap in there. Harry knows them two women and some of his friends like. He reckons they're funny like."

"Oh, people who don't understand artists always have that attitude. He's perfectly harmless. They're going through a bad patch just now. I don't think he eats enough—it affects his moods, you know."

Biddy shook her head. "Harry says he's plenty of money to buy ale."

Clem remained unruffled. "Ale is cheap and there's barley in it."

Biddy frowned. "Are you a student of his, miss?"

"No. He's painting my portrait. I have commissioned him. There is no scandal in that—for my mama, you know. Of course it's to be a surprise, a secret."

Biddy chatted to Jim as they drove by the docks. She pointed to the big sailing ships at anchor in the Circular Quay.

"I wish I could go home on one of them right now."

"You don't want to settle here?" Clem asked.

"Never. I want to see my green village again, and my mother."

"But don't you like New South Wales?"

"Like it? Why should I like it? It's tired out my bones and dried up my face. I sometimes feel like an old woman in this town. Everyone and everything's all wizened up out here, even the trees."

Clem surveyed the line of sun-dappled saplings curving around the bay as Jim whipped up the horses. The road suddenly veered to the west so the sun was directly ahead of them. It was about to drop into the ocean.

It was the gold time again, thought Clem—her time. It would be the gold time at Querilderie, too . . . and at the Brennans'. She imagined Matt riding his horse along the edge of one of the uneven wheat fields, the earth transformed into a rippling sun-drenched sea. She screwed up her eyes against the vision. She shouldn't allow herself such luxuries. He'd told her he was going away, probably forever, and he'd never mentioned taking her with him. She rubbed her eyes with her sleeve, knocking her bonnet to the back of her head, and gazed out into the endless glitter of the wide, saffron sea.

The next morning while Jim was preparing to turn into King Street from George Street, she persuaded him to bypass The Misses Maybright's Academy for Young Presbyterian Ladies and to continue on to Argyle Place instead.

Chapter Eleven

William Purley was in a very black mood that Monday morning. His sister hovered about him like a nurse with a fractious patient. She greeted Clem with a very curt "Good morning."

Clem followed her into the scullery where Hetty was leaning across the black zinc tub. "They say artists are like that, Miss Cameron. Completely self-centered, and that anything that might be said—no matter to whom—must reflect on them. No matter what we say, he—"

"He thinks you criticize him—is that it?"

"Yes, all the time. Some people call it artistic temperament, but I call it childish self-indulgence."

"Hetty!" Clem pulled her hand away from her face. "You have a black eye!"

Hetty started to cry, her body shaking with deep, heavy sobs.

"Did he—?"

"No! It was an accident. But he *does* throw things. Oh dear God, why should I end up like this? What a slattern I've become!"

"There, there." Clem took out her handkerchief and handed it to her. "It will not be so bad when he has some pupils."

Hetty blew her nose. "Pupils!" She laughed queerly. "Bill regards pupils as a dreadful compromise. I wish to God he could get by without pupils."

Clem was about to ask her to explain when William's voice came from the doorway. "Hurry with that tea!"

She was puzzled by William's harsh attitude toward Hetty and didn't know whether to pity or despise her for her weakness. She carried the tea tray into the kitchen.

"If I were your sister, I'd leave you as soon as I possibly could."

"Then I'm glad you're not my sister." Hetty sat down and he ignored her.

Clem ran upstairs ahead of him and arranged herself on the sofa. She steeled herself for more hours of torture. Soon she could no longer feel her body, but remained gazing at William, at his frenzied waltz in front of the canvas. Apart from brief breaks for Hetty's awful tea, she spent the day in a dreaming, lightheaded state, her mind divorced from her body. She was transported into another universe: a world of close white walls continually moving along the spiraling lines of William's raw, harbor sketches, and a world of cloying intimacy intensified by the musky scent of the velvet daybed and the rich thick smell of oil paint.

William's distorted features were sometimes vague in the shadows, sometimes starkly white. When his eyes met hers she would float across the room becoming part of him, and when she lost him he would fade away, his image merging with the fluid lines of the drawings on the walls.

On the way home she studied the rows of mean terraced houses, dark and stifling beneath the hot southern sun, damp and airless in winter. William was a strange creature to be sheltering in a Sydney attic. The more she thought about him, the more he started to assume the shape of a tall black stick-insect trapped in an alien nest. No, it was *she* who was trapped inside *his* nest. She was his prey, but instead of trying to escape, she deliberately offered herself to him.

She stretched her arms and legs, luxuriating in her release from that brightly colored chamber of refined torture. Sitting for a painter was not really *sitting* at all. She stretched her legs as far as the seat would allow and clasped her hands behind her head. How horrified Aunt Margaret would be to hear him mention her money and her *body* so casually! If he really did want her money, he had as much right to it as any of those silly hypocritical young blades of Sydney who'd swear true love to gain their share. The most respectable people were not above *blackmail* when it came to society weddings. . . .

The day was overcast and a chilly breeze blew in from the cove. The little houses were sadly drab without the winter sun glistening on the sandstone. The winter green leaves were dusty from three days without rain. All the little housemaids who dusted all the little parlors ought to be out dusting all the little front gardens too, she thought. The earth churned up by the carriage wheels got into everything. Living in Sydney was like living in a continual dust storm.

They passed the old convict barracks now mainly inhabited by Irish orphans. A few of them, ragged guttersnipes seemingly immune to the cold, played dangerously close to the road and threw stones at the wheels. Driving along the South Head Road she remembered Angus' invitation to go riding there one Sunday afternoon.

He'd called at the house when she was at school, and he and Mrs. Merilees and Aunt Margaret had made all kinds of arrangements for her—including the dreadful possibility of visiting the girls at Parrammatta! She prayed every night for God to rush Angus off to Glen Ross before she would actually be forced to resume their friendship.

Perhaps friendship was too warm a word, she decided as the carriage turned into her aunt's drive. She groaned inwardly as she saw a strange vehicle at the front door. It was a new phaeton, the kind favored by young men who had to do a lot of dashing about town. Surely it couldn't be . . . She raced through the door hoping to escape upstairs before whoever it was would see her, but she was too late. A stocky young man with ginger whiskers was waiting for her at the foot of the stairs. He gaped quite unashamedly when he saw her. "Clem!" He gazed at her in wonder. "You're so—grown-up!"

She watched his whiskers moving toward her. They'd grown so vigorously his head resembled a kola bear's.

"Angus?"

He nodded and clasped her hand. He was like a large red marsupial animal.

Her aunt bustled through the library door. "Clemency—you have exactly ten minutes to change for tea!"

Clem ran upstairs two at a time, pausing at the top to look into the high glass dome above the stairwell. The day was already fading, filling the whole house with a soft gray light.

She appeared quite foreign in her glass and so old. She rubbed her aunt's daily fresh-cut lemon into her face and chest, wondering if her mother would at last be pleased with her. If only her father would let her come to Sydney for just a little while, but her letters had not persuaded him yet. She would just have to keep pleading.

She peered at herself more closely. Yes, she looked quite pale and ethereal, her hair silvery and dark blond—it *was* silver in this evening light! She lowered the shoulders of her dress until most of her bosom was exposed, firm and white above the deep brown velvet of her bodice. Then she pushed back the material, a tiny self-satisfied smile playing around the corners of her mouth. She splashed rose water on her throat and wrists and descended the stairs slowly, wondering if lemons really did dissolve freckles.

The topics of conversation that evening, apart from Angus' recent degree in Natural History from Edinburgh, were Glen Ross and Querilderie, their various childhood pets and japes, and the health and welfare of their respective families. Angus asked a few strange questions about Miss Owen. He seemed more concerned with her relationship to Clem's parents than with Katharine's schooling. Clem, however, couldn't enlighten him, as she heard very little from home—just a brief scrawl from her mother and that only rarely.

They talked late into the night until Aunt Margaret finally fell asleep and, being wakened by the grandfather clock striking midnight, chided them for keeping her up so late, and sent Angus packing.

Clem waved him good-bye from the porch. She'd imagined that going home would have changed him in other ways—turned him into a dandy or a silly young buck as it did to so many others, but Angus had merely grown up. The old resentment of not being born a boy came back to her as she watched him drive off in his phaeton. He'd excluded her from so many of his and the Brennan boys' activities by making fun of her pigtails and dismissing her with "We don't need stupid females!" Well, he'd accepted her as an equal tonight, and from some of his remarks she'd guessed that he preferred her company to that of many of his men friends. He was not so bad really, not nearly as arrogant as she'd remembered.

The next day Jim drove her to Argyle Place with a certain lack of enthusiasm. He was obviously uneasy about her aunt's discovery of their deception and the threat of dismissal. Clem assured him she would take all the blame in the event of such a catastrophe, but he just mumbled something and drove off, forgetting to touch his cap.

He's lost all respect for me, she thought, as she waited by the date palm for the door to open.

It swung back violently and Rupert, wearing an old beaver on his black curls, a thin pipe sticking out from the middle of his wide mouth, grinned at her, ushering her in. "Watch out for Bill today, Clem. He's in an unkind frame of mind. He's a brute, that fellow."

"He doesn't frighten me. I think he's brilliant, don't you?"

Rupert nodded. "Positively, yes."

"I'm sure that portrait will be an excellent likeness."

"Of course. Bill!" he yelled, "She's here!" He took off his hat and scraped it along the floor of the hall.

William was cleaning his brushes. He held a very fine one up in the air for Rupert's inspection. "A pupil brush, that one."

"Do you mean it's for pupils to use?" asked Clem, dropping her bonnet onto the table.

"No, it's for dotting eyes!" Both men laughed uproariously, but Clem failed to see the joke.

Rupert darted out of the room as Hetty's footsteps descended the stairs. He ran down the hall and banged the front door.

"Too sensitive, that's his trouble." William glanced briefly at Hetty as she stood stiffly in the doorway. "He is always uncomfortable in my dear sister's presence. I wonder why that is?" He went on cleaning his brushes.

His dancing was not quite so energetic this morning. He chose the colors very carefully, again without mixing them before they reached the canvas, and executed an almost dainty waltz about the easel.

Clem spent the morning in a trancelike state, floating away from William and the studio, back to Querilderie and to wide oceans of white-brown grass, vast skies, sandstone rocks and caves, and the moon tree. She could smell the tiny white blossoms. She lay beneath it, warm and tranquil, the sun filtering through the dark green leaves and fragile flowers. She could hear Matt's voice coming from miles across the dry plains, calling to her.

"Clemency! Wake up! I'm finishing you off!"

William shook her awake. "I'm almost done. If a thing can be said to be done at all. I could paint you forever and never finish."

Clem yawned. "Like a changing landscape." She studied his face. It was relaxed and happy, his eyes light and wide.

"Your face has changed, even in the short time I've known you." He walked back to the canvas. "Why don't you marry me? You have such an agreeable nature, and we would be so well suited with all your money."

"You couldn't be serious for a minute!"

"But I *am* serious. I *do* want to marry you. It would save poor Hett from having to—to work. We could pension her off *and* her mother! Yes, its a grand idea—Clemency?"

"I wish I were poor like you, then I might have accepted."

William came over to kneel in front of her. He gently lifted the hem of her dusty skirt and pressed it to his lips. "I wouldn't have asked you to marry me, but I would still have loved you." He gazed up at her with dog-like devotion.

Clem laughed. "You don't love me at all, and anyway what would my father say?"

"God knows. As long as he didn't disinherit you, it wouldn't matter what the old tyrant said." He stood up to rearrange a stray strand of her hair. "You ought to consider it." Then his eyes drifted back to his painting. "No, never mind."

"I don't think I'll ever marry—I prefer to be free!"

"That's a pity. I like you as much as I could any woman."

"Perhaps if you had courted me with a little more finesse. . . ."

He came over to her and lifted her from the pile of velvet, and taking her chin in one hand he bent down to kiss her on her still parted lips.

She returned the kiss and was about to put her arms around him when he pushed her away violently. "Go and marry your squatter or whatever he is. This is all fantasy."

"I don't know what you mean," she said thickly, her lips smarting.

"You ought not to have those thoughts—feelings—toward me."

"A moment ago you were talking of marriage!" She tried to smile.

"That is all fantasy, all fantasy. Please sit still."

"I thought, I imagined, you might want to—to—kiss me again. . . ." She felt her cheeks burn.

"I don't want to make love to you—I just want to paint you."

She tried to shrug. "Please continue painting." She rubbed her mouth with the back of her hand. Her limbs had gone weak. She stared at the back of his dark head. She'd wanted him to go on kissing her. She tried to compare his features with Matt's, but Matt's blond head, which she'd often thought of as an extension of her own, had become a vague, smudged image. She could not remember a single detail.

"You can see it now." William beckoned her forward.

She approached hesitantly, standing a long way back from the canvas.

The picture was a mass of yellow and blue paint laid on with tiny brush strokes of bright color, merging to make swirling patterns of light and shade.

Her face—it *was* her face—stared out at her with sad, pale eyes from among the restless golds and greens which formed a million strands of hair.

She moved forward. The colors changed to a dancing square of reflected sunlight, and her eyes watered as she searched for the lost image.

She moved back to the wall and saw that it was a picture of her and of her life—the colors of the paddocks, the trees and the sky, all infused with the warmth of the sun and the broken gold light of the hot evening sky.

He had painted her in the *gold time*.

"How did you know about me?" Her voice was hoarse.

"You are a part of your background and I think I know it well enough to know you—" He took her hand. "I don't mind not having you because I'll have this."

"Oh, yes." She was crying. She would gladly at that moment have given him every Merino sheep she would ever own. She looked up at him, blinking the tears fiercely from her eyes, wanting to tell him how much she admired his genius.

William shrugged, dropping her hand. "It will do. I start another tomorrow."

"What?" She rubbed her eyes. "Another portrait?" The golden changeling stared straight at her with palely glimmering eyes.

"Not exactly. I've been commissioned to paint the Hyde Park Barracks for some fellow, some bigwig in the regiment. Rupert obtained it for me. His wife wants a memento of the colony. Good chap, Rupert."

"Oh." She shut eyes and turned away from the painting. "Will you paint them—like—like this?"

He laughed. "No, I'll regard it as a drawing exercise."

"Then color it in?"

He laughed again, "Yes, you could say that."

She turned her back on the picture. It seemed a sacrilege to talk in such mundane terms of the art which had produced that. His talk of marriage had all been a joke. How could she ever hope to satisfy the man who had created all that beauty.

He walked to the door then stopped, his head half turned to her. "I'm sorry if I upset you, my magnificent Scrub Maiden. You see, an artist cannot possibly marry his muse—or make love to her."

After he'd left the room, she stood gazing into the portrait, into the scattered beams of the late afternoon light. It seemed to be willing her to look for something else. . . .

A loud thud from the room below roused her from her dreamlike state, and she tiptoed to the door. She started to go down the stairs and then stopped, remembering that she'd left something behind. She patted her skirt and bodice trying to find what was missing. She was about to retrace her steps when she pulled up abruptly.

The natives were right. He'd captured more than just her features.

Chapter Twelve

As she passed the first-floor landing her foot struck a loose board.

"Wait!" William shouted.

She went on down the stairs and stood behind the front door. He ran after her and wrenched open the door. He was hatless and wore only his threadbare painting jacket.

"Where are you going?"

"Home," she replied. "You'll catch cold."

He ignored her warning, marching ahead of her toward the docks.

When she caught up to him they walked in silence through the steep narrow streets, descending a long flight of stone stairs which brought them close to the water. The sheds and loading bays were crowded with bronzed men in tattered vests and dirty white convict smocks hauling and loading cargo.

The magnificent red-leather seats of a large carriage were being winched from an enormous vessel, swaying dangerously as they were lowered into a wide barge.

"Look at that thing!" William screamed. "That vulgar great article of prestige!"

Clem waited for someone to notice him, but his voice was lost in the wind from the harbor. "The owner should have bought one of your pictues instead."

"Yes." He stood transfixed by the shining body of the huge, ornate vehicle. "Yes, by God. He could have made a better investment than that monstrous creation—that crude symbol of wealth—for some fat, inflated fellow. Good God!" He wheeled around. "And now I am reduced to painting the damned barracks!"

"It is a pleasant building."

"Thank the Lord for small mercies." He took her arm. "I'm sorry if I appear a boorish fellow to you, little Scrub Maiden; I don't wish to. I'm very fond of you."

"I only hope we can remain friends. Soon my aunt will find me out and that'll be the end of it," she said philosophically.

He was whistling softly, his eyes on the ground.

It was a long walk to the barracks. They went by streets of narrow terraced houses, some tall and freshly painted, the curly cast-iron balconies like enormous cuffs of Brussells lace. Other houses were squat, with peeling paint and mean windows, and had been turned into rows of little shops, every corner one a rum shop. Groups of drunken men and women huddled around their doorways, some of whom tried to push Clem and William into the gutter.

An inebriated aborigine lay outside one of the shops, his head stuck on a pile of filthy rubbish. Not one person spared him a glance, let alone a helping hand. He was like somebody's abandoned dog, run down and kicked into the gutter out of the way. Clem pointed out the sight to William.

"They'll all die of starvation soon or drink," he said.

"Can't someone do something? They are human beings—at least in the sight of God."

"Their own gods'll have to take care of them. Poor fellow, they'll survive for a few more years until the place is settled, then—bang, bang—this greedy crowd'll shoot the lot of them."

"Mathew Brennan says they have a perfectly good religion of their own, and a history and art, and know better how to survive in the bush country than any white man does or ever will do. He admires them enormously."

"He must be a clever chap, this Mathew of yours. But all that won't save them from greed and ignorance. They're doomed." He walked over to the man. "Look at his face."

She saw the wide-boned nose and deeply sunken eyes and bruised lips, slack upon the blue-black face. His hair was the color of red sandstone.

William knelt down by his side, trying to dig a depression so his head would rest more comfortably. "His culture, which as your friend told you is perfectly suited to his country, can't be replaced by ours. He belongs to the past. In fact, he *is* in the past."

The barracks finally came into sight, a handsome building of large blocks of stone, glowing a bright red against the pale gray sky. There were tropical palms and flowering shrubs behind the iron railings, which cut off the well-watered lawn from the dusty footpath.

"Sketching here will be your first lesson. Oh, and by the way, why don't you ask those schoolma'ams of yours about me. I'm sure they could do with a drawing master."

Clem nodded reluctantly. She resented having to share him with the girls at the Misses Maybright's.

"*You* ask them; they would have to meet you."

"Very well, then. Meet me here at nine o'clock sharp tomorrow morning. I don't take on pupils lightly."

They returned by another route, walking toward Darling Harbor, William's eyes all the time glued to the ground.

"Have you lost something?" Clem asked, noticing the paving stones which had become dislodged during the last storm and the virulent weeds and grasses pushing their way up through the space between the stones.

"No, but others might have. The poor don't keep their eyes on the ground because they are humble but because they might find a gold coin or two."

"You'll be taking up the begging bowl soon."

"It will come to that when you finally leave me to marry your rich squatter."

She glanced at his tall straight figure. His coat hung from his shoulders without a bulge. His cravat was loose, too, revealing the very white skin at the base of his strongly sinewed neck. "I won't marry him." She would stock the Purley's pantry for them so they wouldn't starve, and perhaps one of her aunt's friends would employ Hetty as a companion. With a secure position and well-laundered clothes, Hetty might recover some of her looks.

He stopped at the corner of York Street and peered up the long, narrow road, pointing out a church of gray stone in the distance.

"That's what poor old Rupert's reduced to—carving rocks for people's rotting bodies to lie under."

"I sometimes like the angels."

"Mmm. Rupert enjoys the angels, too." He smiled. "The wings are a challenge, he says." He patted his pockets. "Damn, I've run out of tobacco. There's a shop around here, I think." He led the way down King Street across Kent Street and into Sussex Street, then turned down an alleyway leading to Darling Harbor.

She tripped happily along at his side, relishing the freedom from her aunt and her schoolbooks. He was much more erudite than either of the Misses Maybright, and he seemed to enjoy listening to her, too. She had never told anyone so much about herself as she'd told him these last few days.

"It's old Fred Jenkyn's place—the tobacco shop—they say he's a receiver of stolen goods. He was a fourteen year man."

Fred's premises seemed to be the front part of a warehouse. The shop was long and dark with walls completely shelved from floor to ceiling, and each one packed tightly with boxes, all thick with dust.

She studied the old man. His face was as wrinkled and brown as a prune, his eyes tiny bright orbs. His clothes, though of remarkably good quality, hung from his bent old back like so many rags.

"What's 'er doin' in 'ere, Squire?" he inquired, peering at Clem. His chin reached just above the counter.

"She's nothing to worry about. Put that on my bill, will you, Fred?"

The old man chalked a mark on a large slate hanging on the wall.

William hurried Clem out of the shop just as two gentlemen entered through a side door. She glanced at them briefly. One of them was Mr. Michael Pike from the Willawarrha Arms Hotel!

She looked back and caught a glimpse of him again. It *was* he. "William, did you see that man? It was Mr. Pike!"

"Let's get out of here quickly. He's one of those dandies who are all over town. We don't want him to prattle about us."

Clem thought about the extravagant shine on the other man's top hat. Even her aunt would be impressed by that. "Something strange goes on in that place. It's not a shop at all."

"I told you he's a receiver of stolen goods."

She stopped in consternation. "Then Mr. Pike—"

"Probably just buying tobacco. Fred has the best."

"And to think—"

He took hold of her arm. "Come on, stop fussing."

"I was just remembering how he asked me to go to the rum shops with him. And I would have gone!"

"Him, too!" He let her wrist drop and stood still, staring at the row of warehouses opposite with a strange smirk.

"What—"

"You do enjoy the occasional dip into depravity, don't you? Rupert will be disillusioned; he thought you were different, an innocent."

She was frightened. His face was terribly white.

"So, I am equated in your little mind with the dapper Mr. Pike. *I* am *also* allowed to accompany you into your forays into the low life." His eyes had gone black with anger.

"No!"

"You would have let me be your seducer because it would have meant nothing to you! I am merely an amusing episode—someone from a separate stream of life who could never intrude upon your *real* existence."

"You're mad!"

"Yes, possibly. *Your mad artist*—like your rum shop: two naughty japes for you and your fat squatting husband to laugh at over the silver soup tureens." He guffawed loudly. "No, you probably don't even realize it yourself. Will your childhood sweetheart understand? The wise Mathew—Pure Blue Eyes—will he understand?"

"Understand what?"

"That he's just like me—an episode."

"I don't know how pure he is and he's not my sweetheart. He hates words like that."

"The little innocent!" He laughed so wildly some passersby stopped to stare.

She fought back her tears. She suspected he'd hit on some of the truth, and that was the worst of it. Then she managed to make a half-hearted gesture of defiance. Awkwardly throwing her head back she smiled at him. "*You're* being ridiculous. You're the one who keeps insisting on my innocence!"

"You *are innocent*; you *are pure*. A natural creature like you can be nothing else!"

"Matt Brennan is not just an *episode*! And he does not think I am *pure*!" she screamed at him. "*Pure*! What does that mean—*pure*?"

The expression in Matt's eyes that morning in Mrs. Oxley's garden came back to her, and she shouted across to him, "I don't want to be *pure!*"

Walking by his side again, her head held proudly, she noticed through a red blur the two men from Mr. Jenkyn's shop emerge and climb into an elegant barouche. The older man looked behind him. He had the thickest eyebrows she'd ever seen. And they met right in the middle of his nose! "They've gone," she said, her voice weak.

William stared straight through her. "I'm sorry. I forgot myself." He patted her cheek. "Poor little Scrub Maiden, you've had your taste of low life. Was it part of the Misses Maybright's curriculum?"

She pushed his hand away violently and walked ahead of him. "I'm going home." She kept walking ahead, stopping only at the corners to ask the way.

As they turned into Argyle Place a sudden strong gust of wind lifted her skirts. He caught up with her. "Don't be too angry. I'll always be jealous of you despite my lack of claim upon you—or perhaps because of it."

She followed him across the road and into the shelter of the church at the end of the square. Shall I still come tomorrow?"

"I want you to, but you must make up your own mind."

She searched his face, uncomprehending. He had obviously decided to remain distant. She looked away and saw to her horror the tall, gaunt figure of her aunt, followed by the wider, stockier one of Angus Maclean marching down the middle of the road toward them.

"Quickly! It's them!"

William leaned against the wall of the church as he lit his pipe. "So that is your aunt? Fortunately, you do not resemble her in the least."

"What shall I do?"

"You will think of something. Don't forget to introduce me. I may only be a humble artisan, but like your friends the aborigines, I am a man." He gazed up at the church spire for confirmation of this statement.

"I don't care about you! I should be at school! They'll expel me again!"

"And so they ought. School is not a fit place for a frequenter of rum shops." He pulled his coat tightly across his chest as the wind blew around the corner of the church.

"Please don't say anything. Please!"

"Clemency!" Her aunt's voice was a resounding screech. "What is the meaning of this? Who is this fellow?" She held onto the top of her bonnet with both hands. The wind had turned back the brim like a trooper's cap.

Angus walked abreast of Aunt Margaret. "Hullo, Clem. Wagging school?" He held out his hand to William. "How d'ye do, old man. Heard you're a bit of a painter."

William shook his hand and bowed to Aunt Margaret. "That is my profession. Clemency—will you please introduce me to your aunt. And is this Mr. Mathew Brennan?"

"*No!* Aunt—Miss Thorne, and Mr. Maclean, may I present Mr. William Purley. He is the artist I have told you about. He has just finished my portrait. We were strolling in the square. It's so stuffy in the studio."

"The studio! Who was with you, pray?" Aunt Margaret grabbed Angus's arm. "Your mother, sir?"

"Of course. My mama is used to chaperoning young ladies, having been blessed with a daughter of her own, ma'am."

"I see." Aunt Margaret stood firmly between Clem and William. "May we be permitted to view this portrait of my niece, Mr. Purley?"

"It belongs to me, you understand. However you may see it. You will not like it."

Aunt Margaret dismissed his remark by turning her back on him and taking Clem's arm, her fingers clutching at her flesh in desperation. "Your father will know about this. How you have shamed me! And in front of Angus, too!" Her aunt hissed the same angry words over and over again until they reached the little yellow house.

"I don't want anyone to see my portrait. I want to go home." Clem climbed into the carriage, watched by a queer-faced Jim, who stood by the steps.

"I want to see it. I insist on seeing it!" Aunt Margaret started to go up the stairs onto the veranda, her bonnet now raised an inch above her head by the wind.

William jumped up after her and blocked the door. "There is no one at home and I have no key. Therefore, nobody will see it. Good day, ma'am, and to you, sir."

Aunt Margaret was speechless with rage. She clung to the rickety balustrade as she descended the stairs, then heaved herself into the carriage and sat forward in the seat staring at William.

Angus let himself in, pulling up the steps after him, having told Jim to drive away quickly. He sat next to Clem. "What is this portrait like?" He smiled at her as if at a demented child. "Tell me."

"It's so beautiful I can't say what it's like. It's like nothing on earth—a mass of gold and green flame."

"Goodness gracious, the child is insane!" Her aunt mopped her chin with a flimsy square of lace. "I think I need my smelling bottle. Oh, I haven't got it. What shall we do with you?"

"You fuss too much, Aunt. He just wanted to paint my portrait. What harm is there in that, Angus?"

"No harm at all. Miss Thorne, Clemency is seventeen years old. It is perhaps time you started to trust her good judgment."

"What judgment? Oh, how shall I tell John?"

"Don't tell Mr. Cameron. That would only complicate matters. I repeat, there is no harm done." He squinted into Clem's eyes. "That *is* so?"

Clem knew he was looking for signs of lost innocence. "Oh, yes, yes. Please—both of you—leave me alone!"

Angus, hurt, moved a fraction away from her and sat silently studying the buttons in the leather upholstery.

Clem could think only of William. How unfair it was that his father had disowned him, probably because he did not approve of his profession. He could still make a name for himself, of course. One day he would be very famous, unless he starved to death first.

"I do not see why you are looking so distressed, Clemency. I am the one who is distressed!" Her aunt muttered tearfully through her lace handkerchief.

Angus peered into Clem's face. "You *are* very upset. Has that chap said anything to upset you?"

"No. He is such a brilliant painter and he has no money and no patrons. And now his poor family have to work!"

"His sister works! What does she do?" Aunt Margaret's eyes were wide with horror.

"Nothing yet. His father has disinherited him."

"So, he will send his sister out to work to buy his paints and brushes for him. One reads such nonsense in the popular magazines!"

Angus was quietly laughing to himself. "He has certainly wormed his way into your affections. You are not yet well enough acquainted with the ways of the world."

Aunt Margaret sniffed. "*Too* well acquainted!"

"You don't wish me to be friends with Mr. Purley just because he's not successful!"

"It's not because of his lack of a name. Painters are . . . " Angus frowned.

"It is not a manly-enough calling? That's what you mean. If he were a poor and unsuccessful lawyer or doctor, or best of all that paragon of all that is best in society—a squatter! Then you wouldn't have this attitude."

"That house! Those wall hangings Mrs. Merilees spoke about! No decent family would live in a—a *scented* place like that! My friend Mrs. Bland, from the church, you know, she is poor but *unobtrusive!*" Aunt Margaret gasped for breath. "That man was flamboyantly unkempt, and his hair was ridiculously long!" She shuddered with horror of it all.

They were driving past the Cove. A big sailing ship was racing into the Circular Quay, its enormous sails billowing out before the strong wind. They felt the wind even inside the thickly insulated carriage and at the entrance to the harbor they saw that the sky was almost black. Soon odd drops of rain struck the windows with a ferocity which predicted a tropical storm.

"Oh goodness me. This will become worse. The gale is increasing every second!" Aunt Margaret clutched at her coat sleeves.

"It's a gale-force wind to be sure." Angus peered out the window with narrowed eyes. "We struck one of these in the China Seas—a typhoon actually." He moved around in his seat to face Clem. "Everything had to be battened down. Those tea clippers are long and fast but they don't always survive that strength of wind. The waves were higher than—" he pointed to the recently built Customs House—" three times as high as that building."

Clem's eyes widened with admiration. "You didn't tell me. How exciting! What did you do?"

"It was not exciting. I stayed below, battened down like the rest of the cargo, thanking God I was not one of the poor wretches of sailors. Two were lost overboard."

"Oh." Clem subsided into the seat again. She had imagined Angus out on deck with the crew, tying knots in ropes and hanging onto the cargo with his bare hands.

"Whatever shall I say to the Misses Maybright?" Aunt Margaret inquired, unable to look her niece in the eye.

"Say I have been ill."

"Yes. That is not too far from the truth after all. You must promise me—oh, what's the use."

"I shall not promise anything. All this schooling is unnatural—for me, anyway. I would like to go home to Querilderie."

"That's impossible. I've just received a letter from your papa. I had hoped to be able to tell you this under less distressing circumstances: Your poor mama is very ill."

"Well I must—"

"No, you must not go home. Your papa expressly wishes you to stay with me until—until she is well again. Then she will come here to stay—to convalesce."

"Oh, that's wonderful! When do you think?"

"Soon, I imagine. Soon. You must write to her straightaway."

The wind had started to rock the carriage from side to side, and the scenery outside was obliterated by sheets of dark gray water battering at the glass.

"God protect us! It's a hurricane!" Aunt Margaret moved closer to Clem, the bones of her thin body not softened even by her heavy skirt and petticoats. Clem tried to wriggle free of their intimacy.

As the carriage turned into the drive of the house, she could see the dark shapes of the pines bending dangerously beneath the wind.

The three of them ran from the carriage to the front porch, hearing a demonic, high-pitched wail from the tops of the trees, and Clem saw the house in ruins as she followed her aunt through the door.

They stood still for a moment to listen to the wind and had just started to take off their coats and shoes when a sudden thunderous, tearing sound rent the air, followed by a terrible crash. The walls of the house seemed to move inward, and the large chandelier above their heads shook violently. The candles dimmed, then came back to life making wild flickering patterns over the walls and high-domed ceiling. The looked up at the dome, their ears singing.

"A tree! One of the trees has fallen!" Aunt Margaret fell upon the door, and struggling with the handle, wrenched it open, and stumbled outside.

Clem and Angus ran to where she stood. The tallest pine had fallen on the carriage, smashing it into a thousand pieces. Bits of red silk and leather were being pounded into the earth by the rain, and splintered wood littered the entire area in front of the house. Within seconds the carriage wood and the wood of the tree were indistinguishable in the flood.

Jim and the horses had escaped death by only a few inches. He had been leading the horses to the stable and had thrown himself forward onto the ground as the tree fell. The horses stood dazed, apparently unharmed, the shafts wrenched from their shoulders.

"The horses!" Clem jumped over the branches of the tree and held their heads. They shook their manes and started to walk away from the smashed shafts. Jim limped toward them, rubbing his eyes.

"I'll see to it, miss. You'd better go back inside." His thin face was like a white lantern in the dark rain.

"Are you quite all right?" Clem asked.

He nodded and led the horses around the corner of the house, his body bent double into the wind.

Clem stood next to the shattered carriage staring up into the pines. They swayed from side to side in a grand semicircular motion, their branches ripping off each other's boughs and needles, sending them swirling up into the black sky. The wind lifted her skirts and threatened to knock her off her feet. She hung onto a branch of the fallen tree as she studied the pines, wondering which would be the next to go.

Angus was by her side and, taking her arm, propelled her toward the house. "It's too dangerous out here now."

She let him guide her through the door.

Aunt Margaret was sitting on a straight-backed hall chair, her clothes hanging about her like so much wet foliage. "What shall I do? How will I get to church? Will the Westons pick me up and drop me back? How can I ask people?"

"Use the dogcart," Clem said bluntly. She walked up the stairs, holding her dripping skirts about her knees, listening to the wind shrieking in the chimneys.

Chapter Thirteen

Dinner passed without a single reference to Clem's reprehensible behavior. She sat quietly, awaiting her aunt's further criticisms, but Aunt Margaret and Angus, deciding she was definitely a little touched, had resolved to humor her madness instead of aggravating it.

After her favorite pink meringues, her aunt tried to press a particularly bright red apple upon her. "It will do you a world of good, my dear. It's just off the boat today—from Van Diemen's Land."

"Van Diemen's Land! Ugh!" Clem waved it away.

Angus leaned across the table. "If you refuse it, by the same token you will end up refusing just about everything, because almost everything we have here is harvested or built by the convicts." He raised his eyebrows at Aunt Margaret and took the apple from her fingers, putting it in Clem's hand. "There, take it."

"Never! They are treated like animals over there. They are chained together permanently and beaten and flogged like slaves!"

"They receive only the punishment they deserve." Aunt Margaret was busy peeling a red apple, a luxury not to be spoiled by such rebellious talk. "You continually forget that they are criminals—wicked men!"

"They don't all start out being so wicked, but after a few years in chains they become the devil himself. And nobody cares."

Angus coughed politely. "Now, Clem, you know quite well that many people care. There are ideas for bringing over their women-folk to comfort them, and all sorts of clever notions."

Aunt Margaret mumbled something about "newfangled ideas" and bit into her crisp apple.

"To be exiled from home is punishment enough. To be made to work and to be flogged, too, is brutal. The politicians are giving in to Mr. Gladstone too easily. This country should be peopled by *free* men, and free from the *Home* Government also!"

Aunt Margaret almost dropped her apple with indignation. "But *home* is *home!*" She breathed deeply. "One day you will go home, Clemency. How can you say a thing like that?"

"I have just said it. My home is not England, it is Querilderie. And if Biddy Wright had been given her freedom when she arrived here then she, too, would not have wished to go *home* but to stay here. She has been made bitter. And she is such a good person, far better than I."

"You talk such rubbish! Biddy Wright, indeed!"

Angus cleared his throat once more. "I do agree with some of your sentiments, Clem. There are, however, not enough of us to run this country by ourselves. Our politicians are a wild and woolly lot, don't you know. Some are themselves ex-felons. Those newspaper chaps fill the people's heads with exaggerated ideas. You've been talking too much with your artistic friends. Artists are not reason-able men."

"And pastoralists are? They want to rule this country themselves. Or should I say *own* it? Yes, they would like to squat upon the whole colony and run it like a thousand small city states with no interfer-ence from anyone—the Home Government, the Council, anyone."

Angus laughed. "You may be right. I do not think much of city folk, no matter how worldly wise and loudmouthed. They do not un-derstand sheep or cattle. They would like to ruin this country by building factories and roads all over the place, bringing in thousands of free immigrants to work in them, and building their workers rows of little houses and all the rest of it. They want us to be the Manchester of the South Pacific. In a hundred years' time that is ex-actly what we will be."

"I won't like that either. But I do not think that encouraging more convict labor is going to stop it."

Angus grunted and shrugged his shoulders. "Perhaps."

"You are too young to know what you think. Angus, do not encourage her." Aunt Margaret smiled indulgently at Clem, her apple finished down to an evenly bitten white core. The circles of red peel lay upon her fine china plate. "Would you care for a Van Diemen's land apple, Angus?"

Angus laughed and took one, biting into it eagerly, watching the disgusted expression on Clem's face. "You read too many newspapers. The most notorious rag of all is edited by a convict chap."

"He's an emancipist and as free as you or I!" Clem's eyes blazed.

"Yes, of course. And a very clever man he is, too. They are all clever—the journalists." Angus chewed vigorously, then smiled at her condescendingly. "It's not worth upsetting yourself with these problems."

"There you are, Clemency. What did I tell you? Angus also thinks ladies are above these matters; they should concern themselves with domestic activities. Where is your embroidery? May I see it after dinner?" She shot Clem a warning glance while Angus's attention was taken by the port wine bottle.

The wind died down during the night, leaving the harbor area littered with the aftermath. The shoreline was radically altered by huge waves moving tons and tons of sand out to sea and leaving seaweed and driftwood in a great pile along the edge of the water, yards of it stretching as far inland as the streets and gardens of the low-lying properties.

The day dawned gray but fine, and Angus suggested he drive Clem to the Misses Maybright's in his phaeton, which had remained unharmed in the stables overnight.

They drove along the South Head Road, finding little to say to each other. Angus commented on the fallen trees at the roadside without mentioning the gangs of convicts in their white smocks sent out in work parties to make the way safe for passing traffic.

Recalling her conversations with Matt, Clem wondered why more of them didn't escape inland to freedom.

"Don't feel too sorry for them," Angus cautioned.

"I can't help feeling sorry. I would rather resort to bushranging than live on here in such humiliating circumstances."

"That's silly." Angus shook his head at her and looked out at the sea. "The waves are still high."

Clem watched the huge green breakers gathering momentum before galloping into the bay to smash themselves against the piles of weed and driftwood. A cold wind blew clusters of stale yellow foam toward the houses by the shore.

"We had a dray of wool taken only a year or so ago by those fellows." Angus nodded at the convicts. "Bushrangers. My father lost a great deal of money. None of it was ever recovered."

"How did they do it?" Clem asked, hugging herself against the wind.

"In the usual manner—with firearms, and there were four of them to our one driver."

"Where did it happen?"

"Somewhere along the Pringle Road. They hide it thereabouts, then get it to Sydney somehow, where it's sold. One wonders who arranges all that." Angus kicked at a traveling rug lying half obscured by the seat. "Put that around your knees. You look freezing."

She picked it up and laid it flat upon her lap. They were in the narrow streets of the town now, passing the Military Barracks in George Street. Clem remembered William with a pang. "I'm supposed to be sketching with Mr. Purley at Hyde Park this morning. I wish you had dropped me there."

Angus stared at the road ahead, turning right into King Street, then stopping outside the Misses Maybright's Academy for Young Presbyterian Ladies.

"May I be allowed to meet you and take you home after school?" He jumped down, helping her to alight.

"Thank you, Angus. I realize that my aunt has arranged for you to escort me everywhere in case I abscond again, and I am sure it would be very generous of you to drive me back to her house. I hope I will not prove too much of an imposition upon your time."

Angus bowed very low. "On the contrary, my dear; I find all this the perfect excuse for being in your company for as long as possible!" He proffered his arm and led her grandly toward the entrance of the Academy.

The footpath was crowded with people hurrying up the hill to the market place, or downhill toward the docks: well-dressed men and women and people in various stages of shabby dress. Some carried large baskets upon their heads and others plied their trade upon the edge of the footpath.

One man was sharpening knives with the aid of an intricately painted machine. It stood next to a cart piled high with fresh mackerel and flatheads.

Clem stopped before the door of the school and studied the bustling crowd. "Do you realize, Angus, that a hundred years from now each of these people will have been replaced by someone else. How strange it is to think . . ."

Angus pulled at her sleeve. "You are so fey. What funny stuff you talk. Come now, or you'll be late. Have you your aunt's note?"

"Yes, yes, I have it. I'll go in by myself. Thank you, Angus." She released her arm and bolted through the door. Angus was beginning to annoy her.

The Misses Maybright expressed no interest in employing William, much to Clem's consternation, as the image of the Purley family slowly starving to death in the little yellow house was constantly with her. A lady's companion received very little in payment and then mostly in kind, and by the look of Hetty, her health would not allow her to work for long.

She prayed fervently she would not be cut off from William forever. He had proved to be an intriguing source of new ideas to shake her out of her dullness. His many observations on the boring everyday aspects of life kept her mulling over ideas and images which were quite new to her poor starved mind. And how she admired his genius. She was too dull and simple to be a good companion to him. He would soon tire of her. Upon further consideration of the family's plight, she decided to buy the portrait. She had a little money in Sydney—enough for the first payment anyway. At this point, her thoughts were interrupted by the luncheon gong and she was forced to join the line of giggling girls in their bright smocks slowly moving toward the dining room.

There was not one of them in whom she could confide. They all led such sheltered, chaperoned lives. When, as an exercise for her first elocution lesson, she'd been asked to describe her life at Querilderie—her sheep herding and boundary riding—the murmurs of disbelief had been rife throughout the classroom. She'd sat down feeling clumsy and awkward at the others' whispering and staring.

Miss Florence Maybright had explained to the class that Clem's district had been settled rather recently and life there was a little more primitive than in the pastoral areas nearer Sydney. She had gone on to say that most young ladies from such faraway places had governesses whereas Clem, fortunate enough to have a modern and enlightened papa, had been sent to Sydney to finish her education properly.

This little speech singled Clem out as an oddity from the very beginning. Most of the girls ignored her when they did not actively shun her. It had never occurred to Clem that she might put herself out to be friendly with them, as she had long ago convinced herself she preferred the solitary state.

The last few weeks of winter turned into a brief spring and then a hot summer. Clem had not forgotten William. She'd managed to escape from school one luncheon hour during the spring term and had run all the way from King Street to Argyle Place.

No one had answered her insistent knocking at the yellow front door, and peeping through the front window she'd seen that the small drawing room was completely empty. She'd been forced to admit that the house was deserted.

Disappointed, she'd descended the stairs into the street and had wandered along the footpath hoping for the appearance of a friendly neighbor, but all the other houses were empty as well. Even the church had appeared strangely neglected, almost as though awaiting demolition. Only the rapid scurrying of the red worker ants had disturbed the eerie stagnation of the place.

She had stood for a moment to look at the house for the last time. The sun, shining down from the middle of the dusty Sydney sky, had accentuated her finger marks on the front window and turned the grit on the date-palm leaves to silver.

Perhaps he wouldn't have wanted to see me anyway, she'd thought, the memory of that last afternoon now startlingly alive.

The sunny day mocking her distress, she'd walked back to school wondering who might have any idea of his whereabouts.

During the first hot days of November, Clem sat in her aunt's garden trying to draw the summer wildflowers. Seated behind her small sketching easel with the kitchen cat purring at her feet, the memory of William and that strange episode of her life became almost unreal.

The small, darkly colorful house and the thick odor of tobacco and oil paint were a world completely removed from the long grass, yellow daisies and native irises at the bottom of Aunt Margaret's diligently watered terraces. The little green pools of the creek bed were alive with tiny brown frogs and huge dragonflies, their long, watery wings reflecting the blue of the flax lilies which grew in thick clumps by the shallow banks.

She persevered for hours at her drawing, improving a little day by day until eventually she felt skilled enough to attempt watercolors.

Angus visited every afternoon, full of praise for her efforts. They had achieved a lukewarm understanding. He tolerated her views on Sydney society with an affectionate smile while subtly changing the subject to practical matters. He talked at length about his collection of zoological specimens, and every Sunday afternoon they walked in the forest behind the house and down toward the Double Bay to look for opossums and kangaroo rats and other small animals, the smaller marsupials being Angus's special interest.

Christmas drew near with no sign of a visit from Clem's mother or of any improvement in her condition. Clem wrote letter after letter to her father, begging to be allowed home, but she received only two replies. They were brief descriptions of her mother's health, and neither acknowledged her desire to return home.

Twice she managed to escape her aunt's diligent eye while shopping in George Street. Pretending to lose her in the crowds, she hailed a four-wheeler and bribed the driver to convey her at breakneck speed to the house in Argyle Place. Perhaps William had received another country commission and would have returned by now, but the house remained empty, the date palm smothered with dust, and the red ants starved out of their nest.

Returning to George Street upon the second occasion, hoping to persuade her aunt yet again that it was her hopeless sense of direction which had led her so astray, the cab driver was forced to take a roundabout route by the docks.

She stared out at everybody on the footpaths and up every tiny alley, hoping that by some miracle she would catch a glimpse of William or perhaps Mrs. Purley or Hetty. She prayed fervently for each dark head to be William's and each blue bonnet Hetty's.

She was just about to sit back in her seat, her temples throbbing from stretching her neck and straining her eyes, the latter so dust filled that the hope of recognizing anyone was slim, when she was seized with a spasm of incredulous joy. She had not seen William—but there was Matt!

"Stop!" She shrieked at the driver, opening the door and clutching it to her as the cab tried to edge into the gutter.

She jumped from the still-moving carriage, the driver's curses following her as she ran across the busy road and down the opposite footpath, trying to keep the battered hat and faded gray cotton shoulders in sight. She ran heedlessly along the crowded footpath, pushing people aside and racing around them into the gutter and out again.

He turned left at the next corner. She sped along the gutter and cut across the corner in front of two elderly gentlemen, one of whom she sent careening into the wall. With only a cursory glance at the old man, she turned into the little side street between two gray stone warehouses, shouting at Matt to stop.

The man—just for a second she admitted the possibility that it might not be he—stopped and swiveled around on his heel.

She fell back against the wall, completely winded. It was Matt.

He walked toward her, frowning. Perhaps he had not recognized her.

She pulled off her bonnet, her hair falling down her back in long thick yellow corkscrews. "It's me, Clem—don't you know me?"

His step faltered and she looked at his tall, lithe body, every tiny characteristic of form and movement so precisely well-remembered. Then she looked up at his face.

She tried to stop herself from comparing it to William's: his fair, oval face with William's long, dark one. She could almost taste the sun-bleached countryman's clothes, so insubstantial against the somber stone of the city buildings echoed by William's dark and dusty colors. Then William's pale, town face, his sunken, late-night eyes disappeared into the endless rows of gray-brown buildings, eclipsed by the clear, cerulean blue of the other's.

Matt's eyes were as light and artless as the early morning sky. William had called him "Pure Blue Eyes"; how knowing he was. William possessed all the cunning of the city-bred animal, the one who is forced to acquire extra skills, whereas Matt . . . She couldn't meet his gaze when he finally stood only a few inches from her face.

He said something which she didn't catch. She knew the city street did not diminish him or change him, but she was afraid it might do all sorts of awful things to her. When she finally spoke her voice was horribly unnatural. "What a shock!"

"Well, look at me, for God's sake." He slid the top of a lightly clenched fist gently along the underside of her chin.

She tensed all her muscles. Then she tilted her head back and stared at his forehead, then at his cheeks, wondering where his fist was, having a desperate urge to reach for it and to hold on to it.

"Look at me!" Both his hands were on her cheeks. Her eyes looked crookedly into his and he started to laugh, still holding her head. "You look so bloody different I wouldn't have known you, but you're just the bloody same!"

She went quite limp and sagged against the wall. "I'm glad you think that." His hands held her shoulders back against the wall.

"You've been running too fast. You look as though you're going to faint."

"No—just hang onto me. I've lost my breath, that's all."

"What're you doing down here, anyway?" He leaned against the wall and supported her, his arm under her shoulder blades.

He must have taken off his hat at some stage during the last two minutes, for now she could see his untidy blond curls, damp from being squashed inside the soft, sweat-marked crown. The hand which was not digging into the meager flesh of her upper arm was twirling the hat round and round in a kind of frenzy.

"Stop it!"

"What?"

"What you're doing with your hat—it's making me dizzy!"

"Sorry."

"Don't say sorry—don't be sorry for anything. I'm not sorry for anything. Not now."

"What d'you mean?"

"I'm just so glad I saw you."

His fingers tightened on her arm. "That dress is a bit fancy. I mean, d'you always wear dresses like that?" He was smiling.

She looked down at the dress. It was rather ornate: primrose tarlatan with the inevitable rosebuds around the scalloped hem done in gold. "Oh, God—yes!" She started to shake with silent laughter, then broke into spasms of uncontrollable giggles, pushing his arm away and backing into the middle of the deserted alley. She started to pirouette and curtsy in a parody of one of the popular dances of the day. "Dear Mr. Brennan, I do not see your name upon my card!" She subsided into the shelter of the wall as two young men turned into the street. "Yes, it's a stupid dress and so am I."

He did not comment.

"Well, am I stupid?"

"I don't think so. That is, I think I don't want you to really get like that—you know—silly."

"I'm not silly yet." She stepped back from the wall and put her arms around his chest. "I wish we could go home. I'd like us to go home together."

He tried to edge away from her, his arms straight at his sides, his elbows hard into the stone. "You don't really mean it—you bloody well know nothing would work with you, even if —I mean *nothing*."

"When *will* you be home?"

"I don't know. I've got to get enough money to start up on my own. I don't know anything yet."

"Where are you living?"

"Nowhere—that is—nowhere where you could come. I'll see you before I leave Sydney. I'll get in touch. I know where that school is."

"Have you seen my school?"

"Yep, I've seen it plenty of times. I might have seen you, too."

"Why didn't you—?"

"Speak to you? I never got that close."

"But—"

"I couldn't speak to you." He looked down at his shirt and trousers.

"I wouldn't have cared," she said.

"Maybe *I* would have."

"I'm glad you did then. I hate that school; I wouldn't like to think of you being anywhere near it."

"No. Well then, I'll see you."

"Please kiss me."

He let his fingertips rest on her shoulders and kissed her softly on the mouth. "I'll see you again," he whispered, then pushed her to one side and walked away down the street.

She stood watching him, remembering Darling Street and Mrs. Oxley's oranges—their sweet-sour taste, and her mother, and only when she was in the cab again, the irate driver having searched for her and waited at the corner, did she remember telling him she didn't want to see him anywhere near the Misses Maybright's Academy. So where *did* he intend to see her?

Then she pictured herself doing that ridiculous dance. He hadn't thought it funny at all. She must have seemed very foolish to him. The horrid little street *had* changed her.

She cursed the noisy, stinking city streets, then lay back in the leather seat, realizing that he would never try to see her again while she was in Sydney and that he would never return to Querilderie and that she might never have the courage to travel north to find him.

Chapter Fourteen

The Maclean girls visited over Christmas. Una had recently announced her engagement to the son of a wealthy squatter from the Pringle area, much to her mother's joy and relief. This young man was a great friend of the famous Parramatta family, so it was arranged that if Angus could drag himself away from his complicated cataloging of his latest tiny opossum for one evening, the Maclean, Merilees, and Thorne households would attend a musical evening at the Parramatta house the night before Christmas Eve.

Angus drove Clem and his younger sister, Jessie, in the phaeton, while the rest of the party traveled in Aunt Margaret's new carriage. This was a grand affair, made locally, but quite equal to anything imported from *home* and certainly as fine as anything which might be waiting at anybody's house, even in the elegant town of Parramatta.

The first person to catch Clem's eye as she was being presented to her hostess was Mr. Michael Pike! His eyes, darting about the room, had stopped in surprised delight at her entrance. He made a swift beeline for her and, bowing low, kissed her hand in a most familiar manner.

Clem was a little taken aback, and pretended to be more so for the benefit of her hostess and two of her daughters who were astonished at the passion of Mr. Pike's attentions.

"Miss Cameron! I have *dreamed* of this moment! Why have we not met before? You have been in hiding—or perhaps at your home, lost in the wilderness." He relinquished her hand and stepped back, admiring her with his shifty brown eyes.

"You need not have pined for me, for I saw you in York Street with another gentleman some months ago, but you failed to recognize me." Something stopped her from mentioning the true place of the sighting.

"York Street? Can't say I remember being there. . . . "

Clem was just about to jog his memory by recalling his companion with the bushy eyebrows when that same gentleman approached from the door of the music room. "Who is that man?" she whispered urgently.

Mr. Pike's eyes swiveled to the left. "Henry Aspinall's old man, Edward. You probably know Adelaide, his sister."

"I don't know any of them actually."

"You seemed deuced interested in Edward. Why?"

"I think I've seen him before, or someone like him."

"You may have met Henry. They are not unalike."

Clem shook her head. "No, I haven't met anyone, yet."

"In that case, let me introduce you to everyone. Everyone must meet you, or we will have a room full of bitterly frustrated people!" He took her arm and was about to propel her into the drawing room when the sound of discordant strings came from the music room.

Clem breathed a sigh of relief. "The music has started. I must take my seat. Please excuse me." She tried to withdraw her arm, but he held on to it tightly. "Please, Mr. Pike, I—"

"I believe you have been having your portrait painted by that fellow Purley?" His voice was softly insinuating.

"Why, yes. How did you—?" She stopped in confusion as she felt the blood rushing to her neck and face. She opened her fan and covered her cheeks with it.

"I know the fellow somewhat. They tell me that he and his wife and her mother have moved from that house in Argyle Place. There was some sort of to-do about it."

"Really?" She drew in her breath. "But Hetty is his sister."

"Oh? Is that what they told you?"

"They have not left Sydney?" She fanned herself slowly, trying to avoid the anxious glances of her aunt who had just spied her and was standing only a few feet away.

"Rumor has it they are still somewhere about."

"I'm glad. They are such a nice—"

She was interrupted by her aunt who was accompanied by two daughters of the family and Jessie, Angus's little sister. The taller of the two girls, a pale, gray-eyed, fragile creature, shook a soft auburn curl from her cheek and said, "Your aunt tells me you are at the Misses Maybright's. I was there until two years ago. Do you enjoy your studies?"

"Yes." Clem lowered her fan and waited for the other sister to speak. She was small and fair with a perfect complexion. Her ingenuous blue eyes stared into Clem's. "Particularly the *drawing*," she said, the suggestion of a smile in her refined voice.

Clem studied her tiny upturned nose, delicate pink mouth, and petite, trim figure. "Yes," she replied, "I do enjoy the drawing classes." She stood on the tips of her toes in order to look down upon the small, fair girl from a grand height. "Did you?" Then before the other had time to answer, she said with a smile, "But I suppose you were there sometime ago, possibly too long ago to remember?"

Unperturbed, the petite sister moved closer, excluding another two gentlemen who had joined the group. "We never seem to see you, although my brother's friend George Weston speaks quite a deal about you."

The two men elbowed their way politely into the circle. One of them said, "You must be John Cameron's daughter. Everyone has heard of you and yet no one has met you."

Clem nodded and smiled with as much charm as she could muster beneath the sisters' persistant and unnerving gaze, while the two men introduced themselves.

As Jessie was being presented, Clem whispered to the taller sister, "As I have not met your friend Mr. Weston, only his parents, I am surprised that he should speak of me at all."

Both girls started to speak at once, the smaller one silencing the taller with a precautionary finger. "You've caused quite a splash since you arrived in Sydney, not so much with—" she paused, looking around the drawing room full of eagerly gossiping people—

"with our set, as with the—the artistic world, don't you know." She raised her eyebrows very slightly.

"Oh," said Clem, touching her curls as elegantly as possible, "I must meet this Mr. Weston, as he and I seem to have acquaintances in common."

The taller sister shook her delicate auburn head. "He is not really acquainted with that world, but Sydney society is so small, don't you know?"

The petite sister interrupted. "Mama says it's better to keep it small as then one can keep out the undesirable elements." She twirled about to address Clem's aunt. "Don't you agree, Miss Thorne?"

"Indeed I do, my dear. Your mama is very wise—"

Clem interrupted. "Do you mean the criminal or artisitic elements?" she asked bluntly.

One of the men said, laughing, "If there are any artists in Sydney, I do not know of them."

"Clem knows an artist!" Jessie piped, desperately trying to participate in the conversation. "He—"

"Hush, child!" Aunt Margaret pulled at her puffed sleeve, and she subsided for the moment, setting her mouth into a tight pout.

Clem glowered at her, knowing she would not shut up so easily and wondering what her next outburst would reveal. Overanxious to be accepted and admired, her bright eyes twinkling at everyone in sight, Jessie bounced with impatience.

Clem patted her curls again and fanned her face slowly, talking quietly to the two gentlemen of fox hunting, a sport she'd always wanted to try but for which she'd never had the opportunity. Suddenly Jessie opened her mouth wide and flung her head back, emitting a laugh so loud that all those in the vicinity stared at Clem's small group and couldn't help overhearing Jessie's next giggled words.

"Clem hunts kangaroos! With the stockmen! And she rides bareback, with her skirts tucked into her pantal—"

"Jessie!" hissed Aunt Margaret, as she tugged at her sleeve, almost pulling her off her feet, "Hold your tongue!"

But it was too late. Everyone in the room stared at her, then stared at Clem. Clem's knees were quite wobbly and she wondered

if it were possible to faint from embarrassment. She hid her violently coloring face with her fan as the group quickly disbanded.

Clem stayed where she was, studying the faces. The women were
all attractive and viviacious, but the men seemed quite out of place.
Their sunburned features and sun-bleached hair gave them a startling uniformity of appearance, particularly noticeable in their tight
clothes. They all looked so *sandy*, decided Clem, now staring at
them unashamedly.

One or two were still staring at her, and she caught a glimpse of
the smaller sister's fiancé—perhaps the sandiest of all—and remembered Mrs. Merilees's description of the Parramatta girls. Talented
they were, indeed! She listened to everyone's broad accents, harsh
and twanging like the tuning strings accompanying them from the
music room, sometimes interrupted by the sudden and arbitrary use
of clipped English vowel sounds. They were all trying desperately to
be English, yet they looked and sounded awkward and extremely
un-English, almost like clowns! The thought of Matt's reaction to a
gathering like this made her squirm.

Mr. Pike sidled up to her. "You are too lovely to be left all
alone—an exotic wallflower." He took her arm and pushed her gently toward the nearest group. "The music will start in one minute.
Surely you would not mind meeting just a few—"

"No. I would prefer to go straight into the music room."

"That *is* a pity. You see, I am so well acquainted with everyone
here and could arrange such interesting connections for you—"

"Oh, I see." She drew herself up to her full height and looked Mr.
Pike straight in his sly brown eyes. "Well, sir, as you seem to be
such a fellow about town, and as I am imprisoned in my aunt's
house, perhaps you could convey a message to Mr. Purley for me."

Mr. Pike let go her arm and bowed. "Of course, Miss Cameron. I
would be honored by such a trust."

"I'll scribble something on my program and you can deliver it during the week." She smiled and tripped away into the music room,
followed by Aunt Margaret and Angus.

She sat through the recital trying to remember every tiny detail of
her relations with the Purley family. Fancy that silly Mr. Pike assuming Hetty was William's wife. What nonsense that man talked.
She hoped he would not gossip too much about her note.

She found her way to the library during the interval and scratched
a quick note to William on the back of her program, asking him to

reply as soon as possible as she was interested to know the state of Hetty's health and his family's finances. She signed it, "With love," folded it into four and slipped it into her purse.

She didn't have a moment alone with Mr. Pike until it was time to go home. She accosted him just outside the front door, sliding the note into his sleeve. "Thank you, Mr. Pike. I'm sure there will be a reply. You know where my aunt's house is, I think."

Mr. Pike nodded. "Oh, by the way. Have you heard from your sister's governess lately? The one who prefers to bury herself in the country?"

"No. We do not correspond. I'm surprised you should have recalled my speaking of her, it was so long ago."

"Yes, far too long ago. Your being such a stay-at-home is unfair to the rest of us." He took the note from his sleeve and pushed it into his breast pocket. "I have remembered you, and everything about you vividly. I found your observations upon rum shops quite diverting. I hope, despite your desire to remain so solitary, we will meet again. I'm sure you would find me just as amusing as your friend Mr. Purley." He bowed exaggeratedly.

Clem bade him a swift good night and ran to where Angus's phaeton waited at the edge of the drive.

After they'd settled themselves for the ride back to Sydney, Angus asked her why she'd cornered Mr. Pike in such a flagrant manner. "I object to the chap's familiarity. I hope you don't intend to let it continue."

"No. It was a private matter, that is, it wasn't.We shared a joke about the manager of the Willawarrha Hotel, that's all."

Angus grunted and settled himself more comfortably into the driving seat.

"Is he really accepted so wholeheartedly by such families? He's a little mysterious." Clem tucked the traveling rug about Jessie's knees.

"Yes. I've encountered him once before at your aunt's friends the Westons. They are also wool merchants and very well-to-do. He's of good solid Somerset stock, or so I've been told, yet he seems a little—"

Clem nodded. She knew she shouldn't have entrusted him with her note. Perhaps he didn't know William at all!

Angus continued, "He's a great crony of the Aspinall son, Henry, and his father, too."

"The man with the eyebrows?"

Angus frowned. "Yes. They are a peculiar family. The son, Henry, married a woman some years his senior. Deuced funny thing to do. She ran off and left him. The family was relieved, as it turned out she was an emancipist—a thief. She just disappeared one day. They say his father paid her to go. Caused a bit of a shindig at the time."

"What a scandal!"

"Mmm, poor old Henry's still married to the woman!" Angus chortled. "Silly sort of chap really."

"Goodness."

"It's all forgotten now. All happened many years ago."

Jessie sat forward, her hands clasped between her knees, insisting on reviving the topic of the fascinating Mr. Pike.

"He is a bit of a dandy. Don't you think so, Clem?" Jessie went on to describe his clothes in great detail. "I think he is so charming." She sighed with contentment and fell fast asleep, her red curls bobbing in time to the horses' hooves.

Clem laughed ironically. "Jessie has never looked further than outward appearance in her choice of beaux. I hope she was not too impressed by Mr. Pike. He has all the false charm of a remittance man."

"What was the chap doing at Willawarrha?"

"I think he was selling rum to Mr. O'Brien, or so he implied."

"He's a great crony of all the merchants in town. Some say a few of these fellows are not always aboveboard in their commercial practices. Perhaps they use him in some way." Angus frowned and peered into the darkness for potholes. They could just see the faint light from Aunt Margaret's carriage lantern half a mile ahead on the straight road.

Suddenly the light disappeared round a bend and there was nothing to guide them but the few stars visible behind the swiftly moving clouds. There was no moon and the wind was strong. Clem wrapped Jessie more securely in her traveling rug and pulled her own shawl tightly about her shoulders.

Angus did not feel the wind, as he was too busy trying to fathom how Mr. Pike managed to dress so well when rumor had it he was a remittance man from home with very little remittance.

"I think that fellow is to be avoided."

"Yes, I suppose you're right. He's always in the strangest places."

"What strange places?" Angus involuntarily jerked the reins and slowed the horses.

She knew she'd said too much and would now have to explain how she came to be in Mr. Jenkyn's establishment at Darling Harbor.

"I hesitate to mention the name, but William, that is, Mr. Purley, and I were walking along the waterfront and called in at a tobbaco shop which we were surprised to find was something else as well."

"You mean that criminal, Jenkyn's place, do you?"

"I knew you'd be angry. We didn't know. William said he dealt in stolen goods!"

"That's well known. The police turn a blind eye to his activities; they find it too hard to actually prove anything. And you were in that place!"

"Yes."

"That old man is notorious. He has some very interesting sidelines." He laughed and whipped up the horses. They were a fine pair of bays and soon overtook Aunt Margaret's heavy four, reaching the Point Piper Road just after midnight. Angus sent Jessie up to bed and asked Clem to help him with the horses.

"We'll bed them down for the night together. Remember my pony at Glen Ross? You coveted him at one stage. Do you still ride that little piebald?"

"Magpie? Yes, I do. Matt says he's too small for me now. He has a beautiful horse."

"Did he *buy* the animal?"

"Yes." She was surprised at his tone. "He didn't steal it, if that's what you mean."

"No, I assumed he found it unbranded in the hills. Some do that, the ones who can't afford to attend the horse sales."

"He can afford to. He will do very well. He has great ideas." Clem leaned against the stable wall, watching Angus rubbing down the bays. He had flung his coat on the side of the stall and rolled his shirtsleeves up to his shoulders. His ginger-freckled arms were thick with knotted muscle and very pale in the carriage light. Above him, hanging from the rafters and wrapped in torn linen sheets, were four plum puddings. They'd been hanging there since July.

"I will do well, too. Admittedly with the help of my father's land. What I most urgently need now to complete my good fortune is a wife." He straightened up, a piece of old horse blanket in one hand, the other resting on the horse's wet rump. "I wish you would marry me."

Clem gulped. "What?" She felt as if she would burst out laughing.

"Please, Clem, will you marry me?" He let the cloth fall from his hand and took two steps toward her. "You will *have* to marry someone, and we know each other *quite* well and should suit each other."

Despite her still uncontrollable urge to laugh she managed to blurt out, "I'm flattered you should ask me, although I know it's expected of you by our parents, and I would have said yes, but—"

"Not that painter fellow! He's not your lover? I thought—"

"No! No one is my lover. But I don't want to marry anyone yet."

"You couldn't do much better than me. I'm not a romantic kind of chap. I've never brought you flowers or anything like that. I will if you want me to, I—"

"No, Angus. It's not that."

"I though those things didn't impress you. When we live at Glen Ross you will have anything you wish for, as many horses, dogs—"

"Angus!" She looked up at the plum puddings. Like turbaned Indians hanging upside down, they swayed gently in the breeze from the half-opened door.

"And you can help with my research. Your drawing! You can be my illustrator! I intend to concentrate on the smaller tree marsupials, and there are—"

"Dear Angus," she tried not to sound too condescending, "I'm so fond of you—like a brother, I expect. I've never known a brother unless—"

"It's him, isn't it? Matt Brennan. I've been away too long. Why didn't you tell me?"

"I have nothing to tell you about anyone. There is no one else. I don't like the idea of marriage at all. My aunt says, and my mama, too, that—"

"Please, Clemency, I cannot imagine going home without you, please consider me seriously."

"But I don't want to be domesticated or just a mother, you know."

"You will be whatever you like at Glen Ross—just yourself. You may help on the place when you feel inclined or just do nothing at all. Your mother has never lifted a finger at Querilderie, so why should you?"

"She would like to have done some baking, but my father wouldn't let her. There's nothing for her to do, you see. She hates sewing as much as I do and her playing is awful and her drawing too. She was only half alive with boredom and my father kept accusing her of laziness and . . . "

"She could have ridden."

"She was too weak for that."

"You're just talking all the time to put off your answer. *Will* you marry me?"

"No. But thank you very much."

Suddenly Angus grabbed her about the waist and started to kiss her, pressing his teeth and lips into hers. She fought him off frantically, which only increased his ardor. He pulled back a little and took her by the shoulders. "Is that how that chap, that bloody painter kissed you? Is it?" He took a handful of her hair and put his other hand at the back of her neck and kissed her again, this time with extreme passion, his mouth forcing hers open as he tried to imprison her legs between his knees.

She tried to scream, then thought better of it, not wanting to wake the servants. Her fists hit out at him wherever they could. She bit his lips, and he drew back laughing, wiping his bleeding mouth with his bare arm.

"You little vixen! I'll bloody well have you! Be damned to your painters and Irish tinks. I'll have you!" He turned on his heel and, pushing back the stable door with a loud thud, strode off in the direction of the house, still cursing.

Clem watched him more in amazement than anger. He had left his coat. She picked it up and dusted it down. The plum puddings swayed energetically in the wind from the open door. Poor Angus. She walked out into the night wind and shut the stable door.

"It will be a hot, windy day tomorrow," she said aloud to comfort herself. She felt her mouth. It was swelling up on one side. Her head was tender where he'd pulled her hair. She wondered how so much lust could be engendered by family duty. It must have been that, she told herself, as he had not mentioned love.

Her aunt's housekeeper, Sybil, waylaid her at the top of the stairs. "Miss Clemency, would you speak to me for a moment?"

"Certainly, Sybil." Clem tried to hid her bruised lip with a corner of her shawl.

"I think you might guess what it's about."

Clem stiffened. "I couldn't possibly."

"It's that man. Everybody in Sydney knows about you and him. So far your aunt has been spared—"

"For heaven's sake, Sybil. I stopped seeing him or, more correctly, *sitting* for him some weeks ago, and I would be obliged if you would inform your friends and those friends of my aunt's who are so ill-mannered as to discuss my private affairs behind my back, that any relationship which existed between the brilliant, slandered Mr. Purley and myself was strictly a business one. I commissioned him to paint me. That is all!" Her trembling fingers let the shawl go, exposing her swollen lip.

Sybil was smirking. "Of course that was all, Miss Clemency. I never doubted it. But others' minds, you see, are not always so free of wicked fancies and suspicions and such."

"Well, I'm sure your mind is, and my aunt's, and that is all that matters. May I go now?"

"One more thing." Sybil's eyes started to cross alarmingly. "Miss Thorne has not been welcomed at certain Sydney homes of late, and it can only be because of *your* behavior. I wish—"

"What nonsense! My aunt has preferred the company of the Merilees lately. I refuse to hear any more." Clem moved toward her room. "Good night, Sybil."

She noticed that Sybil didn't curtsy but just stood still, her sly eyes following her along the hall.

That poor thing is remarkably ugly, thought Clem, as she shut and locked her bedroom door. What rubbish she talked. It was all the Merileeses' fault; even Angus had mentioned something to that effect. People were not so fond of them as her aunt appeared to be, and as she tended to take them with her on every invitation, people had just cooled a little. Clem flopped down on her bed and unfastened her boots, kicking them into a corner, and massaging her squashed toes, remembered her happy, barefoot days at home.

Chapter Fifteen

Christmas Day dawned hot and still. Aunt Margaret, Clem, and the Maclean girls went to church in the morning, leaving the servants to cook the enormous goose and steam the puddings.

The temperature was just over ninety degrees and Clem was not looking forward to the plate of greasy meat and vegetables and colonial claret followed by the even heavier puddings and rich brandy butter. She felt that Christmas ought to be celebrated in July in the South Pacific.

Angus was there to welcome them back from church, making a point of taking his sister's arm, the other sister, Una, being monopolized by her fiancé, the wealthy Pringle squatter, whose sudden arrival had delighted everybody.

Her family ought to be delighted, mused Clem, as she studied Mr. Gilzean over the goose and prune stuffing. He was not only the picture of grace and conformity, good build, honest eyes, and honest freckled skin, but was also very wealthy. She realized he was a carbon copy of Angus, only a lighter shade all over. His hair was curly but a lighter orange, his freckles, though just as dense, were paler, and his carriage and the dimensions of his person were almost identical. She recalled William's comments about her own chameleon qualities and tried to imagine both men against a backdrop of yellow sandstone. Both would completely disappear. She started to giggle at the picture.

"Clemency, may we share the joke?" Una smiled at her, her slightly buck teeth looking a tiny bit yellow against the bright pink of her lip rouge.

Una was always so determined to be a lady of fashion, yet she never quite succeeded. Each separate article of clothing never quite went with any other.

Clem stared at the tiny lace-trimmed collar fastened with a large blue cameo. The blue of the cameo clashed remarkably with the blue of the dress. "Oh, it's no joke. I was just thinking of something funny." She didn't mean to look at Angus, but unaccountably found herself doing so.

Angus went a deep red. He lifted his wine and drained his glass, then began on his pudding with unseemly haste.

Jessie laughed. "Look at Angus. He has drunk too much wine. Mother says wine is a curse. Only those who understand moderation must indulge in it."

"Angus is a very moderate man." Clem finished her small helping of pudding. She felt rather dizzy with wine. She hoped her face was not red also.

"What do you chaps think of the latest political row? Er, not you, Miss Thorne. I beg your pardon." Mr. Gilzean nudged Una for support.

"What row, Robert?" Una simpered sweetly upon everyone. She was touchingly proud of her Robert. She was transported with bliss whenever he opened his mouth.

Clem had watched her watching him devour every mouthful, as though he was an ailing pet whom she'd promised to succour.

"Oh, all that transportation lark. Went to the meeting a couple of weeks ago. It was killing!"

"Really?" Clem sat forward. "What meeting?"

"Some of the newspaper chappies, you know, that emancipist-ridden lot and a few cronies of theirs—a few free settlers; I was perhaps the only sheep grazier there. They want to stop the *exiles* coming."

"Clem would approve of that." Una simpered again.

"I most certainly would. Do you want slave labor to persist on your property forever, Mr. Gilzean?"

"*Yes,* my dear. And call me Robert. We are about to be in-laws, I think."

There was a strained silence. Angus poured himself another glass of claret which overflowed slightly onto Aunt Margaret's best linen cloth. All eyes were glued to the spot.

"Biddy!" Aunt Margaret screamed for salt to take away the stain, and Mr. Gilzean's remark was forgotten.

"The blighters are better off at Pringle than in a hulk on the Thames. We're doing them a favor by having them here," said Angus ignoring Biddy's efforts to wipe up the pink salt, not bothering to move his arms out of the way.

"Take your elbows off the table." Clem admonished him.

He ignored her.

"You're both like my father. Don't you see that it's the *idea* of forced labor that is so terrible. The Home Government is just using this exile idea to resume the whole transportation thing again. They want to build more convict colonies."

"Well, what's so awful about that?" asked an innocent Mr. Gilzean.

"It's the way they're treated. I've heard terrible things about the Parramatta Factory—those poor women—Biddy will tell you. It degrades people so!"

Biddy had just left the room.

"Call her back and ask her if she's not better off here than in a hulk on the Thames!" Mr. Gilzean struck his knife handle on the table. "Call her!"

"You must refrain from this talk, children," said Aunt Margaret, glowering at Clem. "And you are the worst. I've told you countless times that it's not right for young women to harbor *ideas* or to have *opinions.*"

Clem looked down at the lump of sickly brandy butter on her curly-edged pudding plate and felt almost ill with frustration.

"Clem's friends with all sorts of people," piped Jessie. "Adelaide Aspinall—you know her, I think, Miss Thorne—well, she told me her papa told her not to speak to Clem as she knew some acquaintances of Mr. Pike's who are not nice."

There was another nervous hush around the table. Una looked away from her adored fiancé seeking an explanation from each in turn. Finally, her eyes rested on Clem.

"You should be asking your sister the meaning of all this, not me.

I don't know what she's talking about, unless it's that Mr. Aspinall was in the shop of an old emancipist who deals in stolen property, because I saw him there."

"I don't know where it was, but Adelaide's father saw you walking with a terrible man—a painter! Not the kind of man your mama would wish you to be with."

"Jessie!" Angus shouted. "This is telling tales out of school!"

Clem mustered her most supercilious tone. "I am surprised at you, Jessie. I was under the distinct impression that you had expressed more than just a liking for this smart Mr. Pike."

"I didn't realize what he was like then."

"Rubbish. You have not met him since, have you?"

The table was once again ominously silent.

Jessie stared at Clem with a foolish grin on her childish features. "Yes."

Aunt Margaret drew in her breath with a sharp hissing sound and let her fork fall on the spotless white area in front of her plate. "What did you say?"

"He came into your garden only last evening, Miss Thorne. Just to say how d'ye do. He was passing in his gig. I invited him to sit on the lawn."

"You invited him into *my garden*?"

"Well, he invited himself, and it was so hot on the road I had not the heart to refuse."

"And?" Aunt Margaret had picked up her fork and was pointing it at Jessie's chest.

"That's all. He looked a bit funny. His eyes move about so."

"What did he have to say?" Clem shot Jessie a warning glance, then added casually, "Just the usual Sydney gossip, I suppose."

"Yes. He said nothing of consequence." Jessie carefully extracted a threepence from her plum pudding.

Aunt Margaret called for Biddy once again. She came through the door carrying the second pudding and a bottle of brandy. Mr. Gilzean leaped to his feet and, grabbing the bottle, poured a great deal of the clear brown liquid over the steaming pudding.

"Angus, a light!" He shouted, but Angus was already at his side reaching past Biddy to Sybil who carried a lighted taper high in the air. He lit the brandy and the pudding burst into blue flame, turning Biddy's small brown face into a frightened purple mask.

"Careful!" shouted Clem, but the flames quickly died, and the luncheon quietly resumed.

Clem was in a fever of apprehension. She was sure Jessie would have something further to tell her, or perhaps even a note from William.

During the afternoon walk to the Double Bay, she fell behind the others and was delighted to see Jessie drop something on the track behind her. She hurried to pick it up and secreted it in her purse, meaning to read it when they reached the thicker scrub near the shoreline. Letting the others get far ahead, she dawdled along, looking up at the trees, pretending to be engaged in bird watching.

She stopped and retraced her steps. There had been a nest or something stuck in a paper bark just to the side of the track. She stared up at the thin branches. There were two small lizards and a tiny kangaroo rat impaled on some sharp twigs: the macabre larder of the butcher bird. She studied it for a few moments with a horrified fascination.

Nobody called her to hurry. She took the note from her purse and unfolded it with clumsy fingers, reading the scrawl quickly behind the paper bark.

"Dear Bush Maiden," it read. "How I have missed you. Pike tells me that you miss me too. I shall endeavor to see you as soon as possible. Do not ask when, or how. I cannot leave an address, having only a fraction of one at present. Our circumstances continue to worsen. My sister and mother remain with me, their appetites undiminished. They are insidious creepers affixed to my person and drawing the very sap from my soul. Until we meet again, I shall think of you only with affection. Yours, William."

She stuffed the note into her purse, startled at the sound of a cracking twig.

Angus stood before her. "You have discovered a butcher bird's lair. You see, we do share many interests. I wish you would reconsider."

Clem put her finger to her lips. "Ssh. Not here. Let's catch the others."

Angus looked as though he might try to kiss her again. She sidestepped him with a graceful motion and felt the tips of his fingers upon her back.

"I am sorry for—you know—the stables."

"Oh, that! Never mind. I've told you—" Clem hurried on, keeping well ahead of him—"that I'm flattered." She was panting for breath by the time she reached Aunt Margaret's side. "Aunt! I found a butcher bird's pantry!" She took her arm. "It was horrible. I hear them every morning from my room. What beautiful voices they have for creatures with such horrid habits!" She laughed.

Angus had caught up and was walking just behind them. "The same may be said of some kinds of men—artists, for instance."

Clem dropped her aunt's arm and fell back by his side. "That analogy is a little farfetched," she remarked. "You know nothing of Mr. Purley's character, although his art *is* beautiful."

"I am sure it is." He put his hands in his pockets and stared fixedly down at the track. "I think I'll return home soon. My mother was lonely over Christmas with Marianne gone."

"I don't suppose you've had any news of my mother lately?" Clem asked.

He hesitated. "No, not much really—except that—she is a little less well than you think. I think you ought to come back with me—I—"

"Yes, so do I, but my father will not let me go home!"

Angus bent down to whisper hoarsely into her ear. "I've been warned not to mention it, but your mother is so ill she imagines all kinds of things. She imagines there is something going on between your father and Marianne. It worries me—you *must* go home." He tried to slip his arm beneath hers. "I *will* take you."

"You're already bullying me and we aren't even married, not even engaged! Anyway I can't go home, I've told you. And my mother has always been full of fancies and things. She is so childish."

Angus pursed his lips, "You may be right. I hope so."

"I *am* right. No matter where one is, one is continually surrrounded by rumor and innuendo."

Angus cleared his throat. "Of course *you* would know all about that."

"Oh?"

"Well, you must know what a scandal your *friendship* with this Purley chap has created. People always believe the worst. I'm not saying that I—"

"That's all nonsense! People in Sydney don't have enough to occupy themselves with. I am quite fond of Mr. Purley, although he is—'' She did not want to tell Angus anything about William at all. Talking about him to Angus might somehow lessen her affectionate memories of him. Angus would never understand a man like William. She clutched her purse more tightly. "He is a gentleman, and there is no cause for any scandal whatsoever."

"I'm sure of it. But others are not. Some of your aunt's friends have avoided her lately, you know, because of you. They prefer not to see her in case they're forced to explain why you've been excluded from so many invitations this season."

"I was not aware that I had. Una did not—"

"Una is a kind girl. She wanted to spare your and your aunt's feelings."

"Oh," said Clem, suddenly quite annoyed. "I can understand her delicacy where my aunt is concerned, but she may have no fear of hurting me. I dislike all those evenings and dinners anyway, and I can't wait to get home and away from all of it."

"I know. I wish I could take you. I wish . . ."

"Well, there's no use wishing. Anyway, my mother might still come to Sydney and I must wait for her."

Angus was silent, his eyes exploring the track for more skeletons, Clem supposed. "You know, Clem, we *do* share many interests."

She shook him roughly by the arm. "Don't be silly. I don't want to marry you—not yet, anyway."

"I think that one day soon you might feel the need of a—a— refuge, a home away from all sorts of things." He looked up into the branches of a tall eucalyptus for inspiration; or perhaps to hide his face as he was blushing so deeply, thought Clem, amazed by this emotional outburst. "Er, what I mean is, if you ever do—need what I have just been saying—remember I'll always be there." His words trailed off into a throaty grunting.

"Angus, I'll cry in a minute!" She forced a light laugh and tugged good-naturedly at his hand. "Stop it! Come on, let's catch the others."

He ran heavily by her side, breathless after his speech. "Very well. You seem impervious to scandal or the fate of your reputation, but I am not, not just because I wish to marry you but because I care for your well-being."

She was suddenly quite touched by his concern, no matter on

what ludicrous nonsense it was based, and started to tell him so when he said, "Did you really see Aspinall in that place—that shop at Darling Harbor?"

"Yes. Why?"

"Nothing. Are you sure?"

She nodded, and led Angus past her aunt to walk abreast of the engaged couple as far as the Double Bay.

She confessed to herself that she did feel reasonably comfortable resting on Angus's broad arm and almost envied Una her uncomplicated existence.

She reread her mother's letters many times that night. There was no mention of Miss Owen or of her worsening state of health. Perhaps her father censored her letters, Clem's too. Her mother had never answered any of her questions or asked any of her. It appeared as though she was continually writing to someone from whom she did not expect a reply. She wrote a long and affectionate letter to her mother, resolving to post it directly to Mrs. Oxley.

The letter left for Burrundi the same day Angus set off to drive to Glen Ross, taking Jessie with him. He had offered to deliver the letter personally to her mother, but Clem had refused, much to his surprise, and when she would not be persuaded at all, he had driven off down the drive, whipping the horses angrily.

"I hope he doesn't cause an accident in the South Head Road," her aunt had said. "You've upset him enough already without that."

Clem felt a few pangs of guilt over her behavior toward her suitor, but he had assumed too much, she decided, and during the next two weeks of frenzied shopping to increase Una's already extensive trousseau, the relief of having turned down his proposal became tenfold.

She was beguiled into all kinds of shopping expeditions by the excited Una, obviously as a ploy to persuade her that marriage could be a great deal of fun. No doubt she would be expected to catch the bouquet at Una's wedding.

That event was to be at Glen Ross sometime during February. Mrs. Maclean was very busy arranging all the ceremonies and cooking and accommodations for all the guests. A new chapel was to be built. Clem couldn't see how it would be finished in time, but Una assured her that her father was determined to have it ready as the Gilzeans had a magnificent chapel on their property, and for Una's sake the thing had to be done.

"He has got all the men working on it. It will be of sandstone and wood. Just a small one, but very pretty. Robert has not yet visited Glen Ross. I hope he approves of Mother's arrangements for the wedding. His mother, don't you know, is so particular."

"And so is Robert. Otherwise he would not have chosen you as his bride."

Una blushed at Clem's compliment. On this occasion they were at Mrs. Hordern's shop in King Street looking at materials and ribbons for bridesmaids' dresses. Una was wearing a dress of pink cotton with silk frills inset into the front of the skirt and a brighter pink mantelet to match. The whole had too much lace, and her bonnet suffered from a surfeit of ribbon.

Two other ladies bending to inspect the sewing silks straightened abruptly at the sound of Una's voice.

Una curtsied. "Mrs. Aspinall! And Adelaide! What a lovely surprise! I don't believe you've met my dear friend, Clemency Cameron."

Clem curtsied.

Adelaide Aspinall was a pale-complexioned girl of about Clem's age. Her mother was a short plump lady with highly colored cheeks. She regarded Clem as majestically as she could from her shorter stature with a pair of round watery blue eyes.

"It is a pleasure, Miss Cameron. I've heard that your mother is unwell. Do accept our sympathy." She pushed her daughter forward. "Adelaide!"

"Yes, indeed, Miss Cameron. Please do accept our sympathies for your poor mama."

Clem, slightly taken aback, said, "Then you know more regarding my mother's state of health than her own daughter. From whom did you obtain this information?"

"From the Westons, my dear. They are great friends of ours and of Miss Thorne's."

"My aunt thinks she does me a service by keeping bad news at bay. I'd heard vague reports of my mama's ill health but nothing so definite. Is it common knowledge?"

"Only among those acquainted with your family, my dear." Mrs. Aspinall's eyes moved over her clothes, studying every detail. "I'm so sorry that you cannot be with your mama. Surely your place is at home at this time? Does your aunt not see fit . . . ?"

"No, she does not. Nobody does." Clem turned to Adelaide, who was hiding behind her mother's fat crinoline. "I believe you're an intimate of an acquaintance of mine, someone whom I met briefly at the Willawarrha Arms Hotel one evening?"

"Er, Mr. Pike, I think you mean. We are not such great friends. Oh, no, Mama, that is, I did mention him to Jessie Maclean."

"Yes, you did. And another gentleman of my acquaintance—a gentleman who happened to be painting my portrait at the time. It was commissioned, you know."

"He is very modern, is he not?" Mrs. Aspinall asked.

"Yes. And very good, too." Clem smiled and tried to bow her way back to the silks.

But Mrs. Aspinall would not let her go. "His way of life, too, is modern. Or so I've heard tell."

"I cannot think what your mama means, Miss Aspinall. He is poor, yes. His father has disowned him. He, like so many other narrow-minded people, does not approve of painters."

"I do not disapprove of painters, Miss Cameron. Just this particular one." She lowered her voice. "May we step over here and leave these two girls to choose some silks? I feel strongly that someone must act in the place of your own mama, seeing as your aunt has been spared most of the unsavory details by her good friends. Come."

To Clem's consternation, Mrs. Aspinall took her hand between her short fat fingers and dragged her into a corner of the shop.

They stood hidden behind two dressmakers' dummies, modestly covered in white sheeting. "Now listen, my dear. I would say the same to my own daughter. In fact, I have some years ago said almost as much to my own son in similar circumstances, although that is dead and forgotten now. You have brought your family into disrepute by consorting, that is, mixing with these types. That woman he passes off as his sister is his *mistress*."

Clem gasped and drew back.

Mrs. Aspinall kept a tight grip with her fingers. "No—you *must* know. The older woman was Mr. Purley senior's housekeeper in England, and that young woman is her daughter. His father is a cad, too. He ruined that woman and then threw her and the daughter out when he learned of his son's entanglement with her. They forged some of the old man's papers and embezzled some of his money and fled to Port Philip. They are no better than convicts." She took out a smelling bottle from her purse and waved it in front of Clem's white face. "There, my dear, I knew it would come as a shock. Better you should know now than later."

"Oh, God! It's not true!" Clem held onto Mrs. Aspinall's fat wrists.

"I'm afraid it is, and if I were you, I would buy that portrait before they put it on public show. Are you *clothed* in it?"

"What? Of course. I am not naked, if that's what you mean!"

"Mmm. Well, I've heard of worse things than doctoring a portrait."

"I can't imagine what you mean, Mrs. Aspinall. And I'm amazed you have taken such an interest in my affairs," Clem said weakly, brushing the salts aside.

"We good families must stick together. I met your father once, and I am a great admirer of Charlotte Weston and she of your aunt. I talked to Miss Thorne only the other evening. Do you feel better now?" Mrs. Aspinall took Clem's arm firmly and the two wandered innocently by the ladies' scents and soaps as though they had been talking idly of some gossip.

Adelaide was not so sure. She looked at Clem's pale face with misgiving, obviously regretting her remarks to Jessie and her mother's audacity. She whispered in her mother's ear.

"Quiet, miss." Mrs. Aspinall poked her in the ribs with her fan. "*You* are the busybody in this family. Shall we go?"

The ladies made their farewells and disappeared into the busy street.

"Oh, Una, I feel weak. Can we go home?"

Una suddenly realized that something was amiss. She put her arm about Clem's waist. "Whatever is the matter? You look ill!"

"I shall be all right. I must have some air. I cannot stand the smell of scent and soap any longer. Quick!" Clem stumbled to the door, Una still holding on to her waist.

The air of King Street was not very fresh. It was early afternoon, and although the fish had long since disappeared with the smelly fishmongers who sold it on every street corner in Sydney, the odor was still heavy in the air, mixed with axle grease and sewage. Clem coughed and ran to Aunt Margaret's carriage. She couldn't explain the reason for her distress to poor little innocent Una. If only she could have spoken to William! It wasn't true!

The girls drove back to the Point Piper Road, Clem quickly recovering her composure to spare any further scenes. Her aunt instinctively ignored any change in her mood, resenting any aberration from the softly spoken, domesticated, cultured young lady, whom she imagined Clem had become. This metamorphosis had taken place in Aunt Margaret's mind only because she had so earnestly desired it. She had put the Mr. Purley episode too far behind her to have it dragged out now without being profoundly shaken. Clem sighed, looking up at Aunt Margaret's windows shining in the harsh sunlight. "She'll lock me in my room and tell everybody that I am insane."

"What?" Una was startled out of a dream of Mr. Gilzean. "Why would she do that?"

"Have you noticed, Una, how parents can never admit the wickedness of any of their offspring, as that would reflect upon themselves? Madness, on the other hand, is never their fault. Angus sometimes treats me as though I were a simpleton."

"Why would she lock you up? What do you intend to do?" Una regarded her with bewildered eyes. The two girls climbed out of the carriage, and Una quickly raised her parasol.

"Don't say a thing to anyone, but I want to see Mr. Purley just once more before I go home. My aunt would not approve."

"She certainly would not. I hope it will be only once. I, too, have Angus's interests at heart, don't you know."

"So have I. Mr. Purley is just a friend. No one likes him as he is a bit unusual and invites horrid tales about himself—all *untrue*, of course."

Una shrugged. "I will not say a word, as long as you promise not to do anything silly. Angus told me you have refused him. I told him you were too young and to wait until you'd been home for a while. He hopes to arrange for you to return to Querilderie as soon as possible."

"Then he is a true friend." She took Una's arm, and gently pushing her parasol to one side, whispered into her ear. "Remember, Una not a word!"

Clara Merilees was waiting for them in the library. She bustled over to the two girls, delighted at their early return. "We did not think to see you until tea! Now we have time to talk! You look so pale, Clemency, so unlike you!" She waved her to a chair, then sat down in the chair opposite. "That's better. Una, have you some parcels to put away?"

Una curtsied and tactfully left the room.

"Oh, Mrs. Merilees, a dreadful woman, a Mrs. Aspinall, attacked
me in the soaps and scents! She said the most awful things about
Will—Mr. Purley and his sister. Tell me they aren't true!"

Mrs. Merilees paled, then cleared her throat. "My poor dear. I
had hoped to spare you those details. Did she say that Miss Purley is
not in fact Miss Purley?"

"Yes! It's not true!"

Mrs. Merilees left her chair and came to kneel by Clem's side,
taking her hand. "It is all too true, every word."

"Every word? Even the embezzlement?"

Mrs. Merilees nodded, her eyes moist. "He tells all and sundry
his father owed him his inheritance or some such thing, but—"

Clem just avoided falling over Mrs. Merilees huge skirts as she
fled the room.

Una returned to Glen Ross the following week, bearing gifts for
everyone at Querilderie. Aunt Margaret had taken the trouble to find
Mrs. Cameron's favorite turquoise ribbon and had tied it in a pretty
packet to be presented to her especially from her sister. Lately Clem
had noticed a marked change in her aunt's attitude toward her mother which surprised and worried her.

Mrs. Merilees had been acting as go-between for the sisters, writing to Mrs. Cameron frequently with news of Clem and her aunt,
and on reading aloud the few short replies from Clem's mother in
the presence of Miss Thorne, had finally inspired the latter to write
to her sister for the first time in ten years.

Mrs. Merilees had been very pleased with her diplomacy and had
confided in Clem that it had borne fruit none too soon, as she and
Mr. Merilees were, through unforeseen circumstances, having to return home within the next few weeks.

The couple were invited to dinner almost every evening during
their last month in New South Wales, Mr. Merilees never failing to
amuse Clem with his lively chatter.

He seemed very interested in her notorious acquaintance, Mr.
Pike. One evening he drew her aside and quizzed her at length upon
the fellow's doings. Finally she confessed to having been in Mr. Jenkyn's shop and having seen him there in the company of the heavy-
browed Mr. Aspinall.

Mr. Merilees sat back in his wide armchair and sighed happily.

"Not a word of this to anyone, m'dear; not even Mrs. M. I feel free to tell you now that apart from my brief from my employers at home, I am also engaged in some work for your Governor. I have been acting in the capacity of *agent provocateur* for him. My access to the wool trade here has allowed me into every home, every sphere, and I have formulated some interesting theories on the black market in stolen wool clips. Now, m'dear, I think my brief is completed."

Clem nodded. She wasn't really listening. The thought of Mr. Pike had brought back sudden and very painful memories of William. "Oh, yes. Do go on." She smiled politely.

He leaned backward, reaching for one of the quills on her aunt's bureau, and dipped it into the silver inkwell. "Your fiancé—a most perceptive young man—had acquainted me with some interesting facts, but I could not persuade him to reveal the name of his witness, a young lady, you know. He did not wish to compromise her. But now . . ."

Clem was about to rise and excuse herself when she noticed he was writing something at the bottom of an official-looking document.

"Sign this, m'dear. You will not be called further. It *is* circumstantial, but it will complete the jigsaw."

Clem signed, her mind utterly confused with thoughts of the Purley household, Angus, and Mr. Pike. "But what—?"

"Don't worry too much about all this. From the mouths of babes and sucklings, etc., m'dear. It was you who first put us on to that fellow Pike—something you said about him. Never mind." He patted her hand, taking the quill gently from her fingers.

She was about to ask him to explain further when she was called to her aunt's side.

The last she saw of Mr. Merilees was his fat red cheeks distended while blowing on the wet ink. She was sent to bed hurriedly, the ladies having noticed her pale and fatigued state.

Chapter Sixteen

The weeks passed in a haze of hot days in the garden and sleepless nights beneath a stifling mosquito net. Since school had finished for the summer she had given up any hope of seeing Matt. She knew no matter how many feverish dreams she might have of him he would have gone north by now, gone so far away she would probably never see him again.

The house in Argyle Place was constantly in her thoughts. It stayed half hidden in a dark recess of her mind during the day, but at night, in the heat and stillness of her bedroom, it haunted her. It moved in and out of her dreams, even her dreams of Matt, willing her to enter, to discover the truth for herself.

Then came the terrible letter from her father.

He had had a visit from a certain Mr. Pike, an unpalatable individual who had offered him a portrait, or what purported to be a portrait, of his daughter Clemency! A hideous caricature of his handsome daughter in the brightest most vulgar coloring and painted by a notorious fellow, an artistic cad of the lowest caliber.

The fellow had demanded two hundred pounds for the monstrous thing. He had naturally refused to pay, denying it was a likeness of his daughter and telling the scoundrel to leave his land, or he would beat him to death with his stock whip.

The fellow—obviously a coward—had jumped on his horse and galloped off, much to the relief of the household and Miss Owen in particular. That poor lady had been unfortunate enough to witness the entire incident and had taken some time to recover from a deep faint.

Her father went on to say that he would not be surprised at anything his daughter might get up to, as he knew her to be flighty, thoroughly irresponsible, and quite heedless of the good name of her family. He was, however, convinced that the portrait and neither of these two men had ever had anything to do with her at all, and was not prepared to listen to any information to the contrary.

Her mother was very ill, but still hoped to convalesce in Sydney, therefore there was no need for her to return home until her mother would, much later in the year. He suggested she finish the autumn term at the Misses Maybright's.

Her mother thanked her sister, Margaret, for the turquoise ribbon. Clem was trembling from head to foot by the time she finished the letter. An awful question kept battering at her: "Had William organized this plan?"

She could not eat or sleep for five days, allowing herself to become painfully thin and nervous. Mrs. Merilees, not knowing of the letter, attributed her loss of weight to her recent shock and humiliation regarding the Purley family, coupled with the unbearable heat of the late Sydney summer.

Aunt Margaret, also unaware of the letter's contents, attributed it to the humidity. Sydney was always so muggy in February. The clothes in the closets turned green and in her eyes so did many of the inhabitants.

The doctor was called, a young, elegantly dressed man, newly qualified and very popular with all the best Sydney families, not only for his charming bedside manner but also for his lineage. He was the younger son of one of the oldest and richest pioneering families of the colony.

He listened to Clem's heartbeat, tapped her chest and thumped her back, pronouncing her physically sound, but went on to caution that according to the latest European theories an illness of the mind could produce certain physical symptoms not unlike Clem's general pallor and listlessness. He felt that her condition might worsen as she did seem depressed and off-color, even for someone drooping beneath the oppressive weather.

He asked Aunt Margaret if Clem was suffering from a broken heart, believing this condition to be a genuine physical ailment. When Aunt Margaret shook her head, he nodded wisely and told her to prepare for further symptoms and to call him immediately should they occur. The bill for his brief visit and concerned advice was quite expensive, and Aunt Margaret earnestly requested Clem to pull herself together, as she could no longer afford to be poorly at those prices.

Clem did want to pull herself together, but she felt as though she had fallen apart and the pieces of her were lying scattered around her bedroom.

She was unable to join the Merilees at dinner on their last evening before sailing for home, being too weak to rise from her bed. They ascended the wide staircase to her room, Mrs. Merilees in tears to see her young friend so pale and miserable. She kissed Clem many times and made her promise to visit them in London upon her obligatory trip *home.* Clem nodded and assured Mrs. Merilees that she would miss her very much, as indeed she would, for despite the woman's endless gossiping the two had formed a warm friendship and Mrs. Merilees had shown her nothing but kindness and understanding.

Mr. Merilees stood at the door and blew her a kiss, which she perceived through clouded eyes.

They sailed the following morning. Aunt Margaret and Clem watched the tall sailing ship, its wide white sails just stretched before a lazy wind, tack slowly out of the harbor. Aunt Margaret cried softly into one of her minute handkerchiefs, but Clem remained dry-eyed. She'd cried so much over the last few days that tears for the Merileeses seemed too cheap.

"He was in such a rush to go, almost as if somebody were *chasing* him away!" Aunt Margaret sobbed. "Poor Clara didn't understand it at all! And do you know that nobody—well hardly *anyone*—that is in the *wool* trade, dear, had invited them to their homes for such a time! He seems to have offended them somehow. Poor Clara, she was becoming such friends of the Westons and Aspinalls—poor dear. To have to leave so *suddenly!*"

Clem nodded, wondering how her friendship with William could have produced such intolerance of the Merileeses, and climbed back into bed with her natural history book. She felt obliged to study as much as possible during her last term at school, as her lack of education had somehow become interwoven with her humiliation at the hands of William Purley. He had spoken the truth about one thing—she *was* a simpleminded bush country girl. When it came to common sense, decided Clem, even Fanny Old would have shown a lot more than she did.

She resumed classes at the beginning of March. Her French was now much improved, her embroidery and sketching also, and her knowledge of natural history was exemplary.

The Misses Maybright were extremely impressed with her water-colors. One in particular—a pale study of some native fuchsia which had faded into an insipid pink by the end of summer—caught Miss Florence Maybright's eye, she being the artistic one of the pair.

"It reminds me of those funny paintings that artist fellow brought along to show us. Remember the man, Amy?"

"Yes, very well. Disreputable-looking man, the one with the black whiskers. He wanted us to employ him as a drawing master. The idea!"

Clem stuttered. "What—what was his name?"

"A Mr. Purley. Naturally we refused him, although Florence imagined that his sketches were not without merit."

"Oh." Clem sank down in her chair. "He did not say where he—he is holding his private classes now, did he?" She prayed silently.

"No. I don't think he mentioned classes. Oh, I remember now. He said he had a studio down at the Rocks. Windmill Street—was that it, Florence?"

Florence nodded. "I know it was an address which suited his appearance. Fancy a man like that knowing of our Academy! Not that he was without manners or talent, but . . ." Florence shook her head.

"How interesting," Clem remarked, a catch in her voice. "He is somewhat known, you know," she continued, not mentioning that his fame rested more upon his life-style than upon his works. "I met him on the coach from Willawarrha. He was an established tutor in Port Philip, of course. Aren't most artists a little disreputable?"

Amy Maybright laughed ironically. "Only in the eyes of impressionable young women. They usually look the same as everyone else. In the end, it is their work that counts."

Clem nodded.

"Of course," Miss Florence added, "*some* artists live in such an exaggerated fashion they've produced the myths of starving poets in

garrets and such." She pondered for a moment. "Your acquaintance from the coach did appear a little strange, a bit unreliable."
She looked at her sister for confirmation.

"Oh, yes. I thought so. It was only intutition, you know, but he
was a little strange."

"Probably because he was an artist." Florence smiled wisely at
Clem and followed her sister from the room.

They always managed to contradict themselves whenever they
discussed anything, mused Clem, wondering exactly what qualifica-
tions were necessary for "finishing" young ladies. A little knowledge of French, a shaky grasp of fancy embroidery, and a talent for
pale water colors was apparently considered sufficient by most Sydney parents. She unclasped her fingers from the back of the schoolroom chair. At last she knew where he was. She would visit him tomorrow. She and Biddy would go together in the dogcart.

Biddy was horrified at the plan and begged Clem to reconsider,
referring to the rumors about Mr. Purley now rife in every section of
Sydney society.

Clem decided to confide in her completely in spite of her instincts
to the contrary. She knew that one often ended up hating a con-
fidante for knowing too much about oneself and that women often
practiced the subtlest blackmail upon each other by virtue of these
confidences, nevertheless she went ahead and told Biddy the whole
story of William and the rumors and her father's letter. By the end
of the tale, she felt profoundly relieved.

"Thank you for listening, Biddy," she said. "I feel almost happy!"

"You look much happier. Harry says if you believe it's possible
to be happy then you're halfway there—to being happy." She
blushed.

"Yes, I see. I wish you and I could be friends. I know it's pre-
sumptuous of me to compare our two conditions, but I'm an outcast
from my home, too. At least we have that in common. It's just the
luck of birth that keeps us from being friends."

"Harry says that all this *luck* ought to stop. He's very bitter about
it. It's easy for you to talk about it as you're the lucky one. *You* can
accept me as a friend, but I can never accept you. I can never be
your equal in anyone else's eyes."

"I don't care what anyone else thinks. I *am* your friend, no matter what even you may think."

"With respect, Miss Clem, you don't understand me. I'll always resent you—or what made you—and that's the same. I'il help all I can, though." Biddy waited for her instructions.

"I'll drive the dogcart," Clem said.

"Oh, no! If they found that out I'd be sent back to the Female Factory. Your hands have to be kept soft."

Clem looked at her hands and then took one of Biddy's thin red ones in her own unlined one. Biddy's hand was callused, her fingernails broken short, her knuckles as swollen as Mrs. Brennan's. Clem let it fall.

Biddy left and Clem walked to the window which overlooked the harbor. The water was a deep ink blue, only slightly ruffled by the slight autumn breeze. She looked down at the forest of paper barks between the house and the water, listening to the butcher birds calling to each other from the thin branches. Their cries were suddenly interrupted by the screech of a white parrot. It flew from tree to tree with a mad flapping of wings, sending hundreds of tiny twigs and leaves floating to the ground.

Matt said that parrots were the tormented souls of aborigines evicted from their hunting grounds who flew around forever, screeching demonically to frighten away the white man. She knelt by her bed, trying to conjure up Matt's face. She knew he wouldn't be there when she got back. He would be faraway, perhaps a thousand miles. She had asked again for news of the Brennans in the letter she'd sent to Mrs. Oxley.

Each night she would kneel by her bed and pray, first for her mother, then for God to put an end to the rumors about William, and then for news of Matt. She would also beg God to let Matt be at Querilderie upon her return. He belonged there as much as she did. She sometimes remembered to pray for Angus, too. She wondered if she should ask God to lessen his ardor, but decided against it, remembering that God had never been very successful in trying to influence that area of man's existence.

That night was not as hot as the previous one, and the mosquitos were greatly reduced in number, their buzzing hardly audible with the approach of autumn. She left her window wide open in case it should rain and bring back the scent of the summer boronia. The screech of the parrot persisted for some time, then gradually became fainter until it was lost across the miles of dark forest. It had perhaps decided, thought Clem, that Sydney was too full of tormented souls of its own to be worried by the addition of just one more.

She dreamed of the parrots at Querilderie and of her moon tree, covered with tiny white flowers. The blossoms would be dead now, just dry brown fluff, blowing off into the March winds.

Chapter Seventeen

That following Saturday morning, Clem and Biddy turned the dog-cart into the lower end of Windmill Street. It was a warm, windy day, the dust rising in little whorls from the gutters and tiny white clouds racing across the sky. As they stopped by the curb and Biddy tightened the bow which held her old straw hat firmly on her wispy curls, she said, "There's a boardinghouse down further; they'll know his whereabouts. That family's so well reported among the gentry I doubt they'll not be known about here."

The windmill in Munn's Lane creaked and groaned behind them as they drove slowly toward the other end of the street. Biddy volunteered to go into the boardinghouse, a small building hidden behind a wide veranda which took up most of the footpath. She reappeared, followed by a stout woman in an apron who pointed the way as they turned the dogcart and headed for Munn's Lane.

"It's not much of a house, or so that woman says. Your Mr. Purley's only had two or three commissions in five months! He still drinks far too much, she says. I hope you'll be all right." Biddy maneuvered the horse into the lane, and they stopped outside a small cottage with a tiny attic window in the patched iron roof.

The front door opened straight onto the footpath, and as Clem knocked she looked back at Biddy for moral support. She sat upright, holding onto the reins with two hands as though ready to bolt at a moment's notice. Then Hetty opened the door. She still looked unwell, her face strained and her hair lank about her bony shoulders.

Clem peered at her. "Hetty?"

"Yes, what do you want?" She blinked against the sun, trying to see to whom she was speaking. "Miss Cameron!" She put her hand on Clem's shoulder. "Please go away. I don't want him to see you."

"But I must see him!" Clem pushed past her into the hall and then through a curtained opening. She was in a small parlor full of overstuffed sofas draped with fringed shawls and half-sewn bodices and skirts. The smell of potpourri was overpowering and the creaking of the windmill an ominous sound in the stifling little room. She was suddenly frightened and tugged at the curtain as she backed through the doorway, pulling it to the ground.

She stumbled over it and found a door just to the right of her. It was warped so she had to wrench it open.

At first she could see nothing as the room was so dark. William's voice came from the far corner. "The little Scrub Maiden has condescended to call."

"Yes."

With a great sweep of his arm he pulled back the long red curtains behind him. She saw Hetty's anxious features and his own pale face contorted with a too-wide smile. Then she saw all his sketches and paintings, the thick, wild strokes of color blinding her with their magical incandescence. His eyes mocked her, Hetty's were defiant. The two stood on either side of the window, poised for her attack.

"I have come only to ask for an explanation, to ask why you gave our—my—portrait to Mr. Pike."

"I didn't."

"How did he come by it?" She looked at Hetty for the answer.

"He took it," she said. "Bill didn't know. He thought it might be a good idea and I—"

"You let him?" Clem stared at her in disbelief until she became aware of the tears of hatred in Hetty's eyes. "I see. Why did you?"

"I didn't know he'd do that, I just wanted rid of the thing." Hetty rubbed her eyes with her knuckles. "I didn't care what he did with it."

"I don't know what his motives were," said William, his arm

slowly reaching around Hetty's waist. "The fellow is a mystery to me. Hett thinks they were motives of charity. He hoped to sell it. We are quite poor." He waved his arms about extravagantly. "As you have no doubt seen, my poor mama takes in dressmaking and such, so perhaps he—"

"*Your* mama!"

William smiled glumly, waiting for further recriminations.

"I wish I could believe you—about the painting." She managed to relax a little, her hands slowly sinking into the soft folds of her skirt, pretending he'd lost all fascination for her. No, she could not deceive herself, he *was* fascinating, standing at bay like a naughty schoolboy trying not to laugh. But he was Hetty's *lover.* She wondered if he'd been fond of her at all, had really thought her such a good model, had even for a moment thought of her as his muse. . . .

"I can only say I'm sorry," he said solemnly.

"We are all sorry," Hetty added, her eyes frantically imploring Clem to leave.

"Please—" William put his hand on the flat of Hetty's back and gently pushed her to the door leading onto the back staircase.

Hetty nodded and closed the door quietly.

"Why didn't you tell me that Hetty was your—your—"

"My studio whore? Is that how she is described by polite society?"

"No! She is your mistress—wife—what does it matter?"

"I never led you to believe that our friendship could be anything other than that between master and pupil—never."

"Perhaps not directly, but I did hope for . . . What I mean is I obviously *valued* our friendship more than you did. I told you many things about me—and you, only lies about yourself."

"I told no lies. I occasionally omitted to tell the truth."

"If you had no *designs* upon me, then why didn't you explain about Hetty and you?"

"You might have told everyone, and Hetty would have been upset. She has pride and false notions of propriety. We cannot marry or my father will disinherit me."

"I thought he'd done that already."

"Only temporarily. When he dies, then . . . "

"Then what?"

"Anything—anything could happen. Who knows?" He moved

slightly in her direction, and by the shape of his mouth she knew he was about to say something affectionate.

She smiled ironically at him. "All that talk of—purity—wasn't it?" She backed away from him. "Perhaps I ought to thank Hetty for helping me to retain it—for what it's worth."

He seemed genuinely hurt as he shook his head. "Hetty's existence has nothing to do with you and me—nothing."

She backed further away. "Well, anyway, where's the painting? I want to buy it."

"It's here. Does that mean we'll see you here again?" His voice was mockingly casual.

"No, but I want the portrait."

He called for Hetty to bring it, then said, "Take the bloody thing."

"I intend to." She prayed for the portrait to be ordinary so that she could tell him how his art had also deceived her.

"It's worth a deuced fortune, or should have been."

She would have asked him exactly what he'd meant by that last remark, but Hetty suddenly pushed open the door and let the piece of canvas unroll in front of her.

It was stunningly beautiful. She looked quickly away. If she let her eyes meet the strange, light eyes of the golden apparition, she might have fallen under his spell again. "Here," she said, her voice hoarse, "you'll take these for it." She unclipped her mother's pearls from her neck and threw them at his feet. "They're worth enough." She grabbed the canvas from Hetty and rolled it up again. Then she walked briskly down the hall and, reaching the fallen curtain, stepped gracefully across it and opened the front door. "Make sure you get the right price!" She put her feet precisely together and jumped daintily across the wide doorstep to land in the middle of the footpath in a patch of bright sunlight.

She climbed into the dogcart and they set off toward Windmill Street. The windmill's agonized groans soon became faint sighs and then ceased altogether. Finally Biddy said, "What happened?"

"I don't know. I suppose, like everyone else, you think I'm foolish."

"No—well, mebbe just a little easy to impress."

"Yes, a simple country girl." She saw that Biddy's eyes were watering.

"Are you crying?"

"Not really. I'm just sorry for that woman—the one he lives with. I'd be reduced to that or much worse if I didn't have Harry."

"I envy you your Harry." He had reminded her of Matt. She would like to tell Biddy all about Matt, too, but that would seem even more foolish. She suddenly felt a spasm of intense envy. She would give anything to be as close to Matt as Biddy was to Harry. "I was going to ask you to come to Querilderie with me, until your pardon is through, but I suppose . . . "

"Thanks. But I'd rather wait here and be near him."

Clem nodded. "When is his pardon due?"

"About the same time as mine. We're going to travel home together on one of those. big sailing ships. I think about it every night. I—" She stopped. She was giving too much of herself away.

Clem remembered what she'd said about friendship. Of course she couldn't tell her all about Matt. She could not tell anyone all about Matt. It would be just like telling someone everything about herself. She did not want her most secret and sweetest thoughts plucked from her to be bandied about by other people. Neither did she want to be William's Scrub Maiden, his noble spirit of the forest or whatever poetic notion he had of her. She wanted to be completely real and alive and just to be with Matt. Everything else would be a substitute life, the kind of life to which most people were condemned, but she knew she would need a miracle to deliver her from that.

She leaned back in the seat. "Make the horse go faster!"

Clem insisted on unharnessing and stabling the horse herself. She hid the portrait in the loft, planning to smuggle it into her room after dark.

Her aunt met her at the scullery door clutching a large envelope. "It's your mama's writing." She smiled, pressing the letter into Clem's hand.

The writing was scratched and blotchy. Whole sentences were crudely erased, and even the closest reading produced no real news. Her mother suffered from too many headaches, sleepless nights, and her husband's bad temper. There was only the briefest mention of Miss Owen and then in reference to something quite innocuous. Her mother hoped to travel to Sydney by the end of April and Clem was to await her there and on no account to return home before then, as it would not be suitable. There was a postscript written in such haste it was possible to read only fractions of words. She read

it and reread it a hundred times. It had something to do with someone's scheme. Her father's perhaps or the Macleans' or Marianne's? She finally folded the letter and put it inside the box which
had housed her mother's pearls.

Her aunt and Sybil continually discussed her mother's habit of
drinking too much brandy after dinner, and Clem supposed the letter
had been written late at night when her hand was at its shakiest. Her
aunt had often taken pains to explain to her that many ladies took to
drinking too much brandy as an escape from the loneliness and boredom of life in the far bush country. Clem concluded they would be
less likely to indulge in bad habits were they to spend the days in the
paddocks instead of sitting in hot rooms struggling with badly tuned
pianos and damp thread. She was determined never to be reduced to
such a lowly state. Angus had made all kinds of promises, but when
the time came, he would expect her to stay inside, bearing children
and bullying the servants, sheltered from the rough outside world of
stockmen, shearers, and hot sun, which ruined soft complexions.
Like all the other women, she would be packed off to Sydney during
the hottest part of the year to gossip in overfurnished drawing
rooms.

She sat down at her dressing table and studied her face in the
glass. Most of her freckles were gone and she looked almost white!
Her hair was darker, the gold streaks having faded to a light auburn.
The tiny white lines about her eyes, which had accentuated the gold
brown of her face all summer, had disappeared into the sallow pale-
ness of her skin. She looked like any other Sydney girl. William
probably thought so too. She was quite ordinary. He'd just been flattering her. Her stomach sank with a dreadful humiliation.

She took off her coat and let her hair down, tying it back with a
narrow brown velvet ribbon. It was almost time for luncheon. Eating alone with Aunt Margaret was such an ordeal. Another month of
it would drive her completely inside herself. Her aunt talked cease-
lessly of the virtues of marriage and her hopes for Clem's future,
mentioning the names of many good families on the land who would
be pleased to marry off their sons to Clem if she decided against Angus. She was also full of dire warnings of ending up an old maid.

"But I will have money and the property," Clem assured her that
evening at dinner.

"It is not enough." Aunt Margaret sighed wistfully, suddenly
quite deflated.

That was the first time her aunt had admitted to anything but complete satisfaction with her life, and Clem felt more than just a pang of guilt for the distress her own actions might yet cause her. She was glad her aunt had been spared the truth about the Purley family as she supposed no decent young Sydney bachelor, *on* or *off* the land, would consider marrying her now, and that knowledge would have broken her aunt's heart. At least Angus had seemed unaffected by her disgrace. She was almost looking forward to seeing him when she returned home.

As the term progressed Clem's depression gradually lifted and she devoted all her thoughts and energy to her schoolwork. She had become such a keen student over the past year that the Misses Maybright regarded her as their most promising pupil. Clem realized it was a little late in her academic career to be considered promising and wondered if they were just being kind. It was, however, a more pleasing adjective than *fair*—a word that had dogged her school life until the present term.

The other students at the Misses Maybright's Academy for Young Presbyterian Ladies were only too aware of Clem's disgrace and regarded her with an even greater degree of interest than before, and from a greater distance. Clem would come across them whispering in giggling groups in the corridors and had even discovered a note pinned to her desk with a crudely drawn heart and Mr. Purley's name upon it—misspelled—and smelling of cheap lavender water. She'd carefully unpinned it and torn it up into eight tiny pieces, dropping them one by one into the bin below the blackboard and in full view of the rest of the class. She could never think of anything to say to any of the girls. It was as though they were all actresses in a play she did not understand and in which she had forgotten her part.

In fact, decided Clem, thinking over her life in Sydney, the last months have all been like that. I've done all sorts of things without even thinking about what I was doing, and spoken to all sorts of people without knowing why, or indeed listened to half of what has been said to me. She resolved to talk to no one but her teachers, her aunt, and Biddy, and to concentrate her mind entirely on her studies. Studying is supposed to make one sensible, she thought, and I really must become sensible.

Chapter Eighteen

One cool April morning as she was dressing for school she heard a familiar voice in the front hall. She went out onto the landing. It was Edith's voice! She hurriedly pulled on her dress and ran to the top of the stairs.

Her father's housekeeper was bending over a hall chair, divesting herself of a heavy traveling cloak. She saw Clem from the corner of her eye as she turned to resume her conversation with Aunt Margaret and stopped in midsentence. Then she raised her eyes and stood staring at Clem with a look of stark fear.

Clem's knees suddenly gave way and she clutched the banister to stop herself from falling. She knew what had happened. She walked stiffly down the stairs toward the silent Edith.

"What is it?" Her voice was alarmingly loud in the still house.

"It's your mama, Miss Clem. I'm afraid she is ill. She is very ill. In fact, she is dead."

Clem felt herself trying to hold onto the banister, then the hall began swaying and turned into a million yellow lights, and she dropped into a vast black cavern.

When she awoke, she was lying on a sofa in the library. The curtains were drawn and she could just make out Edith's features in the dark red light of the room. For a second she thought that *she* was the body of her dead mother lying stretched out in the respectfully darkened room; then she tried to talk. "Is my mother really dead?" She sat up, digging her elbows into the hard tapestry cushions.

Edith's face was wet and contorted. "Yes, dear. She died four days ago."

"But I just had her letter! She doesn't say—"

Her aunt's voice came out of the darkness beyond Edith's face. "She died on Monday. Today is Friday. She died a peaceful death, Edith says."

"Please, ma'am." Edith begged her. "She said, 'Give my love, all my love to my daughter Clemency.' Then she passed away." Edith wept copiously.

Clem reached out to find her hand. "How is my sister taking it?" she asked, her tongue thick and unmanageable.

"Well—quite well. They were not so close. They did not have the affinity you both had."

Clem nodded. Edith had noticed this affinity—it must have been there all the time. Now that her mother was no more it became painfully apparent.

"My father?"

"Oh, he has Miss Owen—that is, your sister does."

"Yes. They must all be close by now. If only I'd seen her before she died. There was so much to tell her, you see, I—" To lose her mother just when she'd started to understand her, and when she needed her most, was too unjust. She felt again the anguish of not having said something—anything—just to let her know that she was not unloved. That anguish was unbearable now. She broke down completely and had to be carried to her room.

Edith stayed on for some days, expressing a wish to take Clem back with her. Clem knew that it would be too soon. She couldn't have faced either her father or Miss Owen. She knew now that the affair was no rumor.

The May holiday was a time of black dresses, veils and church. The minister's sermons grew more meaningless with every service. His funny chanting in a precise English intonation made the whole performance like an overacted play, and she found herself smiling nervously at his antics. Her aunt and Sybil looked on this as merely another symptom of her bereavement and gently tolerated her wicked blasphemies. Aunt Margaret was enjoying a new found indulgence. Her kindness and patience had increased her weight, fattened her cheeks, slowed her reflexes, decreased the pace of the household routine, and turned disgruntled servants into contented ones.

Clem decided her hated sister's death had roused disturbing emotions in her aunt's heart. Unable to feign grief or even to shed one tear on her sister's behalf, she lavished attention on Clem and thus expiated her profound, life-long guilt over her lack of feeling for her dead sister.

Aunt Margaret instructed the cook to prepare a feast for every meal: Clem's favorite jellies, cakes and the little meringues she had always loved—and oysters, mud oysters brought all the way from Botany Bay and hawked around the harbor shores by ragged creatures who made a living by cutting them from the rocks and selling them at popular beauty spots. Jim would drive out every morning for a quart to encourage Miss Clemency's appetite.

Biddy made up for all her former remarks about friendship by being always at Clem's side, listening for hours to her tearful diatribes against God and the minister, her father, Miss Owen, and everybody at home and in Sydney who had concealed the true nature of her mother's illness.

Biddy countered all this by her own tales of sorrow and humiliation, her early, degrading convict days and her years of hard labor in the Female Factory. Through this strange bond of anger and resentment they at least managed something akin to friendship.

Finally Clem's anger subsided and she was left with only grief— milder now—and the occasional return of an overpowering urge to avenge herself upon everyone at Querilderie. They had *known* her mother was dying and had cold-bloodedly denied her her rightful place at her mother's bedside.

She decided to finish the winter term at school and return home in September. She would be eighteen then, old enough for her father to treat her as an adult.

She said as much to her aunt one Sunday over luncheon, in the process of finishing yet another quince jelly. "It's very kind of you to be ordering all these delicacies for me, Aunt, but the time for regarding strawberry meringues and quince jellies as the be-all and end-all of existence must pass!" She giggled for the first time in twelve weeks and her aunt beamed.

"My dear girl! You laughed! The quince always did tempt you."

"Yes. I don't know what could be *better* than oysters and strawberry meringues, but I must try to find it. I'll start by returning home at the beginning of September. Perhaps my father can use my labor on the property. I was always a good boundary rider." She smiled ruefully. "It kept me out of his way."

"Oh? You really wish to go home? I thought I might have you here with me forever. I flatter myself I am your true guardian now that your mama—"

"I must go home. If things don't work out as planned, then I don't know what I'll do." She shrugged and scraped the remaining jelly from her plate.

"You must marry Angus. It is the right and proper thing for you to do."

"Oh, Aunt Margaret! We've been through all that before. I don't love him. I *am* fond of him, but only as a brother."

"There is no harm in that, my dear. Better to marry for a deep abiding love of that nature than for a brief passion of another kind. That usually does not last—with the man at any rate."

"Why not with the man?" For once her aunt had aroused Clem's interest.

"Babies. Women must bear the children. It ages them, tires them, and leaves them uninterested in—you know—er—that men require a great deal of love. The passionate kind. I mean—oh, dear me."

Clem laughed. "Yes, I know what you mean. I understand. It's unfair, isn't it?"

"Yes. Terrible that women must submit to all that!"

"No, I mean that women must give it all up for the sake of screaming babies!"

"You are immoral! No, you can't possibly understand what I mean. Young women's ideas of love are a thousand times removed from the reality of married life and love." Aunt Margaret shook her head sadly.

Clem wondered how she knew anything about married love. Perhaps her ideas were sadly removed from reality too. She did not say so however, but begged to be excused on account of a French prose which had to be completed by Monday.

* * *

Three weeks later on the first warm days of August, Clem was driving slowly along George Street with Biddy, both girls engrossed in tales of their childhood, when Biddy suddenly turned a deep pink and stuttered over her next word. She quickly turned her head away from the nearest footpath.

Clem automatically slowed the horse and turned to look.

William Purley stood halfway off the footpath, talking and laughing with an extremely well-dressed young woman who was definitely not a model or anyone remotely connected with the artistic world.

Clem could not resist calling to him.

He looked up at them, puzzled. He seemed very well, and his clothes were new and well cut.

"I see the pearls did fetch a good price. And patrons, too. Well done, William, you will paint the Sistine Chapel yet!" She whipped up the horse before he could reply, and when she looked back he was staring after her, his mouth twisted into that annoying little smile she knew so well.

She left the Misses Maybright's the following week. She thanked the ladies profusely for her newfound interest in things of the mind and her new cultured accent, which for some reason seemed to go hand in hand, and drove back to the Point Piper Road with not a little regret at her departure.

The next two weeks were spent shopping and packing. Her aunt insisted on extravagant wedding presents for Una to make up for their absence at her wedding, which had by all accounts been a huge success. The chapel had been finished in time and had been embellished by the addition of two magnificent stained-glass windows from a demolished Sydney church. These had been transported from Sydney at great expense and had so impressed Mr. Gilzean's mother that she was heard to declare that Una Maclean would make her son a perfect wife.

Clem's summer wardrobe was more trousseaulike than anything else. Her aunt was determined she should not refuse Angus again and had almost worn Clem down into agreeing with her just to save everyone a lot of fuss and bother.

"If you go on like this I shall marry him just for some peace and quiet! Or is that how all marriages are arranged?"

Her aunt touched her on the cheek with her fan. "Quite a few," she said, choosing yet another piece of dark blue velvet for yet another afternoon coat.

"But who is there to visit in all these afternoon coats?" Clem asked. "The local aborigine mission?"

"Is there one?"

Clem nodded, fingering the pile of thick velvets, and remembering the hot brown paddocks and the dusty main street of Burrundi.

"Well, why not? There are missionaries there to talk to. No, silly girl, Querilderie, of course, as you will be resident at Glen Ross, and many others, the Gilzeans of Pringle, for instance."

Clem nodded again, imagining herself visiting her father and Katharine wearing a long blue velvet coat and could not repress a giggle. She remembered her mother's turquoise finery for Mrs. Oxley. Perhaps she ought to visit Mrs. Oxley, but not in a velvet afternoon coat.

By the time Clem was packed for home she had acquired two new trunks, a smart portmanteau, and a hat box in which rested a large wide-brimmed straw hat. It was trimmed with tiny daisies and brown velvet ribbons. The only good thing to come out of this shopping spree, thought Clem, as she stared once more at the daisies and ribbons, is my aunt's decision to change my colors to brown and blue.

The coach hired to take her and two other families to Willawarrha started at six o'clock on a Monday morning, arriving at its destination on Wednesday evening, when Jock would be awaiting her in the family carriage.

She didn't shed a tear as she bade farewell to her aunt, in spite of the fact that she'd become almost fond of her since her mother's death, but she was very distressed at her departure from Biddy. The last she ever saw of her friend was her thin back in the now soiled pink dress, as she climbed up to sit next to the groom at the front of her aunt's carriage.

She would later discover some clothes and books which Clem had left on her narrow bed in the servants' quarters at the top of the house and the portrait, with a note explaining its possible value and its presence as a wedding gift for Harry and herself. "The money for this will secure two passages on a grand clipper," she'd written. Then she'd gone on to beg Biddy "not to regard the gifts as charity, but to accept them as the tokens of a friendship which I value deeply, the only real friendship I have ever had with another girl."

She remained aloof during the journey home, trying to concen-

trate on coming to terms with her mother's death. She knew that
Miss Owen would have brought about many changes at Querilderie
but was not sure how many she should be prepared for.

She received a hint at the Pringle Hotel, another more obvious
one at the Willawarrha Arms.

The effeminate manager met her at the door. He mentioned that
her father had come in person to arrange for her coach journey and
to book her room for the night, believing it safer for her to travel by
daylight, as there were quite a few bushrangers working the local
roads.

"But we all know that *you* are aware of that, Miss Cameron."

Clem regarded him with surprise. "No, why should I be?"

"Oh, no reason." He coughed politely. "I suppose the new circumstances at your home will disturb you a little at first, Miss Cameron. But, one manges to get used to anything in time."

Clem was about to inquire further, when he started to offer his
condolences for the loss of her mother, which she was obliged to accept, reminding her once more that her mother would not be at home
to greet her.

She walked through the town again that evening, discovering two
more streets of new wooden cottages with gravel paths and geraniums and a schoolhouse. She thought of Mr. Pike, and returning to
the hotel, inquired of the manager whether he had been seen recently in the district.

The manager was unusually perturbed at her question. He stammered, "You did not hear?" Then he looked at her slyly. "Really—
you did not hear?"

"No! Do tell me!" She was agog.

"He was arrested for highway robbery. He was buying stolen
wool clips and selling them to some Sydney wool merchants. There
is proof against them, too. But they have friends in all the right
places. He—that young Pike—was caught red-handed."

"Oh, my goodness! Will they hang him?"

"I believe the merchants, one or two of them, have hired him a
good lawyer. He will be blackmailing them, of course, to get him off
the charge. He has *friends*, too, you see."

Clem gasped, remembering who his friends were. Surely not the
exemplary Westons, the Aspinalls—and the Parramatta family!

"Do you know the names of these—these receivers of stolen
goods?" That had been William's phrase.

"No. Nobody does. Or ever will. They have a lot of power—the

wool merchants, almost as much as the squatters. Wool is everything in this colony, Miss Cameron."

"Ah, yes, so it is." Her mind was wildly ticking over, trying to remember what Mr. Merilees had been talking about in the drawing
room of her aunt's house when the manager's insidious voice interrupted her alarming thoughts.

"They say somebody—a lady—informed upon him. I cannot imagine who it could be. Could you?"

"No, I'm afraid I could not."

"She was the mistress of his friend. They had played some trick
upon her, not in the best of taste—I think that is how the story goes.
She informed some fellow working as a spy for the Governor, so
they say."

"Really!"

"Yes. This fellow, the Governor's man, has had to flee the colony. The wool merchants would cheerfully lynch him."

"Oh, yes. Indeed they would. . . . "

The manager waited for her to continue. She stood regarding him
with bewilderment for a few seconds, then blinked her eyes twice.
"Goodness gracious." She smiled ingenuously and left him, making
her way slowly to the dining room, feeling slightly lost. She had just
uncovered a labyrinth disturbingly close to home, the existence of
which she had been entirely unaware of until that moment.

She did not look up from her plate during dinner, having resolved
never again to make the acquaintance of any passing stranger. The
colony was far too small for such games.

She prayed Mr. Pike would not hang. She didn't suppose anyone
deserved that, no matter how heinous the crime. It had always been
a mystery to her why property was valued so far above life, as far as
the law was concerned, and a convict's life less than both. People
were not hanged for killing convicts unless they happened to be a
convict, too; and aborigines were hunted for sport!

Jock arrived at ten o'clock the next morning. The furrowed,
weatherbeaten face and heavy-lidded eyes were a comfortingly familiar sight. He doffed his hat, then quickly pushed it back onto the
damp and flattened gray curls.

They set off on the road to Burrundi. Spring had come unnoticed
to the wide brown fields, the monotonous gray-brown only rarely re-

lieved by a tuft of green sword grass or verge of yellow paspalum
left from the previous summer.

"You haven't had much rain, Jock."

He didn't reply, so she repeated the remark.

He merely shrugged, then took off his hat to scratch his head.

"I've been away for over a year and a half and it seems like ten
years."

"Mmmm? When you're young, it does that," he mumbled. He
spoke as though she'd been gone for two days' shopping in Pringle.
She didn't know how people were supposed to react when one had
been away for so long—with a little more enthusiasm perhaps.

As they drove through Burrundi Clem saw the bright green of
Mrs. Oxley's orange trees. "Jock, have you heard anything of Mrs.
Oxley, since—" She couldn't say it.

"She's gorn."

"Where?"

"Dunno. Your father bought the house. Jim's retired there. She's
gorn."

"Oh. Who's the new cook?"

He did not hear her. He was staring ahead at the long dirt road out
of town, as though in a trance.

Clem looked around at the horizon, following it from the west to
east, scanning it for any sign of a living thing. Nothing moved. The
sun was hot and the sky cloudless. She looked down at her clothes.
Her formal outfit looked so silly squashed into the narrow driving
seat of the carriage. Once again she was reminded of her mother and
Mrs. Oxley. Her mother had been a little touched, thought Clem
fondly. How she wished . . .

A lump stayed in her throat for the next few miles as she fought
back her tears. Perhaps Katharine would be glad to see her. Surely
she must miss her mother, too. At least they might talk about her
together. That would be some relief. She wondered where she was
buried. Probably by the old chapel.

There were six graves there: four convicts who had died as the result of ill treatment before they'd arrived at Querilderie, a stockman
who'd been mistaken for a kangaroo during a hunting party, and an
old woman, somebody's mother, who'd followed her transported
son all the way to Querilderie from Birmingham, only to discover
that he'd disappeared on his way back from town one day and had
never been seen since. She had waited in vain for his return and had

died brokenhearted after three years spent scrubbing the floors of the men's cottages and cleaning the kitchen stoves.

The memory of the pathetic old woman brought the tears flooding down Clem's cheeks. She tried to wipe them away, glancing surreptitiously at Jock in case she was embarrassing him, but he still stared ahead, entirely unaware of the young woman huddled by his side on the small seat, the tears flowing from her swollen green eyes.

By the time they'd reached their own road, her tears had dried in the sun and had been replaced by a nervous sinking in her stomach. The nerves increased tenfold as they neared the home paddock.

The outline of the house appeared, the sun just a few feet above it in the white afternoon sky. She was breathing deeply, trying to stop herself from shaking. Her armpits were wet and her body trembled with a strange apprehension as she climbed down from the seat.

There was nobody to greet her. The place was utterly silent. The wattles had just started to bud and the young pines looked down upon her disdainfully, as if she were a stranger.

"I am not a stranger. This is my house! My home!" She repeated the words until they had the desired effect. Her knees stopped tingling and her voice was almost normal. "Jock, will you take my trunks to my room?" While Clem spoke she stared up into the pines, then she noticed an extraordinary thing. They'd built another story onto the house! She ran backward. There was a top story built onto the house—with windows, shutters, and a perfectly good roof!

She pointed wordlessly, turning to Jock for some kind of explanation.

He picked up two trunks and the portmanteau all at once with very little effort. "That's *'er*, like." He wouldn't be drawn further but disappeared around the side of the house. Clem rushed through the front door and down the hall to her room.

She passed her mother's room, then the first guest room, then as she turned the corner to *her* room she realized she'd run up against something. The hall was quite dark, and the sun, still so bright in her eyes, had almost blinded her.

Chapter Nineteen

There was a huge staircase blocking the way to her room!

"Where is my room?" She ran halfway up the stairs and peered over the side, but there was nothing there, just the part beneath the staircase and the back wall of the house. She ran down again. "Where is it? My room?" She started running around in circles.

Suddenly an arm grabbed her and she was being held close to somebody's firm bosom. Edith's voice echoed strangely inside her head. "There, there, don't fret. Your room is upstairs—they've moved it upstairs. Come, I'll take—"

"But my room's not upstairs! It's downstairs! It's here! Where's my wallpaper and my rugs and my view of the wattles? Have they moved all that too?"

"Yes, yes. Come." Edith led her upstairs.

Clem didn't see the new hall or pretty porcelain door handles or the new hall chairs and carpets; she didn't see Miss Owen's watercolors adorning the brightly papered walls; she saw her old room, the walls and floors and furniture, covered in a pile of bricks and rubble.

She was led into a room papered with embossed pink flowers and furnished with some of her old furniture, a new bath, and a beautiful rosewood bookcase. Miss Owen's wildflower sketches covered one wall.

She ran to her dressing table. The crystal bowl was gone. "My quartz! Where's my quartz? And my bird book?"

"Hush. Your books are there. Miss Owen had a beautiful little rosewood case made for you and a tallboy. She is so thoughtful. She wants you to feel *so* at home."

"But I *am* at home!"

"I meant to say just as you would feel if your dear mama were with you."

"I know now that she is truly dead. My mother is dead. And so is my life. This isn't my room! It's a strange house. I can't stay here. Where's Katharine?" She sat on the bed and sobbed into her new pink brocade quilt. "Where's my old quilt?"

"You're being silly. Control yourself. And I thought we would be welcoming back a grown lady—not the wild girl who left."

Clem wiped her eyes. She *was* being childish. She stood up and put her hand on Edith's comfortable arm. "You're right. I'm just tired. The sun is still in my eyes. Tell Jock to bring in my trunks. Lizzie and I will unpack."

"Yes, dear. Lizzie has left us, though. She ran off with that Matthew Brennan. The oldest one anyway."

Clem sank down on the bed again, gripping the new quilt with clenched fists. "Goodness," she croaked. "Are you sure?"

"That simple Fanny says they ran off together. They've left their place. All the Brennans have gone. The father near drank himself to death on cheap rum, and they had to sell out to your papa. He wanted the water anyway. It suited him fine."

"Where did they go?"

Matt didn't tell her . . . He didn't tell her *anything*.

"To Sydney. Packed up a bullock cart and left, some months ago now, nigh on a year."

"He didn't say that," she whispered. She felt as though she were floating above the house, looking down upon it from a great distance. She could see a tiny figure sitting on a pink bed. She started to giggle, then to shriek with uncontrollable laughter. Edith slapped her hard across the face and she stopped.

She saw herself in perspective again, only this time from much closer. Gradually the vision and her body merged.

Edith was still shaking her. Clem removed her hands from her shoulders calmly. "Thank you, Edith. My head aches. But I'm perfectly all right now. Please ask Fanny to help me."

Edith stayed by the door for a few seconds, watching Clem move around the room inspecting the new furniture. She went after Clem had smiled at her and, fingering the new bookcase, said, "It's such a beautiful bookcase. Such a fine grain, don't you think?"

Edith nodded and hurried away to find Fanny.

Clem went over to the washstand and splashed water on her face and neck. It was her mother's stand, bowl and basin. It was painted with faded pink violets. Miss Owen must have picked that for her room, too. She had always exhibited such delicate taste while at the Macleans', and now she was leaving her mark here. Clem wondered why her father had bothered to add another story to the house. It had always been big enough for just the four of them.

She placed her bird book, having found it in the top shelf of the almost empty bookcase, on her rosewood table, then proceeded to search every drawer and cupboard for her crystal bowl and quartz. It was nowhere to be found.

Jock brought the four trunks and portmanteau to her room, and was followed by an excited, shy, lopsided Fanny Old, curtseying in her comic manner as she came through the door. "It's right nice to see you back, Miss Clem." She was blushing furiously all over her speckled face and neck.

"Fanny! It's lovely to see you—all of you—again. Have you seen my father or Miss Owen?"

"No, I haven't."

"Well, never mind that now. Let's get on with all this unpacking. I have something for all of you in my trunks."

Fanny went a deeper red and helped Jock undo the trunks. Clem found two blue ribbons and a pair of silk gloves for the poor thing. She could wear the gloves to chapel.

Fanny just nodded and stuttered her thanks after a few seconds, tucking the ribbons into her flat bosom, then went on to help Clem hang some of her dresses in the tallboy and to fold the chemises and petticoats and pantaloons and nightgowns into the drawers of the large mahogany chests. She had inherited those from her mother too. Her mother had preferred mahogany to rosewood, even for the bedroom. It faded to a delicate gold in the bright New South Wales sun.

By teatime the two had finished and Jock had stored three of the trunks, leaving the fourth at the foot of Clem's bed for her evening gowns. They were laid gently on top of each other, separated by the finest Chinese rice paper.

As Fanny was about to leave, Clem casually mentioned Lizzie's name.

"Lizzie Bell? Oh, her. She ran off with that Matt Brennan. She might have gone to Sydney with 'im. Her final pardon came through. She was right hoity-toity with yer father, like. She was screamin' something about her pardon bein' signed by the Governor 'imself and such—at his face! We all laughed. Oh, don't be tellin' 'im, Miss Clem."

"No. I won't mention it. And if ever, if *ever* you hear anything at all about the whereabouts of Matthew Brennan, you let me know immediately. But do not mention it to my father. And if you can keep secrets I will give you more ribbons."

Fanny went toward the door, dragging her left foot slightly. It caught on the rug and she bent to straighten it. "He had a fight with your father."

"Who?"

"Matt Brennan. He told 'im he was a tyrant or some such name."

"What did my father say?"

"He never said nothin'. He hit him with this riding crop and Matt dragged 'im from his horse and punched him! In front of everyone, Miss Clem!" Fanny giggled. "Your poor mama, she was so ill. She just stared. She didn't say nothin' either. Not a soul did. Matt just walked away and never came back. That was when she, Lizzie, left too."

"Was my mother happy before she died?" Clem knew the poor creature would probably not know anything about her at all.

"Yes, she was happy to see your father *hit*. I swear it!"

"But what about just before she died? Did she manage to see Mrs. Oxley?"

Fanny stuttered and stammered, then blurted out, "He got rid of her. He bought her house and made her go. Soon as your mother died. She saw her just a few days before she went. She was too far gone to be unhappy. Too ill and hazylike—for months."

"Thank you." Clem dismissed Fanny with an awkward wave. How she *hated* her father.

She put on an elegant dress for tea, taking care to look very grown-up. She did her hair in a chignon low on her neck and touched her cheeks with powder. If she looked like someone else, then her father might treat her as a strange young woman and not his erring child.

He'd always managed to reduce her to a confused and angry state whenever she'd been in his presence, obviating any need for reasoned argument from either side. It had been his instinctive contrivance for never having to take responsibility for her behavior. Her mother had just retreated to her room and left him to deal with everything.

She heard the front door open. Miss Owen's voice was a murmur in the distance. Clem stopped, then tiptoed the rest of the way down.

The voice was audible now. "We must tell her immediately, John."

She heard her father grunt a reply, then their footsteps faded into the drawing room.

She followed, the nervous tingling returning to her stomach. She stepped inside the door, not sure whether she'd entered the right room.

The entire decor had changed. The wallpaper, the furniture, and even the curtains. Everything was light and sunny, and there was a strong scent of some exotic tropical flower.

Miss Owen stood stiffly at attention, her hands held in front of her, making her wide yellow crinoline billow out strongly from just below the waist. Her hair was fairer than Clem had remembered, or perhaps it was the effect of the sunlight filtering through the half-drawn silk curtains. There was something else about her, too, which Clem was trying to fathom, when her father, who'd been leaning over a small tea table, straightened his tall frame and turned to face her.

"Well, Clemency, you are quite grown-up." He smiled. His face was so transformed that for a moment she didn't realize it was he.

"Good evening, Father, and Miss Owen." She curtsied, then looked from one to the other, trying to hide her amazement.

"Clemency has noticed your new coat, John."

"Marianne, Clemency is too like her papa to notice such things. Or so you tell me." He beamed at Miss Owen. "Shall we get it over with now, Marianne?"

"Yes, please." Miss Owen moved majestically across the room, her hands still together, crushing the top of her fragile silk skirt.

"What a beautiful dress!" Clem blushed. Miss Owen was a stranger to her. She didn't quite know how to feel about her. It was obvious that she'd usurped her mother's position in the house as well as in her father's heart, thought Clem, trying to stop the awkward little surges of jealousy she felt rising to the surface. It seemed that some other person inside her was trying to emerge. Soon she felt an almost physical need to push it—or her—back.

"You tell her, Marianne." Each time he said her name, his lips formed the word with a surprised delight, as though he were still relishing the privilege of using her Christian name. He sat down on the edge of a high-backed armchair upholstered in light brown velvet. It matched his coat perfectly. Miss Owen had refurbished Clem's father, too, to complement the furniture.

Clem smiled. "Everything in the room is so beautiful! How it all goes together!"

"Thank you. I arranged it so. My dear, we must tell you our news immediately, as you will hear it from others if we do not—others who might not have taken it as kindly as I know *you* will."

"Yes?" Clem still stood in the doorway. She felt excluded from all this grandeur.

"Your papa and I were married two weeks ago." She remained with her mouth slightly open, staring at Clem, then slowly turned her head around to Clem's father. "Weren't we, John?"

"We were, indeed. Indeed we were." He nodded and kept nodding until Miss Owen took one step forward and opened her mouth wide to speak again.

Clem, by now quite numb, managed to forestall her. "I guessed you would be married. I'd heard rumors, and my mother knew about my father's feelings."

Her father was about to remonstrate, but Clem stopped him. "It doesn't upset me. It has nothing to do with me. I hope you will be very happy here—both of you. Will you let me stay for a little while?"

"Oh, my dear!" Miss Owen sank elegantly into the nearest seat, which was a small chair in front of a walnut bureau. The hem of her voluminous skirt caught at the top of the heavy protruding legs of the piece, and she had trouble pushing it down. Clem noticed how thin her legs were.

"This horsehair! This is your home!" She looked near to tears.

"Of course it is. She was always an unreasonable child. Well, Clemency," he stood to help Miss Owen from her ludicrous perch, "did you accept Angus?"

"No. I do not think I want to be married. I must think a great deal about it. It's not a thing to be taken lightly. Even my aunt says so." Clem was amazed at her own absolute calm.

"We'll discuss all that later. You already know my opinion of the matter, I think." He smiled down at Miss Owen, who had quickly recovered her composure. "My dear wife, Marianne, has thoughts upon the subject of matrimony not unlike your own. Perhaps you two ladies might discuss the matter together." He bowed to each of them in turn and added, "May I change out of this deuced rigout now? Can't abide all this stiff stuff. Done m'duty, have I?" He winked at Clem.

She blinked at him. It was the first time in his life that he'd winked. She gazed after him as he left the room.

"My father is a changed man. You've made him into a different person. I will not ask how you've done it. It is a miracle."

"And one must not delve too deeply into miracles." Miss Owen's mood had altered completely during the few seconds since her father had left them. She no longer sat edgily on her chair but had pushed herself back and rested her wrists upon the soft gold velvet of its cushioned arms.

"When was the second story added?" Clem inquired. She would not ask *why* just yet.

"Your father had started it to please your mama, God rest her soul, just before we lost her, and therefore was obliged to finish it. It was only completed a month or so ago. We—he—wanted it to be a surprise for you. That is why, when you suggested returning in March, or was it February? he advised you not to. The place was such a —" she looked around in despair at the newly papered walls. "Such a mess, don't you know. It would not have done for you to return then."

"I wish I had, for then I would have been with my poor mother when she died." The baffling change in Miss Owen was that she not only appeared ten years younger, but had also developed an enormous amount of self-assurance and authority, neither of which had been obvious at Glen Ross. She was proving herself the mistress of

Maud Lang

the house with every sentence she uttered. She had a quiet strength
in her voice and a clear confidence in her large gray eyes.

Clem stared straight back at them. "No one has been able to tell
me why my mother died. What did she have?"

"What illness? I believe it was one of those wasting diseases.
They are always such a mystery to the doctors. Your poor mama
was prescribed so much brandy that by the end she was nearly in-
sensible."

"Was that to stop the pain?"

"I believe the pain came during the last few days. The brandy
would be prescribed for that, yes." Miss Owen poured the tea,
which by now was less than warm. "Sugar?"

"No, thank you. No cream either." Clem took the dainty cup and
saucer from the other woman's cool thin fingers, noticing the narrow
gold band on her left hand. "It would suit you and my father for me
to marry Angus Maclean."

"Only if you were absolutely sure of your happiness in doing so.
You know I cannot fault Angus. I have a very soft spot for him, and
I'm sure you could do no better. He is educated, too." She raised
her fine eyebrows, offering a plate of seed cakes.

Clem took one, then surveyed the room properly for the first
time. It was very pretty—all golds and creams and golden browns.
The furniture had been polished energetically and where possible
moved away from direct sunlight. The Chinese rugs had been
washed and turned about. The Scottish lochs still adorned the walls,
together with a few of Miss Owen's Sydney landscapes.

"Did you hear about all that fuss over my portrait?" Clem asked,
returning her cup and saucer to the table.

"Yes, I have only the vaguest memory, however. I apparently
succumbed to a fainting fit. I did not see the painting, nor the young
man who brought it."

"Did Mama?" Clem retreated to her seat, her eyes still warily
studying the other's face.

"Why yes, I think she did. Your father said she actually admired
it." Miss Owen smiled a soft smile of benevolent toleration.

Clem was suffused with joy. Her mother *had* liked it. She knew
she would. "She was *right* to admire it. It was an excellent portrait,
excellent! The Sydney artists—the professional ones, of course—
admire him a great deal. He is a painter's painter."

Miss Owen seemed singularly impressed with Rupert's phrase.

She quickly recoverd her subtly patronizing air, however, and remarked, "I see you've picked up a little of the jargon of the painting
student." She studied her exquisitely polished fingernails for a moment, then said, "I have never heard of him. I wonder why that is?"
Her eyes crinkled in mock surprise.

Clem glanced at Miss Owen's insipid watercolors hanging in their
ornate gold frames upon the heavily embossed wallpaper. "Perhaps
you and he do not share the same ideas. He is not very convention-
al."

"They say that all great art is beyond its time. One must only hope
that the time will dawn when your friend's work will come into its
own."

"Yes. And for his sake I hope it dawns soon." Clem affected a
gay laugh. "I have further unpacking to do!" She got up and made a
brief curtsy. "I intend to ride all day tomorrow. Is my pony still in
the stables?"

"You'll have to ask Katharine that. She rides the animal occasionally. You won't know her. She is such a young lady." Miss
Owen rose also, ringing for Edith. "Katharine has always respond-
ed so well to learning. She is so amenable." This praise of her sister,
said with such a gush of fondness, was meant more as a criticism of
herself, thought Clem.

She couldn't be bothered to defend herself. She left the room
straightaway in search of Katharine.

She didn't have to go far, as Katharine was descending the stairs.
"Clem! Quick, hide me! I'm late for tea!" She giggled and ran into
Clem, kissing her on the cheek. "You're home!" She saw Miss
Owen at the drawing-room door. "I'm sorry, Marianne. I was held
up, I mean, pinned up! Edith could not unpin me in time!" She
rushed down the hall and kissed Miss Owen—with extraordinary
affection, thought Clem. "Isn't it lovely to have her back?"

Clem realized that she had not meant a word she'd said. She kept
trying to glance at herself in the hall mirror behind Miss Owen. "Is
the bodice right?"

"Yes, I think so. Turn around."' Miss Owen pinched and pulled
at the waistband. "That will do nicely."

They both turned to face Clem. She was stunned. Katharine was
not yet sixteen yet looked nineteen and was behaving just like all the
girls at the Misses Maybright's!

"Have you been riding Magpie?" Clem blurted out.

"Only a few times. I was told to exercise him. You don't mind, do you?"

"No, why should I? He enjoys being ridden. Do you ride much?"

"No, not really. I prefer other things, you know. Marianne says that girls ought to do lots of other things beside riding and such."

"I'm sure Clemency agrees with that." Marianne tempted her to differ.

"One must do anything one likes doing, unless it interferes with someone else's happiniess." Clem knew she sounded terribly pompous. She had not meant to say that at all. "I mean, do what you like—I don't care." That was even worse!

Katharine frowned.

"Don't worry, Kathy. I'll not thrust my ideas down your throat the way I used to. I see you are very happy now. I won't interfere with all this—" She waved her arm in a circle above her head. "All this feminine grandeur! It's very pretty and becomes you both."

She still sounded terribly resentful. She *was* resentful. She was jealous of their happiness in each other and in their surroundings. She was an outsider. She would never forgive that woman for making the last few months of her mother's life so miserable, or for wooing her sister from her as well. She realized that she was crying.

"It is your *room!*" Miss Owen looked genuinely distressed. "We had to move it. We knew you might be upset. Please try to understand." She came toward her, holding out her hands in supplication.

"I'm trying to understand! I don't blame my father for marrying you and changing the house. I know it's not just *my* house. Perhaps it was never my house. I didn't build it—I just lived here. But my room was my own! And my mother—"

"And they are both gone!" Katharine cried. "I'm so sorry I wasn't able to greet you outside the house, but Edith had put tongs in my hair and was fitting me. I couldn't move!"

"Never mind, Katharine. Sisters are never the best of friends. Aunt Margaret has told me that many times. I hope we *can* be friends, well, at least not enemies. I'm not such a ragamuffin as I was."

"No! You are beautiful! Jessie Maclean says that you were thought of as the most beautiful girl in Sydney!"

Clem was uncomfortably touched by her sister's outburst, but just for a moment. Then she felt herself overwhelmed with a violent, passionate anger. She could not control it, and lifting her skirts roughly, she pushed past the two of them and ran up the stairs to her room.

She was shaking with anger and jealousy, emotions too strong to conquer by weeping into the pillow. She didn't know exactly of whom she was jealous, and the not knowing made her even more angry. She was angry because they'd deprived her of her mother's last few months of life. She was gripped by a spasm of violent frustration. She wanted to murder them all! To wring their selfish hypocritical necks!

She banged her fists and head against the wall until Miss Owen's wildflower sketches dropped one by one onto the carpet. They'd taken so little *notice* of her! Her head throbbed alarmingly, forcing her to sit on the floor. She rocked back and forth, the rhythmic movement calming her. She sat for some minutes trying to reason out her position in their lives, in their house, and all the time there was something else—another dark disturbing patch in the back of her mind.

She stood up and went to the window. A great flood of sorrow suddenly drowned the remaining frustration, and she wept loudly and bitterly, staring out at the brown paddocks, the flat brown land stretching in its familiar landscape to the Brennan house.

She had come back hoping to return to her *childhood*. The grass and the trees were there, but *she* was not. She was a stranger to this house, and she feared—with a fear that had become a gnawing physical pain—that she might also be a stranger to her beloved land.

She tore at her clothes, pulling them from her like an insect that has stayed too long inside its hated and sticky chrysalis; wrenching open the bottom drawer of one of the chests she found her old riding habit and got into it in such haste that her hair was falling down her back and half the buttons of the jacket were left undone.

She would ride out now, as far as the horse paddock, to *prove* that she was home. Nobody had the right to usurp her home—or her childhood!

"I *must* conquer it! I *must*!" She kicked aside the broken glass from Miss Owen's delicately framed sketches and marched out onto the landing.

She met Miss Owen halfway down the stairs. "It is too late for riding. Where—"

"I must go out before dinner. I feel locked in. I—"

"We could walk together." Miss Owen looked behind her. There was a scurrying and scuffling in the hall. "The servants. What were you doing?"

"Nothing. I'm sorry, I want to get out!"

"I understand. Don't rush off. I wish to say something." She looked down the stairs again. "They've gone." Then she took a step backward and barred Clem's way.

Clem pushed at her arms. They were incredibly strong for such a slender woman.

"You are no longer a child. You must conquer this willfulness. Look at yourself. You look like a madwoman!"

Clem started to protest, but the other woman flexed the muscles in her strong straight arms. "No! You must hear me out! It is always a blow to return home after a long absence, at your age in particular."

Clem slumped into the banister. She was exhausted. "Go on."

"What I'm trying to say is that in your case it's doubly hard. I've noticed with some of you bush country girls that it's harder for you to grow up than for others. You have to change—not from girlhood into womanhood—but from *boyhood* into womanhood, which is sometimes almost impossible."

Clem breathed painfully. What was the woman saying?

"Do you understand me?"

"No, I don't."

"It's an awkward life out here for a female. She feels she must be accepted wholeheartedly by the men, as it is their country. And where there is little female influence for her to follow . . ."

"My mother—"

"I don't mean to belittle your mother. She had other qualities, removed, however, from the knowledge of how to bring up young women. No, you have always been like a wild boy. That is why your father has never understood you or your sister. I wish you would let me—"

"No! I don't want to talk to you!"

"Will you at least think about what I've said? And do try to control yourself—the servants think we've brought an insane creature into the house. Please?" Miss Owen backed down the stairs, her hands still holding fast to the banister. "Please?"

"All right!" Clem rushed out the front door and ran down to the stables. The grapevine on the back veranda had tight unfurled leaves which danced at the very edge of her vision like light green butterflies against the dark sandstone wall.

Everywhere she looked the colors were heightened, blinding her with their brilliance. She stopped running and held her head in her hands. She was insane. Everything about her was moving wildly. She seemed to be in another world. She covered her eyes, waiting until the dizziness left her. She had been walking in the portrait, walking in the brilliant and fragmented world of William's vision.

The cool darkness of the stables gradually restored her composure. Magpie was happy to see her. He snuffled at her hands for oats and followed her meekly into the yard.

They rode to the horse paddock, Clem feeling the heat through her thick skirt and jacket, enjoying the proximity of the other horses who gathered around, nuzzling her for food. They had obviously recognized her and whinnied as she rode away.

On the way back she gazed continually at the house. Although the second story had altered the outline, the familiar feeling of the place returned as they advanced slowly toward it. She galloped Magpie across the home paddock, then walked him slowly down to the cottages.

It was nearly sundown, and the men would be eating in the kitchen. She decided to look in to say hello to the few whom she knew well. She jumped off Magpie, leaving him untethered in the kitchen yard and entered the long smoke-filled room.

There were about twelve men sitting at the table, drinking tea and smoking variously shaped handmade pipes. They were talking in loud voices, interspersed with sudden guffaws and exaggerated gesticulations.

As she stood in the doorway, the voices gradually ceased. They all looked at her. Some didn't know her; some didn't recognize her, but the few who did stood up and pushed their hats to the back of their heads.

One spoke. "It's Miss Clemency, isn't it? From the house?"

"Yes. I've just returned from Sydney. I've come to meet the new cook. Where is he?" She blushed profusely. She didn't really know why she'd come at all. She hardly knew any of them, not any more.

"He's in the slaughterhouse, miss. You're a big lass now."

"Yes." She stood stiffly in the complete silence for a few moments, then said, "Well, just tell him I was here."

They all nodded as she turned and walked away. Halfway across the yard, she could hear them conferring together in low voices.

None of them had ever really noticed her before. Yet now they looked at her in the same way they used to regard her mother—with a feigned politeness—followed no doubt by a series of frank comments on her appearance.

Walking Magpie to the stables, she watched the sun start to set. The ground and the house were pink and gold, and as she watched, they gradually changed into a softer, darker pink. Then the sun went down, and the house was left tall and isolated on the flat purple land.

Dinner was a feast that night, and now that she was too old to be refused wine by her father, she became quite giddy, her feelings superficially warm toward the three people whom she still could not bring herself to trust. Their awkward overtures of friendship now ceased to worry her and she sat eating meringues until she felt she would burst.

Later Miss Owen and Katharine played duets upon a magnificent new grand piano, and Clem was persuaded to fetch her watercolors for the family's admiration. Miss Owen was genuinely impressed, and her father patted her on the head and rewarded her by summoning Edith to share his pride at his daughter's newly flowered talent. Edith made all the right noises, then was dispatched for the brandy.

Mr. Cameron drank a large glass, cradling and fondling the wide-bottomed tumbler with his two great brown hands. Clem watched them, their sensuous movements gradually lulling her into a gentle sleep.

Katharine woke her by tugging at her hair. "Clem! You were asleep! Father wants to know why you're not wearing our mother's pearls."

"What? Oh, the pearls. I shall wear them some other time."

Her father nodded, then dismissed his offspring with the customary lowering of his forehead. Katharine ran to kiss him. Clem followed reluctantly, brushing her forehead against his, finding her old posture of standing on tiptoe too ridiculous.

She could hardly sleep for worrying about the pearls. What on earth would she tell him? Her mother had left her most of her jewelry, of which there was very little. The pearls, apart from the sapphire ring and the jade brooch, were the most valuable stones. He would never understand why she'd had to part with them. She hardly understood it herself.

The next morning Angus arrived, his horse covered in white foam from galloping the miles between the two homesteads.

Clem greeted him affectionately. He was, after all, the one constant factor in her life. He seemed to recognize this, and gradually his voice and mannerisms took on the character of an overprotective parent. She played up to him quite unconsciously, and the two spent the day talking in whispers in a corner of the drawing room.

She couldn't stop herself from telling him all about her homecoming, and he was appropriately sympathetic. His ginger eyes took on a benign and kindly glow beneath the bushy red brows, and his broad-framed, capable body became a confortable refuge.

At the end of the day, though a little more resigned to her circumstances, Clem was still sufficiently disoriented and demoralized to be swayed by Angus's gentle persuasion, and when he asked the inevitable question she was unable to refuse him.

I *am* very fond of him, she assured herself as he rode away that night. And he is quite right—about time and habit being important. As my aunt said: a deep and abiding friendship is a better basis for marriage than a romantic dream.

She had realized long ago the sheer futility of imagining any kind of life with Matt Brennan. His ideas were the same as Biddy's. She was a member of the privileged class, and he of the underprivileged, and he would ultimately feel the same way about her as Biddy did despite any love which might exist between them.

William and Matt had both said she was born to be rich and spoiled, so she may as well remain that way; besides, all of her efforts to become anything better had so far been ignored or ridiculed by both. As her only alternative now was to be an unwanted old maid, a figure of fun, and a hanger-on at Querilderie, she may as well marry her squatter and bore herself to death over the silver soup tureens. She smiled, remembering William's description.

No, she would marry Angus and not have too many offspring and still ride and help on the property. He'd promised her he would never curtail her freedom.

She stood on the veranda gazing out at the diminishing image of Angus riding away into the darkness with a slight feeling of unease and a suggestion of guilt. She *was* very fond of him.

Chapter Twenty

The early summer days extended into one infinite sunny morning in the drawing room and the library. She would sit and sew with Katharine and Marianne (she was finally able to address her by her Christian name) or read by herself in the library—her mother's old room—now richly paneled with native red cedar and stocked with shelves of uniformly bound classics.

The only variation from this tranquil domestic routine was her afternoon ride when she would gallop her tall handsome gelding out into the far paddocks to race over hastily devised courses of log piles and makeshift jumps. Her father had given her the horse—a three-year-old with a magnificent pedigree—only two days after her homecoming.

To refuse such a gift would have been churlish, decided Clem, concluding after a few moments of soul searching that most gifts were bribes of some sort. On reflection she'd thought it possible that Mulga—so-called because his coat was the color of polished mulga wood—had been more in the nature of an olive branch.

Marianne did not encourage visitors other than the Macleans and the infrequent visitor from *home*, yet each evening would be arranged with the exactitude reserved for a full-scale formal dinner.

Mr. and Mrs. Maclean, Angus, Jessie, or all of them, would arrive at tea time, stay the night, and be gone by midmorning at least once a week. Clem would sit and talk politely of life in Sydney and other people's visits home. Katharine and Marianne would play, and Clem and Marianne would produce their latest watercolors for the inevitable sighs of surprised delight.

John Cameron viewed all this with a benign eye, sometimes making an appearance at luncheon with face and hands scrubbed and a clean shirt, and always dressing with great care for dinner. Clem noticed how irritated he would become at bedtime, especially when the visitors did not appear to want to retire. Marianne would humor him with promises of future early nights.

The Camerons frequently returned the Macleans' visits, as it was now accepted that Clem and Angus were soon to be married. The two spent many hours together as the Christmas season approached, usually riding to the western boundaries of Glen Ross to take up Angus's favorite occupation of fossil hunting.

His pet fossicking place was a particularly arid region, almost a desert. Even the trees were like fossils. They were paper barks in clumps of four or five, standing crookedly in depressions of powdery soil, their trunks white with loose layers of fine bark. These ghostly trees followed the course of a dry creek bed for ten miles to the north where they disappeared abruptly, giving way to an endless, featureless plain.

"Aborigine country," Angus always remarked, each time they reached this particular spot. "Better not go further." He would lead the way back to his usual resting place—a native orange tree. The hard bitter fruit it bore was devoured by the aborigines when they could find nothing better. Clem enjoyed biting into the small woody fruit, picking out the flat seeds one by one and digging each into the dry earth with her fingers. The bitter taste of native oranges would always bring back the sound of Angus's voice, lecturing her on one of his latest finds.

One early November day, the two had reached the tree by late morning and Angus, taking out his most recent treasure from his specimen bag, began to turn the tiny skeleton around slowly to see if it was completely intact. Clem sat gazing at the nearest paper bark. Its tiny creamy flowers, growing in loose clusters at the end of the dry branches never failed to bloom in early summer, no matter how dry the water course. She signed contentedly. These outings with

Angus had made her feel a part of her own country again. In spite of the constant threat of his emotional outbursts, she was indebted to him and constrained to keep her promise.

He watched as she leaned over to touch the tiny sun-dried bones of the animal, then took it from her and wrapped it, laying it to one side. "I wish you were as interested in me as you pretend to be in that creature. I wish—"

"Surely you don't intend to go over all *that* again!"

"This will be the last time. I have come to dislike, no *hate,*, this tree because of you. It represents everything—"

"Please, Angus! It's no use telling you I love you! You *do* want me to pretend—is that it?"

"No, I just want you to name a day—*any* day. My mother says—"

"I'm thinking about it."

"That's not enough. And love does come, it will come, with marriage. It always does."

"I don't believe that, that's nonsense."

"You talk too much. I'm sick of listening to you. I don't care about love. We've been together for as many years as I can remember."

"But—"

"You can't deny that!"

"But that was when we were children. And you were never nice to me."

She stared at the earth and the brown ants crawling in and out of the fallen fruit.

His eyes followed hers. "It's stupid of me to pretend that artist fellow didn't exist. I don't even care that he was your lover. Other men—I mean, it makes no difference to me." He flicked a pebble at the ants.

"He was never my lover. I've had no lover, except perhaps you."

Angus laughed joylessly. "I wish that were true! I can't go on seeing you all the time without wanting to—to kiss you—"

She sighed, trying to dampen his passion with her indifference.

"You don't know how beautiful you are! But you're so cold!" He got up and knelt before her, staring at her with his funny ginger eyes. Then he hugged her to him. She was too tired and too hot to protest. He kissed her and kissed her until her face was chaffed with his beard.

Finally he fell upon her and kissed her throat and her breasts until she thought she would suffocate. She tried to respond with an equal desire but found it impossible to feel anything but a heavy and overwhelming fatigue. She *wanted* to be able to return his frenzied caresses, but she kept seeing Angus's familiar wiry hair and hearing his anguished breathing and passionate epithets, all of which utterly repelled her. Again, as in her aunt's stables, she was overcome with an urge to break out into hysterical laughter.

The smell of sweat and tobacco and saddle leather was thick in her nose and mouth. For an instant she pretended it was Matt who was kissing her and immediately opened her eyes. She oughtn't to have such silly fantasies, and she was being so cruel to poor Angus. She had to get used to the idea of being married to him.

For a second she returned his embrace, kissing him awkwardly on the side of the mouth. He relaxed his hold and she drew back, knowing that she would never be able to kiss that mouth again without being forced to. She pushed him away violently. "I'm sorry!"

"Don't be stupid! Don't be so damn stupid!" His face was red, his pupils large and bright, and his mouth distorted into a bitter smile. "If that man was your lover, then it will make no difference if you have me too."

"He was not my lover! And even if—"

He tried to take hold of her again, but she scrambled to her feet and ran to the other side of the tree. "You won't! You have no right!"

He lunged at her suddenly, pulling her down on top of him, holding both her arms behind her back, then he rolled them both over until he was on top of her, still pinning her arms. She tried to kick him, but he'd somehow managed to trap her legs.

Now she was pushed flat on the ground. She felt the hard bones of his hips bruising the soft skin between her thighs as he forced his body upward, pushing her skirt into a stubborn lump, the only barrier between his urgent body and her stiff, protesting form.

She felt the earth press cruelly into the back of her head, the sharp little stones digging into her scalp like a thousand miniature daggers. She couldn't even cry out with the pain. Her mouth wouldn't open. Nothing would move at all. She was like an animal caught in a steel trap.

Her feeble attempts to move only increased the pressure, intensifying his brutal hold, until her body, burning with pain, became numb, and she feared that her limbs would be torn from their sockets.

Her skin was wet and loose, like an outer garment. She felt as if it would come off in his hands.

He was writhing maniacally, the stench of his saliva making her retch. He raised his head for an instant. She froze, petrified with loathing. Then her body involuntarily jerked upward, her knee colliding violently with his groin. He screamed in agony and rolled off her onto the the ground.

She found herself loosening her horse's reins from the orange tree with slippery fingers. She heaved herself into the saddle and urged him on, glancing back only once as he broke into a gallop. Angus was lying flat on his back, holding his groin with both hands.

Mulga galloped wildly through the paper barks. She raised one weak hand to attempt to clean her face. The earth and warm slime from his mouth had hardened to a viscous second skin.

She had ridden for three miles before she sensed him behind her. She looked back and saw him racing after her through the slim white trees.

The brittle branches cracked like gun fire, falling on their shoulders and glancing off the horses' rumps as they careened down the dry creek bed. She reined in her horse as they neared a small flock of sheep, huddled together in fear.

The sight of the thin dusty animals quelled her terror: the creature behind her was only Angus.

She'd lost her hat and felt clumsily at the back of her neck for the ribbon. Her hand shook; soon her whole body was shaking violently.

She thought about the hat and started to laugh, a jerky high-pitched sound which gradually subsided into heavy sobs. Her stepmother had told her to wear the hat as a precaution against freckles. Should she tell her how she'd lost it?

Suddenly the horror and disgust left her and she felt only humiliated and ridiculous. She tried to stop sobbing, taking deep rasping breaths and letting her head drop onto her chest. She knew she was as much to blame as anyone for his outrageous behavior. She should have put an end to it long ago. Her mind had tolerated his desire, though her body had continually repulsed him. Now this would finish everything.

Angus had reached her, he and his horse both gasping for air.

"You've lost your hat. D'you want me to go back and look for it?" He lay forward in the saddle, his eyes closed.

He looked so foolish, so red and winded, she felt nothing but a contemptuous pity for him.

Through dry dusty lips she said, "I've heard of men who compromise women into marrying them." Her head was throbbing relentlessly. She lifted it a little, staring at him as she rubbed her cheeks and forehead. She could smell him still, even at that distance.

"And I've heard it told the other way around, near home, too." He raised his eyes to her face, waiting for her reaction.

She stared straight back at him. He was harmless now. "I've heard nothing of the kind." She was still shaking. She didn't know quite what he was talking about—unless her father had seduced Marianne—which was unthinkable! She shook her head slowly. "You're only guessing."

"Not at all. It happens all the time. Your father was tricked into marrying your mother, believing marriage necessary when it was not. Women, you see, are just as dishonorable."

"How dare you slander my mother!" The pain in her head was so intense she thought she might faint. "Your own dear Miss Owen has no doubt played the same trick on him!"

"No, she isn't the type. Your father has wanted to marry her for years. You were too naive to see it. The baby would have come anyway."

"What? What baby?" She grabbed the horse's mane to steady herself. The sun seemed to be shining from inside her head.

"Haven't you noticed? She's going to have a baby. Quite soon, I should think."

"No, I haven't noticed," she whispered hoarsely. "If it's a boy—"

"It may very well be a boy." He grinned at her, his eyes colorless in the harsh light. "You will not be so self-sufficient then."

"I wouldn't marry for money, even if I were destitute." She hated him then. Despite everything, he was still so sure of himself. She shut her eyes and licked her lips with a dry tongue.

"That's easy to say when one *has* money. People's characters have been known to change alarmingly when suddenly deprived of it. You're just like my sisters. You take everything for granted. It's all talk with you."

"Unlike you—you only take *people* for granted. You know nothing about me. I've seen how the poor and despised live. I wouldn't care to live like that, but I would survive." Her throat was thick and dry.

"A woman can't survive on her own in this country. You live in a kind of fairyland. If that child is a boy, then you'll have a taste of real life."

"If it is—it'll make no difference in my feelings for you!" She turned her horse's head in the direction of home, hoping he'd keep going south to Glen Ross. She rode straight toward the line of coolibahs growing in the low-lying watered area which divided the Macleans' property from her father's.

The trees were visible for miles, towering above the paper barks and water bushes growing in patches by their sides. The eighteen trees, at a distance of about half a mile from each other, formed a natural boundary between the two properties. From far away the water bushes looked blue. Their shimmering leaves created the illusion of a long wave of water on the horizon, promising to roll toward her and engulf the hundreds of acres of brown grass.

She rode slowly toward the nearest coolibah, taking sips of warm water from her water bag, feeling so devoid of substance she imagined she was floating above the land. So they were going to deprive her of *that*, too. Eventually she would belong nowhere at all!

She rested beneath the coolibah's branches, her head against the rough bark. The tree must have been struck by lightning, as one of its two main branches lay rotting on the ground, leaving just one thick low-spread branch. This hung near the earth and was so heavy it seemed about to fall. She finished the warm water, swilling it around her mouth and wiping it over her face.

The rotting branch was full of insects—thousands of ants in all shapes and colors. Soon the wood would be just a heap of soft dust on the dry soil. The next rain would wash it out of existence.

Clem turned to look back across the paddock. There was no movement. It lay brown and gold beneath the sun for miles and miles until the earth curved and the sky touched it with an imaginary green line.

If her father *did* have a son, she *would* be disinherited, and her position would become untenable. Whereas Katharine was accepted totally by Marianne as a friend and dutiful daughter, she, Clem, had no rank or security in the household at all.

If she didn't leave or marry Angus, she would spend the rest of her life as the spinster aunt, occasionally called from her room to sew and patch or to mind the children—an unpaid seamstress and nanny. She'd prefer Hetty's life to that! She wondered how much the rest of her mother's jewelry would fetch. She stared at the pale green of the water bush flowers and remembered how her mother had always made her wear green. Perhaps her father hated her, not only because she was not a son but also because she was her mother's daughter.

A bee buzzed excitedly inside a cluster of little flowers, the only sound in the still, hot air. She felt the back of her head gingerly. The throbbing had stopped, leaving a dull ache where Angus had banged it repeatedly on the ground. She rolled up her sleeves to look for scratches and found only a slight graze.

He imagines as I'm already soiled by the terrible William it will make no difference if I compound the felony. I wish William *had* made love to me, I wish—Matt . . . She stood up wearily, stretching her arms above her head.

As she mounted Mulga she thought of Biddy and squirmed with shame at the memory of her soppy letter. Biddy would have even less respect for her after reading that. She *was* right, of course, there *was* too great a barrier, despite its occasional blurring. No matter what you said or did you could never completely transcend it. Somehow she would have to get used to Angus. Perhaps it was not always as horrible as the first time. . . . Perhaps she could bring herself to kiss him. She pulled the petals from one of the tiny flowers and crushed them between sticky fingers.

The next few days saw no answer to her problems, and Clem suffered alone. Even a Mrs. Merilees would have been of some comfort. She wrote to her and then to Biddy, the letter so full of questions about her and Harry, she would *have* to reply.

Then Clem wrote to her aunt, telling her of the forthcoming happy event and suggesting that although it was still a secret, she might try to engage a nanny as they were so scarce in the Pringle area and not always the right type.

She wrote almost in a spirit of perversity, feeling a little uncomfortable as she signed her name, but shook off her uneasiness with a rush of self-righteousness. It was merely the beginning of an unselfish interest in the welfare of her father's wife. She admitted to herself that she *was* jealous. But she wasn't jealous of the baby; it was of her father and Marianne's happiness. How she envied them that.

Marianne eventually informed Clem of the good news, and together with an excited Katharine they planned the infant's nursery and clothes. Clem had determined to rise above her detestable envy and to enter wholeheartedly into family affairs. She and Marianne became quite friendly and had reached the stage of kissing each other good morning and good night with a degree of fondness, when she mentioned the letter to her aunt.

Marianne had entered those long weeks of prenatal bliss when one becomes entirely self-absorbed. That morning she sat by the tall windows at the end of the library, gazing out onto Clem's mother's garden, while Clem and Katharine chatted with each other. She ignored them until Clem repeated her plans for a nanny to be engaged from Sydney.

Marianne suddenly broke out of her dreamlike state, her face deathly pale, her eyes wide with terror. "What—?" She lurched forward, her long fingers clutching at the gold velvet arms of the chair.

Katharine gaped at her while Clem stuttered, "There is nobody suitable in this area . . ." Her voice faded.

Marianne stood up, holding her enormous skirts in front of her as if to stop herself from toppling to her knees. "You had no right to ask your aunt! You must tell her to stop it immediately!"

The shock of seeing her so violently disturbed had gone, and Clem now felt the same unaccountable anxiety which had overtaken her while writing the letter. She stood up, unable to look at Marianne. "It's too late. Somebody is already engaged—an elderly woman—"

"Is she recently from *home*? Has she been employed in Sydney? Who has employed her? Do we know them? What do we know about her—what!"

Katharine helped her to sit down. Marianne was trembling with a passionate anger. "You!" She screamed at Clem, "You—why did you interfere!"

"I—I'm terribly sorry, but she is entirely responsible. She has worked for a family called—I cannot remember their name—and other families before that, both here and at home. I assure you that—"

"Why are you suddenly so concerned? It used to be just your habit of talking out of turn that made you so much of a nuisance!" Marianne rose and walked stiffly to the door. "You must try to stop that woman from coming here. I do not want a stranger in this house. I will hire someone from Willawarrha."

Katharine glanced at Clem. They both knew that that idea was entirely unreasonable.

Marianne's two stepdaughters concluded that she was not in a fit state to know what was best for her. She was obviously overtired. They decided Clem should not stop the woman from coming and that Angus, who'd planned to attend a natural history conference in Sydney at about the same time the child was due, ought to be entrusted with the woman's traveling arrangements.

"When have I talked out of turn, Katharine?" Clem asked, still puzzled by Marianne's words.

"You mentioned her to that awful man who was here. I promised not to say anything, but she had to bribe him to keep him quiet, and had nothing to give him. It was all too terrible!"

"Why did she have to bribe him? What had she done?" Clem was blushing furiously, remembering that Mr. Pike had talked of Marianne months after she'd told him of her desire to stay buried at Glen Ross. "I merely said that she preferred to remain a mystery or something of the kind."

"Yes. That gave him the idea. Your portrait was only an excuse for his coming here. He came here to blackmail Marianne. She had an unfortunate youth, you see. She had to leave home, as she was accused of trying to win her brother-in-law's affections. He found out all about that and said he would tell Papa."

"Did he keep silent?"

"Yes. She gave him some gold. Yours, actually."

"My quartz!" Clem was about to protest vehemently but then remembered it was all her fault anyway. "Well, I suppose that was a kind of justice." She shrugged.

Katharine was regarding her with an expression halfway between pity and vexation. "There is no happy medium with you, Clem. You're either completely withdrawn or too garrulous by far." She paused. "I know it's none of my business, but you've almost destroyed poor Angus with your madness."

"Katharine, you're too young to understand. Just because you feel so educated does not give you the right to pronounce verdicts.

Music and French and poetry may induce a certain poise, but not necessarily wisdom.''

"I know, but all that is irrelevant to how the heart feels!"

"Oh. So you think you know about love do you?"

"You're so pompous, Clem!" Katharine was now almost as tall as she. Her face was taut, her gray eyes bright with anger. "You've always treated me like a simpleton. Well, I'm not! And you've treated Angus in the same way!" She strode out of the room.

Clem caught up with her in the hall. "I'm sorry. I suppose I know nothing about you at all. But you're wrong about Angus and me."

Katharine continued toward the stairs.

"Wait!" Clem grabbed her arm. "How did Mr. Pike know about Marianne?"

"You told him! How else!"

"No, I mean about her past."

"Some people in Sydney knew of her I think. I'm not sure."

"Katharine, I'm sorry to have been so unfriendly at first—really."

"That's all right." Katharine forced a smile.

Clem studied her sister as she mounted the wide staircase. She was so graceful and so attractive, and above all so happy.

She wondered what would become of her. Perhaps she would be packed off to Sydney to find the equivalent of a Mr. Gilzean or an Angus. She would have no trouble, as men just adored such gay, lighthearted creatures. And Katharine was so accomplished. Clem sighed, remembering her own awkwardness at Katharine's age.

When Christmas was only two weeks away, Clem decided that she'd put off riding to the Brennans' for too long. She'd dreaded reaching their deserted house, knowing that yet another part of her childhood was gone. She sometimes pretended they were still there, that the boys were harvesting the second crop or grubbing up the iron-bark stumps in front of the small house. It was time she saw for herself that they were no longer there.

One evening, while the family was sitting quietly in the drawing room and her father was in a good mood, being without visitors to entertain, she asked his permission to ride out to the boundary fences near the quartz ridge.

"You intend to take up your old profession of boundary riding?"

her father asked, blowing thick cigar smoke toward the wire-screened french windows.

"Why not? I must be useful."

"Do you intend to camp overnight?" He knocked his ash off loudly into the small brass bowl at the foot of his chair.

"Good heavens!" Marianne lapsed from her serenity for a moment, horrified. "You cannot be serious! The snakes and natives and such!"

"Clem does not fear any of that, Aunt Marianne. She often used to stay out in the paddocks. There are no aborigines about here now."

"No. That's right. The men have frightened them off. She can camp out. Those Brennan lads have gone now, too." He looked at Clem with a self-satisfied grimace, as if Matt Brennan's attack upon him had had something to do with her.

"I know." She stared at his cravat. "Is the creek dry?"

"I don't know. I haven't been there for over a year. You can find out for me and look at the well and the fences too. Won't do you any harm." He grunted his approval.

Marianne leaned across from the chaise longue where she rested precariously in a wide dress with a raised waistline and put her hand gently on her husband's arm. "John, dear, may she look for plants in the garden too? Edith tells me the old woman had many cuttings from us. They ought to have taken well by now. She might make a list for my perusal."

"She might indeed." Clem's father patted his wife's pale hand, his great brown fingers covering her fragile white ones.

Marianne smiled benignly upon Clem. "That would be very thoughtful of you, my dear." Her every word, these days, thought Clem, was a pathetic plea from a sorely tried woman, one whose proper place was in bed, but whose high standards of housekeeping bade her forsake her rest for her duty. She wanted her glowing state of expectancy to be fully appreciated by all and not wasted within the four walls of her bed chamber.

Her husband was enjoying his role of expectant father and could not do enough for his beautiful wife, thought Clem. She scolded herself for her bitter thoughts—she was still envious of them.

Clem brusquely refused Katharine's request to accompany her. Her continuous chatter would ruin the expedition.

Katharine had taken to questioning Clem in some detail about Angus and his intentions and even wanted to know what they talked of when they were alone. The subject had become painful to Clem after her last encounter with him and she preferred not to think about him at all, let alone discuss him with her little sister.

Clem retired to her room early that night in preparation for her long excursion, though she was not unaware of plans afoot to finally unite her with Angus. She'd guessed they would be thrown together at Christmas, and that their parents hoped for a date to be set during the informal festive season of the New South Wales bush country.

Liberal doses of colonial wine and brandy had often been known to effect profitable liaisons during the hot nights of Christmas week.

Chapter Twenty-one

The heat rose in shimmering layers before her as she rode toward the eastern boundary of her father's land. The drought would probably not break until February, and herds of red kangaroo had been seen as far east as the property adjoining the Macleans'. As the dry weather continued, so would the large herds in their push toward the watered pastures of the east. Three men had been employed to ride the boundaries continually throughout the summer to shoot the kangaroos on sight. It was hoped that the sound of gunfire would keep any stray aborigine also at bay. For this reason, Marianne's fears for Clem's safety were considered unjustified by John Cameron, who had never before objected to her camping overnight.

She reached the water hole by midmorning. The sheep were gathered around it, mostly lying down, their filthy, dust-covered bodies devoid of life. A few huddled in the shade of the emu bushes, bleating weakly. Clem dipped her fingers and licked them; the water seemed salty.

She rode on slowly to the Brennans', looking out for the white flowers of the Christmas tree on the horizon. She still couldn't believe they would be gone. Just the house, the Christmas tree, and the boronia would be there. She wondered if they'd all settled down happily in Sydney. If she'd known they were all there she could have visited them. No—Matt would have accused her of playing the lady bountiful.

She stared at the horizon, shading her eyes with her hand. There it was—the Christmas tree—just a small white dot above the brown land; it had been there for as long as she could remember. She spurred her horse and cantered over the sun-baked earth.

The bark roof appeared first, the dry moss a deep gold beneath the midday sky, then the veranda posts, still standing, and the iron-bark stumps.

The white tree rose above the house, its tiny star flowers clustered upon upright stems, their fragrance sweet upon the still air.

She tethered her horse to the willow nearest the well and tried the pump. It had rusted. She pushed harder. It wouldn't go. She brushed the thick pieces of rust from her hands and walked through the iron-bark stumps—the only remaining evidence of the years of hard labor by the Brennan boys—and up to the house.

The screen door lay half open, and the calico walls of the kitchen sagged into the middle of the room. The table had started to rot. No doubt the termites were bsuily working outward from inside the thick slabs of wood. The stove was pale red with dust, the floor, too. She walked into the boys' room. One iron bedstead stood against the wall. A swaggy must have lit a fire under it and used the wire mesh as a grill. The wall and ceiling were black with smoke.

Clem looked into Mary's room, and instead of the dark square patch on the far wall, she saw the Irish lake and the purple hills. She stood perfectly still, staring at the patch. Some people said that if you listened hard enough you could hear the sound of termites boring into wood, but there was not the tiniest sound to disturb the silence. The scent of the Christmas tree pervaded the house. She walked out of Mary's room and through the kitchen into the garden.

It was overgrown with flannel flowers. The creamy velour petals covered the rose beds, and the rose bushes were shriveled with the heat. Two dry red buds clung to a climbing branch which had managed to reach the kitchen window. Edith's English garden flowers were destroyed. Only a strangled clump of forget-me-nots lay crookedly beneath an outcrop of strong pink boronia.

Clem knelt to sniff the boronia, which mingled with the scent of the Christmas tree. She stood up and looked about for suitable cuttings for Marianne, but there was nothing left.

Her horse watched her intently as she wandered round to the front of the house. She poured a little water into the billy lid and held it for him. He guzzled greedily, knocking the lid onto the ground with a loud clatter.

It was met by a frightening screech. A cockatoo flew out of the Christmas tree, squawking at them, its enormous white wings creating a swift wind. Clem felt the air move coldly against her cheek and just glimpsed the yellow feathers in its crown as it disappeared into the iron barks. It was the soul of an aborigine who had once held this piece of land sacred to his tribe. The land had defeated the Brennans; she wondered if it would ever defeat her father.

Clem left the yard and rode down to the creek, now just a narrow strip of dust. The iron barks echoed with tiny scratchings and flappings: more parrots, their nests high in the solid branches.

The trees were sparser now. When they reached the top of the next rise she stopped her horse and looked back at the iron barks. They were a dense forest from that distance, their black trunks and gray leaves dark and somber beneath the light sky.

It was not far to the quartz ridge, so she decided to stop there to boil the billy and eat some of her salt beef and Edith's gingerbread. She could almost smell it now. She *could* smell it—no, it was the smell of wood smoke!

It was coming from the quartz ridge. Someone was there. It was too far from the boundary to be one of her father's men. She hoped it wasn't an aborigine, as she wouldn't know what to do. She decided to skirt around to the east where the ground was a little higher, and to spy on the intruder from there. She rode to the high ridge about half a mile to the east and got off to lead Mulga up the side of a sandstone outcrop on the edge of a low plateau.

The curl of the black smoke was visible from there. When they reached the top Clem saw one small figure sitting by the fire. It was a white man. She breathed a deep sigh of relief and led the horse back down the slope.

As they neared the quartz ridge, the smell of burned flour was strong in the stifling heat of the day and the wood smoke stung her eyes.

The man must have heard them coming. He stood a few feet from the fire, his gun half raised as they came over the next rise.

Chapter Twenty-two

Clem's eyes suddenly filled with water. She pulled up her horse and stared at him—a blurred and contorted figure. His face was burned almost black and his hair was bright yellow and fell to his shoulders. His eyes were slits of startling blue.

Then she saw his gun drop to the ground. They both remained perfectly still for an instant before he started to run toward her. She jumped from the horse and ran to meet him.

His eyes and hair dazzled her with their unearthly brilliance. He was a golden specter—the Sun God—come to claim her. She flung her arms around his neck as he lifted her off the ground, and in the white heat of the day their bodies, saturated with the sun and sweat and an ecstatic joy, clung together.

They finally drew back, the space between them still warm with the heat of their embrace. His face glowed, reflecting the sun and reflecting *her* face, too. *He was the portrait.* She stepped back.

He said nothing.

He was the portrait.

He smiled, his mouth stretching into a wide grin that crinkled up the hard skin around his eyes. "I've been wondering when you'd come and find me." He waited for her to say something.

She opened her mouth to speak, but could think of nothing to say. "I've been digging for gold." He pulled her gently toward him. "There's plenty of it—pure, too."
She pulled back, wanting to keep looking at his face.
"I showed it to a bloke in Pringle. Said he'd sell it for me."
"Oh."
"I'm going north soon. Soon as I finish here."
"Oh, yes." She sat down on the ground, her limbs weak.
"I heard you were goin' to marry Maclean. Suppose you have to. I understand." He grinned at her again, sinking to his knees beside her.
"I don't *want* you to understand! I'm not marrying him anyway."
He took her hand. His was rough and blistered, the nails black and torn below the hard skin. He leaned over and took her by the shoulders. "I never thought—"
"What?"
"That it would be the same. That you wouldn't change or something."
"We're always the same. We have a separate time from anyone else."
They embraced again and slowly stretched out on the hard gritty earth. Neither felt the sharp stones or the blades of dry grass attacking their already tormented flesh as they made love beneath the brilliant rays of the midday sun.

The jagged sandstone cliffs, glinting with gold quartz, sent shadows to cool them as they slept, their limbs still tangled. Nothing disturbed them, not even the screech of a parrot or the lizards continually slithering from boulder to boulder. Their exhausted bodies, like one creature, rested on the hard earth, late into the afternoon, their breathing peaceful in the shade of the soft red stone.
Clem stirred first. She opened her eyes to the glittering quartz touched by the setting sun. The air was cooler. Matt's breath filtered gently through her hair. She sat up to gaze at him while he slept. His face was mottled with pink sunlight, his hair, half in the shade and half in the sun, steaked with copper light.
He opened his eyes. "Don't move." He grabbed a fistful of her hair.
She winced with pain.

"You *are* here." He lay down with his arm behind his head, staring at her, his eyes a strange light purple, reflecting the red sky. "Your hair's darker." He reached up to pull her down gently by a tuft of hair. "It's full of sand." He started to pick out the pebbles and insects, blowing each handful of damp hair free of dust.

"I've never stopped thinking of you." Clem knew that everything she said would, just by her saying it, be inadequate. Angus had been right about time being important. But he didn't share the same time they did. "Remember the moon tree?"

"Your tea tree? I remember. You used to go on about the flowers. It'll be in flower now."

"I want to stay there—tonight."

"I wanted to ask you if you were marrying Maclean—that last time. I'm glad you're not going to marry him."

"I'm glad, too."

He shook out the last strand of her hair and pulled her to her feet. He turned away to look at her horse. "I'll bet he can't beat Caesar."

Clem was straightening her riding skirt and blouse. "We'll see." She carefully buttoned each tiny covered button. Her fingers were dark against the glistening white silk.

"I'll race you three miles—from here to the next lot of wood."

The sun started to set just as they mounted the horses. It left two long bright green streaks above the vivid pink land. As they spurred their horses into the darkening landscape it disappeared, and the paddocks turned into a wide plum-colored sea.

There was no moon. Only the stars relieved the density of the close black night.

Clem stared straight ahead, trying to see the moon tree.

A soft glow appeared on the horizon, and as they rode toward it, it slowly changed into a large, white ball. "It's the moon . . . it's fallen from the sky," she whispered.

"When the sky's as black as this, it's because the moon's dropped out of it. That's what the Euragalla tribe says." Matt felt for the back of her neck in the darkness.

Clem wondered how many thoughts which Matt attributed to the aborigines were really his own. He was so averse to talking; perhaps he felt obliged to deny his thoughts, too.

They rode in silence as it loomed closer, bewitching them, drawing them to it like moths to a light. An enormous, glimmering ball of soft white wool, it rested just above the unending black plain.

Clem gazed up into the sky. The stars, puncturing the thick ebony wall with their million-year-old beams of straight white light existed only to increase the shining splendor of her tree. She knew she was dreaming, perhaps still lying in her bed in Aunt Margaret's house. She dared not look behind in case he wasn't there.

The tree was moving toward them, its flowers dividing into separate candles with brilliant black spaces in between. She could hear Matt's breathing, yet she still did not look back. The tree was only a few yards from them. A twig cracked beneath the horse's foot.

Matt dismounted and began to gather sticks. They let the horses graze free. She carried the gun and the heavy saddles to the tree. Its branches divided close to the ground, leaving a large cleft in the trunk where Clem placed the saddles. She hung the bridles from the higher branches and felt the dark rough bark with her fingertips. The branches spread so wide and low to the ground that once underneath the tree, one was completely enveloped within it—almost like being inside a temple, thought Clem, a temple with a floating roof.

Matt scraped a patch of earth flat with his fingernails and constructed a tiny pyramid of twigs, placing each one as delicately as might a builder of intricate card houses. Clem watched him. He sat on his haunches, his knees splayed like a native, his elbows resting on them as he carefully selected each twig.

He sat back and felt along the ground for the billy. "Here! Catch!" He threw the billy at her and she caught it with both arms. "Fill that up. There's water in my bag."

By the time she found his water bag the fire was a flaming pyre. He'd stuck two forked sticks into the ground on either side and hung the billy from the cross stick. Matt's face was dark red in the firelight, his eyes narrowed against the heat, his mouth a hard line of concentration.

The fire spat drops of hot liquid at them—the juice of tiny insects caught on the sticks. He put his arm about her shoulders and they sat gazing into the fire until the water boiled.

They drank the burning black liquid in silence, then Matt threw the dregs onto the fire, and stamped on it heavily, scattering the ashes and grinding them into the earth with his heels.

Clem sat back against the tree, feeling the hard stiff bark in the small of her back. "I wish this night could go on forever."

"Yes." He lay down with his head resting on her thigh.

She could feel his wet curls through the limp material of her skirt. A delicious weakness flooded her limbs. One whole night with him beside her was too much to have prayed for. It could surely never happen again like this. She shut her eyes, sensitive to the tiniest movement of his body. The tree was perfectly still, not even one late bee moved in its branches. The white flowers had the faintest scent; it would drift about them and then waft away. She opened her eyes and looked up into the tree. They were floating inside a strange moon, divorced from the paddocks and the bush life around them. She pressed herself hard against the bark at her back. She knew that as long as they stayed inside their moon, nothing could hurt them or cause them to part. She prayed that the night would last forever.

"I'm afraid."

"Of what?" Matt whispered, smoothing the material of her skirt along her calf and holding her ankle between his thumb and forefinger.

"Something will keep us apart again. It's all too good."

"I won't let it."

"But it *will* happen."

"When we've got enough gold, we'll go. It's as simple as that."

"Yes." Clem tried to sound convinced. She bent forward to try to kiss his forehead, but he sat up and pinned her against the tree. "I love you," she said.

Chapter Twenty-three

Christmas with Angus had come and gone and not succeeded in reuniting the estranged couple. Angus had left Querilderie a sad and sober man. Clem had avoided him wherever possible and paid him scant attention when forced into his company.

Katharine, however, had been kind to him. Her lively chatter and feminine accomplishments had kept him from sinking into complete gloom and had saved the season from disaster.

Marianne was now confined to her room for most of the day and retired so early that everyone but Clem's father, who'd prayed for a quieter existence, missed the long, musical evenings in the pretty gold and brown drawing room.

Matt remained at the quartz ridge. His diggings had multiplied and his pile of gold mounted steadily. The quartz was on Cameron property, and legally the gold belonged to Clem's father, but Matt believed he was entitled to profit from his own labor and had no qualms of conscience about selling Cameron property. He'd worked at Querilderie for nothing for many years just to keep his family in flour and salt; and then John Cameron had paid his father half of what the Brennans' three hundred acres would have fetched on the open market. He believed John Cameron owed him the gold.

Clem agreed Matt had a moral right to it. It had not been a part of the original land grant, and if it were anyone's property by natural law it belonged to the Euragalla tribe.

She'd listened with horror to Matt's version of his fight with her father. He'd ridden to the house to refuse his offer for the land only to find that Mr. Brennan had already accepted the sum and had squandered most of it on rum. "I would have killed the tyrannical bastard if four of his tame convicts hadn't dragged me off him."

Later, one morning while he and Clem were chipping the tiny pieces of dull yellow mineral from the quartz, he'd suddenly stopped working and stared at her with a strange new depth to his pale eyes, a kind of hard, metallic glint. "Your father was bloody pleased to pay me so little. He never liked you and me being friends, and he gave my old man the money when he knew the coot hadn't told us anything. He got his revenge—he got rid of us all in one go."

She'd been about to ask him how soon they would be leaving, wondering also what she would tell them at Querilderie, when suddenly she was afraid to ask him, afraid even to contemplate the future. The present will have to do, she comforted herself. I can think about leaving when he tells me to, she decided, wondering for the millionth time how Angus would react to her departure. He would no doubt be dreadfully hurt. Poor Angus; she suffered awful pangs of remorse when she tried to imagine his feelings.

The baby was born at the end of January—a big, healthy boy with a mass of dark hair and John Cameron's long-boned nose.

Clem was pleased he was a boy and happy for her father and Marianne. She would enjoy playing nursemaid with Katharine until the nanny's arrival. Marianne had finally been persuaded that a well-recommended person from Sydney would be far superior to anyone local, and although she'd expressed a wish to actually look after the child herself rather than have a stranger in the house, she had gradually succumbed to Clem and Katharine's gentle persuasion, being too weak after the birth to do otherwise.

She'd begged them not to mention her previous distraught behavior to her husband, as he wouldn't understand such a fuss over a mere nursemaid. On the contrary, when Clem had asked him if he approved of her writing to her aunt, he'd insisted on reading the

woman's references himself, as he was not going to have another
convict woman in *his* house.

"These so-called emancipist creatures—criminals they are in
fact—are no good at all in the house. They either steal or refuse to
work properly, or what is worse are actually insolent to their employers. Ungrateful wretches!" She assumed he was alluding to Lizzie Bell.

He had finally approved the woman's references. They were not
shown to Marianne, as she was considered too tired to be bothered.

Normally her father's remarks about emancipists, some of whom
Clem regarded as her friends, would have roused her to angry argument, but she was in love and entirely unconcerned with any other
kind of passion.

She sat demurely at the dining-room table, no longer hearing his
loud denunciations of emancipist journalists and council members,
but daydreaming of being with Matt, lying beneath their tree or just
talking together at the quartz ridge. Matt's hatred of her father had
eclipsed her own to the extent that she no longer hated him at all.
She could not understand his dour, unforgiving soul, but she ceased
to fight it or even to think about it. She was on too high a plane for
bitterness of any kind.

Marianne, on the other hand, seemed beset by fears and anxieties.
She would jump at the slightest sound and become short tempered,
even with Katharine.

Katharine confessed to Clem that she was very worried about her.
Marianne seemed to have a terrible fear of something or someone
unknown. She had always spied on guests before allowing herself to
be seen, but now, if anyone—even Mrs. Maclean or Jessie—arrived
for tea, she would refuse to come out of her room until it was time
for them to go.

Clem advised Katharine not to worry, as nursing one's own baby
often had that effect upon mothers, especially those in their thirties.

Angus was still a frequent visitor despite Clem's distant attitude.
Though his manner had cooled toward her, his emotions apparently
had not. Many times she caught him watching her gloomily from
across the room. He would often try to corner her away from the
rest of the family and at times, trapped her for a few moments when
he would become tongue-tied and red in the face, unable to blurt out

his feelings. She tried to be pleasant, and having forgiven him for his dreadful behavior in the past, would have found his company quite tolerable if it hadn't been for his excessive self-pity.

Her guilt intensified until her nights at home became unbearable. She lay awake listening for Angus's horse and dreamed frightening dreams in which Angus and her father and Matt would all become confused tangled images, and she would be left, a solitary figure, in a black alien landscape.

Matt never mentioned Angus now, and she was glad. She didn't want Angus's misery to intrude on them. She'd become two different people, and the shock of one of her lives overlapping the other would have been too great.

The days Clem spent with Matt, helping him to extract the tiny pieces of gold from the quartz, and the nights beneath their tree were like a succession of vivid dreams, each detail of which she would take back with her into her other existence. At home, every moment would be spent planning an excuse for the next prolonged excursion into the paddocks.

She hadn't asked him about Lizzie Bell and tried not to pay any heed to all the rumors about her. Edith had seen someone very like her in Willawarrha, but Clem knew it could not be she, and asking Matt about it would have been petty, even a kind of sacrilege.

But at night, alone in her room, she sometimes remembered her nightmare at the Willawarrha Hotel and was haunted once more with images of them together. All her life the hot, muggy nights of late summer had bewitched her with groundless anxieties and dark forebodings, and now they seemed to portend a catastrophe.

One particular night, late in February, tortured by Lizzie's face and the increasing stories of her presence in the district, and finding it impossible to sleep in the airless tent of her mosquito net, she got out of bed and walked down the stairs and onto the veranda.

The moon was a half circle floating in a larger, hollow moon of soft, transparent gray. It had turned the paddocks into wide pellucid lakes and the little puffs of browned wattle into heavy clusters of iridescent dewdrops.

She wandered—a barefoot white wraith—around to the back of

Maud Lang

the house. The grapes, which always ripened too quickly in midsummer, still clung to the dry sticks like shriveled black beetles. A few lights shone from the windows of the men's cottages. Behind them was the graveyard.

She ran lightly over the warm ground to the cottages. She must see her mother's grave once more before she left.

Each mound was marked by a squat wooden cross and overgrown with tall grass and a creeping weed which had blossomed into bell-shaped purple flowers at Christmas. The creeper and the grass were both now dead, increasing the desolation of the neglected little graveyard.

Her mother's cross was at the far end. The long shape was still evident despite the entwined spirals of brown creeper. The cross was cracked and gray. She wondered why her mother's grave had not been dug closer to the tree. She tiptoed to its edge.

"Tomorrow I'll plant some flannel flowers," she whispered, her voice flat and foreign. She knew her mother would object strongly to being put out here in the sun, as she'd always wanted to escape from it to Sydney or to Mrs. Oxley's dim little sitting room.

She had a clear vision of her mother walking between Mrs. Oxley's orange trees. But Mrs. Oxley was gone too. Neither of them had belonged here.

She was going to cry. She ran back to the cottages. A light was still burning in one window. Something made her creep up and peer inside.

Clem blinked in amazement to see Angus sitting hunchbacked on a wooden stool holding a glass of ale. He was supposed to be in Sydney at his natural history conference. He was talking to a woman at the other end of the room.

Clem tiptoed around to the door and put her ear to the crack between the rough wood and the frame.

"What do you think?" Angus said.

She strained to hear the woman's reply. "Dunno, Mr. Angus. Does the mistress know?" It was Fanny's voice.

"She guesses at it, I believe. How can I tell them?"

She missed Fanny's reply. She could see one side of Angus's face through the crack. He looked anxious and pale in the lamplight. Fanny crossed the room, standing between him and the door.

"She wouldn't have me anyway. If only I'd behaved differently from the beginning."

"It's past now and you didn't die of love over . . ." Fanny
paused. "Over her."

"No. I used not to believe in it—love, that is. But that's changed
too. How I love her! I would give my life for her. Do you understand
that?"

"I hope not, Mr. Angus. That is, don't do anything daft."

"She's too honorable."

"Yes, sir. And what about her and that Matt? And him with Lizzie Bell waiting in Willawarrha. I saw her there myself—spoke to
her I did."

Clem went cold with fear. What did she mean—how did she
know?

She heard only the end of Angus's next question. "They are not
married?"

"No one knows, least of all Miss Clem."

"I wonder what she's playing at?"

"Her sister wonders that, too." Fanny refilled Angus's glass.

"Revenge is sweet," he said bitterly.

"What?"

"And what would they talk about together?"

Fanny giggled. "Just the time of day I suppose. What did you
mean about revenge?"

"The man has taken John Cameron's gold and his daughter too."

Clem didn't catch Fanny's reply. She moved back from the window, quivering with shock and fear and anger. She ran back to the
house, deciding to ride out to confront Matt at dawn. It could not
possibly be true. And Angus—poor Angus—dying for love of her
and she too selfish to see it. He loved her enough to confide in a half-
witted serving girl!

She would write to Angus. No, that was not enough. *Nothing* was
enough.

The rest of that night was one long nightmare. She would go off
into a fitful sleep then wake to the loud buzzing of mosquitoes and
the sound of Fanny's words, which made her shake with a fierce
jealousy. Then she would remember Angus's face and be suffused
with guilt. Her mind kept moving rapidly from scene to scene and
face to face, recalling each word and gesture until finally everything
and everyone became confused. Close to dawn she fell into a deep,
troubled sleep.

Chapter Twenty-four

The next morning somebody was banging loudly on her door. It was Katharine. "Clem! Quickly! Wake up!" She didn't wait for a reply but rushed into the room and flung back Clem's net. "Quick! Something's happened!"

Still dazed from her sleepless night, Clem threw on her dressing gown and followed Katharine to the window.

Katharine seemed quite deranged. "It's Marianne, look!"

The two girls peered out the window to see the carriage piled high with the second Mrs. Cameron's paintings and trunks and a woman wearing a black bonnet standing by the carriage steps.

Clem turned wide-eyed to Katharine, who was dreadfully distressed. "What is it?" she asked.

"Oh, Clem!" Katharine collapsed onto Clem's shoulder. "He's sending her away! Angus arrived last night, late, with that woman, that nanny, who said—Oh, Clem!" Katharine began to sob hysterically.

Clem held her tightly by the shoulders, rubbing her cheek against hers, but she sobbed on, catching her breath only to gasp a few strangled words of explanation.

Clem gripped her tightly, growing increasingly alarmed. The nanny had been employed by a Parramatta family until the previous week and had been conveyed in Angus's phaeton to Querilderie late last night. He'd left the woman with Katharine and her father and gone to stable the horses. When Marianne had been summoned to greet the new arrival she'd taken one look at her and fallen prostrate into a hall chair.

The nanny had then related the most fantastic story to John Cameron about his wife being already married to the eldest son of one of her previous employers and being an ex-convict and a well-known thief to boot! Seven or eight years ago she'd disappeared with some of her husband's money into the far bush country, thus ruining the young man's life. He'd already been partly disinherited by his father for marrying this emancipist, as she was not only a convicted criminal but also some years older than his innocent son.

The nanny then went on to relate the story of Miss Owen's life—a very colorful history—which so horrified John Cameron that he grabbed the old woman by the throat and threatened her with strangulation unless she retracted every word she'd spoken. The old woman refused and promised to send for the husband by the next post.

Upon hearing this, Marianne, who seemed to have succumbed to a fit of nervous giggling, readily admitted, with some relish, to the whole story. She said she would leave only if he gave her a large sum of money!

Katharine stopped sobbing. "Money!" She broke away from Clem and stared out the window. "If he'd any doubts, that is what put paid to them. He shouted at her that she was a blackmailing— oh, I couldn't repeat the word—and she laughed. Clem—she laughed!"

"What happened then?" Clem was stunned.

"I don't know. I ran away. Marianne was—she was—Clem! How could he send her away? And the baby, too?"

"But it's *his!*" Clem ran out of the room and down the stairs three at a time. She heard voices from the dining room.

Marianne was sitting at the table in her usual place, the baby lying in a small wooden cradle by her feet. "I was waiting for you and Katharine to bid me farewell. Well, are you going to?"

"It's all true then?" Clem sank into the chair next to her. "Poor Marianne, I'm so sorry, I—is there anything I can do?"

"*You! You're* sorry?" Marianne smiled her soft, tolerant smile.

"I would never have thought that you could be sorry, especially about my departure. It was you who arranged it all so well, was it not?"

"No! I was happy for you and my father, after my mother—and you—" How she wished she hadn't written to her aunt or had stopped the thing when Marianne wished it. "I wish I had told my aunt not to bother—"

"Indeed? But it was my impression that you took a perverse pleasure in at last being able to impose your will upon mine. I was so weak at the time. If only I had been stronger . . ."

"It did *not* give me pleasure." Clem's voice faded. Perhaps it was true. Marianne had sensed it, so perhaps there *had* been a kind of pleasure in so blatantly contradicting her wishes. "Oh, Marianne . . ."

"Oh dear, yes. And are you sorry for Angus, too? You have treated him monstrously. To lead him on so. However, that is none of my concern, thank God."

"I will fetch him—he will stick up for you!"

"Stick up for me? Is that all I need—a champion? You silly infant; your father has a heart of granite. I managed to scratch only the surface of it. The effort has almost finished me and I'm not about to try again. And for heaven's sake, girl, don't feel *sorry* for me. I always fall on my feet." She started. "I can hear your father's voice now." She shrugged, then smiled secretively, rocking the baby's cradle with the point of her tiny boot. "Strangely enough, I've never liked it . . . too harsh." She sat up straight as his footsteps approached, smoothing the silky hair back from her forehead. "Better to say nothing, Clemency." She glanced once more at the baby. "In fact, Clemency, you ought to apply that bit of advice to every sphere of your life: Better to say nothing."

Clem gazed at her serene features. "I am terribly sorry; I don't know what to say."

"Then don't say anything." Marianne spoke without moving her lips.

John Cameron came swiftly through the door. "Clemency! Back to your room! Dress yourself, your sister, too! I'll see you both later in the library. Out!"

Clem gathered her dressing gown about her. She felt terribly weak in the face of her father's temper. She hadn't seen him in that state

for such a long time she'd forgotten her old fear of him. She sidled
out of the room.

The old nanny was standing just outside the door—a wizened old
woman with kind brown eyes. She smiled at Clem and tried to take
her hand as she fled down the hall. She didn't look as she'd imagined
her to. Clem came to an abrupt halt halfway up the stairs. But what
about the baby? What would he do about the baby?

She turned around and ran down the stairs and back into the dining room. "You *must* let her take the baby!"

Her father was standing by the table. As he turned to face her,
Clem saw that his eyes were red. "What? The boy? He is hers."

Marianne had been about to speak. She looked straight through
Clem, then swiveled around in her seat to face the window.

Clem wanted to try to stop him from sending her away, but she
didn't know how. She had no idea what to say. She hadn't even succeeded in telling Marianne how very sorry she was. She merely
backed out of the door and stuttered a weak, "Good-bye."

When Clem reached her bedroom, the old woman was there trying
to comfort Katharine.

Clem stood in the doorway. "You shouldn't have said anything."
She walked over to her bed and turned back the covers. "Would you
mind leaving now? I'm going to dress. Stay here, Katharine."

"Miss Clemency, is it? I *had* to say it. From your fiancé's description of your stepmother I knew it was her, even before we reached
that big town. And it *was* her. She is a wicked woman—she almost
ruined my dear Henry's life. Your father had to know."

"But why?" Katharine's eyes were dry, but her face was devoid
of color.

"Because she might do it again—run off. She is weak and untrust-
worthy. She stole from Henry, and she was transported for stealing
from her brother's wife. It was jewels—jewels and heirlooms worth
a fortune. She was unrepentant, too. A thoroughly wicked person."

"The Macleans loved her." Clem combed her hair, taking a long
time with each waist-length strand.

"They didn't know her as I did." She looked Clem up and down.
"You have beautiful hair."

"Thank you." Clem remembered Matt's fingers playing with her
curls. *She could not possibly leave with him now.*

The old woman was still speaking. "And then she had the gall to ask your father for money. If she hadn't done that, then he might have kept her here. She threatened to tell everybody in Sydney what a fool she'd made of him unless he paid her."

"Who would she tell? Who would care?"

"The Aspinalls would be interested—and your aunt!"

"Mrs. Aspinall? What has she to do with it?" Clem stared at the old woman, her hairbrush still high in the air.

"They were my employers when it all happened. I was little Adelaide's nanny. Henry had been one of my charges, too. Such a lovely boy. And then he got involved with that woman!"

"I see." Clem gazed at her in amazement. She hadn't bothered to read the references. Dear God! If only she had shown them to Marianne all this would never have happened.

The old woman picked up a half-sewn baby's sunbonnet, painstakingly embroidered by Clem and said, "What's the matter?"

"I know the family, in a manner of speaking." She stared at the bonnet, thinking Marianne had been quite right. She remembered her strange feeling as she wrote to her aunt and Marianne's subsequent behavior. She *had* arranged the whole thing out of a deep and cruel spite which she hadn't even guessed at until now. "Will he have her back—do you think?"

"Never! His pride is too damaged. Not *that* man. I saw how he looked at her."

Katharine started to sob again. "She shouldn't have mentioned money." She wiped at her eyes viciously with the sleeve of her gown. "If only we had not been so persuasive about engaging—" she looked at the old woman despairingly—"you!"

"It was all my fault," whispered Clem.

"No—how could you possibly have known?"

"I don't know, yet I must have known. There was something in the back of my mind without my even realizing it."

"No!" Katharine rushed out of the room. "I must say good-bye!"

They listened to her quick footsteps on the wooden stairs. "I hope she will understand. Do you?" The old nanny begged Clem's forgiveness with her eyes.

"You've behaved properly by your own principles. What else can one do?" She wanted to ask this woman what she should do about Matt—and Angus, and now Katharine. She knew the only honest advice the woman could give her would be to tell her to stay and not to run away.

"Yes. I couldn't have left, made some excuse and gone back to Sydney. One ought not to leave such a situation. Your father deserves more consideration than that. He is a fellow human being."

And so is Angus, thought Clem. So is Angus.

"Some would say they deserved each other," Clem commented. She smiled ruefully, almost laughing, remembering how little credence she'd given to her mother's ramblings in the coach that afternoon. At least *she* would be sweetly avenged by all this. Then she remembered the child. "What does he intend to do about the baby?"

"It is a bastard. He bears no responsibility for that. She must look after it."

"Bastards still have a sex," Clem admonished the old woman. "And this one has a name: John Joseph Cameron."

"Ah, yes. I wonder if she will keep that name."

Clem fervently hoped she would. It had been such a great joy to her to have that hated name bestowed upon someone else, releasing her at last from her father's disappointed eyes.

They heard voices from the veranda. The old woman bade her farewell and bustled off downstairs, straightening her cap and cloak. Clem watched the scene from her window.

Marianne got into the carriage, assisted by Jock, who handed her the baby and then the cradle. The old woman mounted the steps stiffly, looking back at John Cameron as though she expected some kind of support.

None was forthcoming. He shut the door of the carriage before Jock had lifted the steps and, turning his back on his "wife," strode off in the direction of the stables.

The carriage moved slowly down the drive. Katharine ran after it, coughing at the dust in its wake and waving frantically with her linen nightcap. She was still in her nightdress, one of Marianne's castoffs, a flimsy cotton thing embroidered with primroses.

Clem backed away from the window. The sight of Katharine behaving in that manner was too painful. She went out into the hall. It was bare. "All her watercolors have gone," she said to herself. She went downstairs to the drawing room. They were gone from there, too. Only the dark lochs remained.

Katharine was talking to somebody on the veranda. Clem recognized Angus's voice. He was comforting her. She peeped out from one of the long windows opening onto the veranda. He had his arm about her and was patting her gently, soothing away her tears as one might placate a distressed child.

That's all she is, thought Clem, a child. I must go to her.

She walked through the drawing room. The curtains were still drawn, and the only light in the room came from the hall door which fell on the back of one of Marianne's gold velvet chairs. She had left so much more of herself in this house than Clem's mother had, mused Clem. Even without her paintings the place was still hers.

Katharine drew back from Angus as Clem stepped out onto the veranda.

"Oh, it's you." Angus was disheveled from a night's drinking.

"You were up very late last night," Clem said to him, as she took Katharine's hand to lead her inside. "I saw you at the cottages with the men," she lied.

"Yes. I was upset about all this business. However, it was no concern of mine. I had always guessed as much of Marianne when she was with us. My mother had had her doubts, but kept her on as we children were so fond of her. Your father was besotted with her." He looked meaningfully at Katharine who returned his gaze with a pale smile.

Clem winced. He'd told her all about his own passion for her. A spasm of unbearable guilt came over her. "I'll stay here now—for a bit, Katharine. I think I can understand what you feel."

Angus's arm shot out from his side and his hand gripped her wrist. "But we thought—that is—Fanny Old said that you and the Brennan chap—"

"Matt? How do you know so much about us, you and Fanny?" She shook herself free of Angus's grasp.

"One of the men saw you both near the boundary. We have all known for some time," explained Katharine.

"Not Father?"

"No. Of course not." Katharine pulled her toward the door. "Please, let's go inside." She dropped her eyes from Angus's puzzled face. "Angus, you had better go home."

"Yes." Angus walked quickly away, his head down, staring at the dead lawn, kicking at the tufts of dry wild grass at its borders.

'He's sulking." Katharine looked back from inside the wire-screen door.

"He has every right to," said Clem.

Katharine looked at her in a rather quizzical manner, almost like an older sister, thought Clem. Then she said, "We are all surprised about you and Matt. At first I thought Angus would either kill him or do himself an injury, you know, with rage, jealousy, or whatever, but—"

Clem interrupted her. "I don't know what to do about it all. I'll stay with you and Father; you can't be left alone with him. It would be dreadful for you."

"Oh, Clem—"

"Don't say any more. It's the least I owe you." She didn't deserve their thanks; she deserved nothing.

As she was helping Katharine to do her hair she said, "I was relieved to hear Father hadn't heard about Matt."

Katharine shook her head. "No one knows anything at all really. One of the boundary riders saw you at the quartz ridge. And you've been gone so often, we put two and two together. Everyone knew it would be him because Lizzie has been seen so often in Willawarrha. Is she waiting for him?"

Clem's legs went weak. She tried to fight off the despair that always attacked her at the mention of Lizzie's name. "No, it's not true—they're friends—he feels sorry for her." She breathed deeply. "All that's over between him and me. I'll stay here—for the family's sake, you know."

"Oh." Katharine did not seem so sure. She was fiddling with her silver brush and comb set, another Marianne castoff. "You mean Father."

"Yes, poor man, and you—and—well, anyway, my place is at Querilderie." She wondered how she could possibly explain all that to Matt.

"What about Angus?" Katharine lifted the heavy hand mirror and wrinkled up her nose.

"I shall have to think about that."

Katharine put down the mirror and stared at a picture on the far wall. "I wish she'd left me just one of her paintings. I'm sure we're still good friends, despite everything. Did you really know that young man with your portrait very well?"

"No, of course not. Why do you ask?"

"You have such funny friends."

"I suppose it's a fault of the colony. We are all such a mixture."

Katharine nodded. "Will he hang for the wool business?"

"That might please Marianne. No, I'm sure it wouldn't. It's too horrible. The Aspinalls are mixed up in all of that, I'm sure."

Katharine wasn't really interested. She was examining her teeth in the hand mirror.

"What hypocrites those people are!" Clem exclaimed.

"Oh, Clem." Katharine dropped the mirror again. "I still can't believe all of this. Poor Marianne. Father called her a criminal! He said that convict women never change. Now he despises her, and yesterday he loved her! How is that possible?"

"That's his nature. He is unable to forgive." Clem laughed. "He would never have forgiven me if I'd run off with Matt."

Katharine's small tearful voice said, "Perhaps you ought to."

Clem reassured her with a motherly kiss and then patted her hand. "Not while you are here with *him*."

Katharine opened her mouth to remonstrate, but Clem put her finger to her lips. "Please don't say anything."

"But you have no—"

"Hush, my mind is made up." Just for a second Clem felt a great warm surge of martyrdom travel though her body. She hoped that God—if He was looking on—would appreciate it. Then at least there might be some reward for her somewhere.

Suddenly, however, the true horror of her decision struck her. Matt would never understand. And how could she ask him about Lizzie now—when she was about to desert him!

She drew herself up to her full height. "Don't fret. You'll be able to visit Marianne in Sydney. I'll make sure of that." She ran her fingers along the top of Katharine's smooth well-brushed hair and then went down to breakfast.

Her father disappeared into the paddocks that day while Edith fussed about the house, quite pleased to be in complete charge again. Clem came across her in the library dusting the books.

"This is all a dreadful shame, a dreadful thing, Miss Clemency. You must be the mistress now. I'll help as much as I can, of course."

"Goodness, what must I do?" Clem had no idea how to be mistress of anything—except perhaps a horse.

"You must order the meals for a start and you must give us our instructions—not me—I know how to keep this house, but Fanny and the two new lasses."

"Please, Edith, won't you do it all?"

"No, you must. After breakfast the girls must be told what to do. You will have given me the lists for Cook the day before."

Clem sat down at the desk and took a sharp quill, writing down every suggestion of Edith's.

"You sister's favorite is a burnt cream—no, that's too festive."

Clem starred at Edith. What was she saying? She dug the quill into the margin trying to control her shaking fingers.

"Will an almond flory do?"

Clem nodded, blotting the page. How on earth would she tell him she could not go with him? Perhaps he'd never really wanted her to go . . . "I beg your pardon, Edith?"

"The dinner—tomorrow's dinner!"

Clem handed her the quill, "You do it." She ran to the door, noticing Edith's curtsy. Edith was obsessively fastidious and well groomed. Her tightly laced body and her eternal dressmaking and tatting had not endeared her to Clem. She had bitterly resented her parents' continual advocacy of Edith as someone to emulate—probably because she'd secretly envied her accomplishments. Also she'd always despised her servility.

"Please don't curtsy to me, Edith. I am younger than you. I ought to curtsy to you."

"Miss Clemency!"

"I'm sorry, but please don't."

Edith left, her back painfully straight. Clem giggled, then found that she was crying. Katharine looked round the door. "I'm going riding—to visit Angus. I—"

"Yes, yes—I know. I must go now. Have a nice ride." She rushed upstairs and slammed her door, whispering to herself as she pulled on her old riding clothes. "He came back for *me and* the gold, not just the gold. He couldn't love her like he loves me. I'm a traitor having those thoughts—"

She saddled Mulga hurriedly, forgetting to take a water bottle, and rode off toward the water hole at a canter. Her mind was a buzz of unconnected thoughts and half-remembered conversations. People from different backgrounds could not always be friends, Biddy had said, but they might be lovers. Anyway, Matt and she were from the same background: the same hot sky, the same dry-leafed trees, the same dusty soil beneath their feet.

It was because she was that man's daughter—that monster's offspring—that she was forced to leave him. She had to go back to Katharine.

She would be going back to this, too. She gazed around her at the familiar landmarks. This was her land—Querilderie—the land also needed her. Her home, her father, her sister, and . . . Angus.

She couldn't just walk away and leave them. One could not build one's whole life on everyone else's unhappiness.

Matt had never told her he meant their liaison to last forever. Underneath their tree he'd said he would never let anything part them . . .

She kept trying to remember everything he'd ever said to her. Perhaps he'd changed—perhaps Lizzie . . .

He probably meant to go back to Lizzie all the time! He'll have enough money to buy his own land or squat on a fair acreage. He'll be off to Moreton Bay or wherever he's going—and with her! He'll soon forget about me.

She reached the water hole in a state of dehydrated fatigue. She stumbled from her horse and lay down with her head half immersed in the shallow brown water. After a few seconds she sat up and splashed water over her face and throat, gazing out at the arid land. The sheep had cropped the ground bare and left wide gray patches of loose dust behind them.

As she neared the Brennan place she couldn't see the house at all. Without the white flowers of the Christmas tree to lift it from the surrounding plain, it had sunk into the paddocks, to disappear, perhaps to crumble into layers of soft ant-ridden wood. The iron barks gradually formed a long black line on the horizon and she rode into them, her anguish increasing beneath their dark metallic leaves.

He'd be pleased. She shouted aloud. "He'll be pleased!" Salty tears stung her cheeks as she spurred the horse to zigzag between the thick trunked trees. "He doesn't love me! He's never said so, never!" She urged the horse to a wild gallop as they approached the quartz ridge. "He'll be well rid of me!"

Chapter Twenty-five

Matt was standing by a two-wheeled cart. He pushed his hat back from his brow as she pulled up the horse.

She stayed in the saddle. "I'm not coming with you," she shouted, trembling violently, her voice thick with dust.

He walked very slowly toward her. "What?"

"I know you'll be happy to hear it—that I don't want to come. You couldn't have taken both of us anyway."

He kept walking toward her, his eyes compelling her to stop.

"I have to stay at home. She'll be better for you. I know she will."

He took her horse's reins. "Who?"

"Lizzie, of course. She's been here all the time. I knew it, I knew none of this was true."

He suddenly reached up and pulled her from the horse with such violence that they both fell to the ground. "For God's sake, will you stop!" His face, so close to hers, was white beneath the hard tanned skin. She stared through his freckles at the strange frightening pallor.

"She *is* here! Everyone says she is!"

He grabbed hold of her head with his two hands. "And everyone says that your and Maclean's wedding is already arranged. I didn't believe them, but I do now."

For a moment she thought he was going to hit her. He dropped his hands and got to his feet, pulling her up roughly with him.

"Marianne's gone—I have to stay with my sister," she stammered, not daring to look at his face.

"You're right about Lizzie. She is in Willawarrha, but what was between us is over, has been for a long time. I don't care if you don't believe me. Believe what you like." His face, still pale, was a stranger's face.

"I'm not marrying anybody. I can't imagine—" her voice caught at the back of her throat as he took a step toward her.

"All this is an excuse. You're not up to it—to leaving all this. You people always revert to your background. You—"

"I've got just as much courage as anyone! And I'm not one of *those people*—how can you say that after—after—"

"After what? Your nights with me? In some kind of little girl's paradise?" He seemed to be smiling.

She fought back her tears and looked straight into his eyes. "Yes. It was paradise. I shall never forget it."

He did smile at her, his dry bottom lip caught against his top teeth. "Even when you're making love to him—to Maclean?"

"I've told you—" Her voice started to rise to a scream as he lifted his right arm and slapped her viciously across both cheeks.

"Don't try to deny it," he hissed. "I know!"

She rocked backward and forward slowly, hugging her cheeks with her grazed palms. There was nothing more she could say. She raised her head and tried to open her mouth, imagining that something would issue from her lips, some magic syllable that would explain to him . . .

"If you tell me more lies I'll kill you!" He backed away from her, then turned and ran to the cart, shouting, "I'm going now. Go home!"

Her hands were still stuck to her cheeks and she was still swaying. He would kill her if she ran to him, she knew he would.

He piled all his belongings into the cart, leaving a small pile of her books next to the ashes of the fire. Then he harnessed the horse to the short shafts and drove off without looking back.

She heard her voice screaming his name from a thousand miles away across the barren plain.

When she looked again he had disappeared over the edge of the plateau.

She let her hands fall to her sides and walked stiffly, like an old woman, to the fire. She stared at the quartz ridge. Despite his pillaging of it, the quartz still glinted gold. She picked up the books one by one, brushing the dust from them slowly and carefully. "He's left the bird book," she said aloud, frightening the tiny gray lizards, who scurried into the cracks in the sandstone. "That was the one I *gave* him. It was a *gift*." She spoke clearly, as though expecting an answer from the rocks.

She rode back to Querilderie, staring at the ground ahead with narrowed eyes beneath lids swollen with sticky salt. Her cheeks still ached from his blows. She laid the flat of her hand on either cheek every few seconds, remembering his hatred.

She went back over all the years she had known him and realized it would never end. He would not come back to her, but she would go after him—one day. She smiled. His hatred was better than his contempt.

Mulga trotted across the dusty paddocks, his hooves making little sound on the powdery soil. Matt thought she was returning to her father, but she was returning to Katharine. It was her fault Marianne had left. She could not let Katharine stay there with that madman. "If only . . . if only." She held her temples with her clenched fists. If only what? She'd not written to her aunt? She'd been born someone else? She'd not been born at all?

The lump in her throat was painful. She tried to cry but only heaved with great dry sobs. They persisted until she was almost home.

She heard the sound of galloping hooves behind her. It was him!

She swung round in the saddle. It was a strange man, one of the boundary riders, his shirt wringing wet and his horse covered in foam.

Clem rode with him and they jumped the home paddock fence together. He raced ahead of her waving his hat in the air.

Her horse whinnied softly, seeing the house, just visible in front of the evening sky.

The half moon hung in a dark gray sky, the same gray of the paddocks. They lay desolate beneath the cold moon, the house too.

She looked behind her. There was nothing there—just the deserted ashen ground of the late summer night.

Chapter Twenty-six

For the next two weeks it rained every day. The paddocks sprouted tufts of long green grass, and strange wildflowers grew there, tiny orchids and daisies, some of which Clem had never seen before.

Her father spent his time away from the house, driving the sheep onto higher ground and looking for strays. Clem was obliged to talk to him very little during this fortnight and found it a great relief, as even talking to Katharine was becoming rather a strain.

She would hover at her side all the time, often asking the most peculiar questions about Matt and Angus. She came into Clem's room one morning, uninvited, and sat down on the bed, looking a little disheveled. "Clem, I must talk to you. Angus is coming over today. We have something important to say to you—and I hope you will hear us out. Will you be here?"

"Yes. I'm always here. I have nowhere else to go."

Katharine looked troubled.

"Oh, I'm sorry, Katharine. I didn't mean it as a reflection on your company; Edith's either, as long as she doesn't curtsy to me."

"Clem, I wish you would listen!"

"I am listening. What is it? What do you want to know?"

"Nothing. I want to know nothing. Just *listen* to Angus when he arrives—please!"

"It seems I have spent two years listening to Angus."

"Not recently!"

"You can't expect me to marry him now!" She laughed. "For *duty's* sake and *affection*. You see, Kathy, it is *that* which matters so much to him and the *land!*"

Katharine swore violently under her breath. "No! I do not see!" She flounced out of the room.

Clem was amazed. She had never heard her sister swear before. Seventeen was quite old enough to swear, she decided, and smiled to herself, although she couldn't fathom what she'd been swearing about.

She had smiled! It was possible to be amused in the midst of utter despair! Perhaps the moments of amusement would increase. Each ordinary moment so far had meant dragging on from day to day in a limbo of misery. Matt's face was always in front of her. He followed her into every room and out into the sodden garden. His still shape would appear at the end of the garden and she would run toward him through the heavy rain to find only the sandstone wall.

Whenever she heard the sound of wheels squelching in the muddy drive, she would rush to the nearest window. Once, when it had been a tinker on his yearly round, she'd stumbled down the stairs and out onto the veranda to be greeted by an old brown man, laughing at her through toothless gums.

She'd sat down heavily on the veranda steps, oblivious to the water dripping from the guttering and cried uncontrollably, her body shaken by violent spasms. The old tinker had tapped her on the shoulder.

"What's up, love?" His breath had smelled of axle grease and rum.

"Nothing. I thought it was—"

"Well, it ain't. It's just old Hannon, the tink. Want any pots or such, me love?"

"Yes. I think—please go to the kitchen. It's . . . " She had pointed vaguely in the right direction.

"You be mistress 'ere now, eh? Since that last lot scarpered? They say she smashed 'is 'eart ter smithereens."

"Yes. So she did. The cook is in the kitchen."

The tinker had driven off to the kitchen, his copper pots and pans clanking dully in the rain.

Clem had not even thought for one second of the state of her father's heart. He might be almost as miserable as she. She tried to feel sorry for him and managed a slight twinge of pity, before she rose to go downstairs. She'd written letter after letter to Matt, having no idea where to send them. She had torn each one up as soon as it was written. They did not even clear her mind, let alone serve any other purpose. She felt utterly useless, empty.

Her father had spoken only a few words to her after Marianne's departure, and they were in the form of a brief lecture on the importance of retaining land. Land was, according to him, ninety percent of one's identity. He'd advised her to marry Angus and stop shilly-shallying around. He'd hoped that the rumors of her and some chap in Pringle or Burrundi or wherever were unfounded, as he intended to put a stop to it, whatever it was, if they were not.

"Stay on the land, at all cost! Angus is the man for you. He has his feet on the ground—and on his own land." He'd looked at her as though she weren't quite real.

She had naturally denied the rumors and had given a half promise to consider Angus more seriously, at which point her father had left her abruptly. He had been unshaven and covered with thinly caked mud; his hair had been too long, his face gaunt, and his cheekbones too prominent.

"Wretched man," she sighed. "He was almost human when she was here." She walked slowly through all the rooms of the house. They no longer had Marianne's spirit or Katharine's gaiety to bring them to life. They were a fitting mausoleum for her own dead heart.

Edith followed her from the drawing room into the library. "These rooms would not be half so empty if you were to marry. He would give you this house and retire to one of the cottages."

"I already have enough of this house, Edith."

"Mr. Maclean is visiting today. I wish you'd fix a date—for all our sakes. The place is so lonely."

"I know what you mean. But I can't marry him, not yet anyway. And he won't wait forever."

Edith polished the green leather top of a large desk with long methodical strokes. "No, that he may not." She looked up at Clem, her eyes catching Clem's for a second. "It just might be too late now, Miss Clemency."

Katharine was unusually quiet at breakfast, which meant that hardly a word was spoken. John Cameron picked at his food silently and Clem ate a small portion of grilled lamb cutlet, refusing the thick slices of brown bread and the cook's orange marmalade, and passing them to her father, knowing that marmalade was one of his favorite dishes.

"No, thank you," he growled, his head buried in an old Sydney journal. "These damned emancipist hacks! These people!"

Katharine raised her eyebrows nervously. "What people, Father?"

"Nothing you'd understand. Why aren't you eating?"

Katharine didn't answer, but got up from the table and curtsied to him before she left the room.

"I'm surprised you let yourself get worked up over these things, Father. You ought to try to forget emancipists and convicts for a while." Clem felt something slither down into the pit of her stomach. She'd made a dreadful blunder. She'd only meant that he ought to try to be calmer—for the sake of his health. She opened her mouth to attempt an explanation, but it was too late.

"My God! She talks about convicts! *She* does. *She* with her tinker lover and her artist remittance man, and her little blackmailing thief!"

Clem froze with fear. He was crying with rage!

"You gave him Edwina's pearls! Gave them to that charlatan, that filthy seducer of young girls—that painter of obscene pictures!"

"No! Stop! It was not like that—he was not—"

Her father's face was beetroot. A tiny vein pulsated at the side of his forehead.

Clem got up and stood over her chair, shaking with anger. "I love Mathew Brennan. I *love* him!" She pulled her chair aside and held onto the two corners of the table. "And I would have left with him if *she* had stayed!"

He seemed about to rise. He threw his napkin into the marmalade dish, screaming at her, "Get out—get out!" Then he slumped forward onto the table.

Clem rushed to his side. "Father—I—I—" She laid the tips of her fingers on his shoulder. "Are you all right?"

"No. Don't go. She needs you. Your sister needs you." He looked up at her. He should have been crying by the expression on his face, but there were no tears. "You were a good girl to stay—a good girl."

"No—I won't go. I wouldn't have gone—for you, too." She avoided his eyes. "I'd better go and see Fanny about—"

"Yes." He composed his face and retrieved his napkin from the marmalade. "I believe Angus is . . . ?"

"Yes." Clem forced a smile. It was the first time in her life that he'd called her a good girl. *A good girl!* She left the room quickly and hurried out to the veranda to breathe the fresh air.

Katharine stood by the rail, staring out at the paddocks, waiting for Angus.

"You're so fond of Angus, I'm surprised *you* don't marry him," joked Clem, seeing the anxious expression in her eyes.

Katharine ignored her. "There he is!"

Katharine's nervous mood puzzled Clem. Perhaps her behavior was even more embarrassing to her family than she'd supposed. She would definitely put an end to all that now; tell Angus she couldn't marry him in front of the whole family, explain about Matt—that would finish it.

Angus tethered his horse to the veranda rail. "Good morning, Clem. How are you?"

"Well. And you?" Such formality was so silly between them, she thought. She remembered his advances without resentment. In the light of her passion for Matt she could be quite magnanimous. In fact, she felt almost fond of him again, almost hurt that he'd spoken so formally to her. She said, "You'd better come into the drawing room, both of you. I have something important to say to you."

"Oh?" Angus took off his heavy riding cloak, while Katharine and she went inside.

"And he has something to say to you," said Katharine quietly.

"Indeed." Clem sat upon the chaise longue, remembering Marianne's habit of spreading her crinoline over each end. She did the same, hoping to create an imposing figure.

"You *are* funny, Clem." Katharine sat on the piano stool, touching the keys with her long pale fingers.

"Your fingers are trembling," remarked Clem.

Katharine removed them from the keyboard and sat immobile, her hands clasped tightly in her lap. She was wearing a dress of pale blue silk, her hair parted in the middle and drawn back into a loose knot behind. She suddenly appeared quite grown-up.

As Angus walked into the room Clem saw her with his eyes—as a beautiful young woman. And then she knew what Angus was about to say. Of course! All this time and she had been too self-centered to notice! She sat forward on the chaise longue, her elegant pose entirely forgotten.

"Katharine!"

"Clem, I do not know how to say it," blurted out Angus, "Katharine and I are engaged. We are going to be married!"

"Soon!" Katharine interjected, a radiant smile on her face. She jumped up and hugged Angus quite ardently. "She doesn't mind. She loves Matt Brennan." Katharine ran over to her and knelt by her side. "Say you don't mind, Clem!"

"Oh . . . yes . . . no." Clem was transfixed by their joy.

Angus glowed with pleasure and pride in his beautiful bride. He advanced across the room, a huge grin on his freckled face. "You were right about love being important. It *is* the most important thing. There can be nothing without love."

"Oh, no." Katharine hugged him again, and Angus reciprocated by crushing her to him.

Clem said, "Oh, yes. Love is the thing. Indeed it is." There was an ache in her chest and behind her eyes. She stared at them. They seemed too happy, like a pair of dancing puppets. She tried to say the right thing, but she couldn't think what it might be. She had given up *love* to come back here—and all for nothing.

"For nothing!" She cried and stood up, holding onto the back of her seat. "For *nothing!*"

"What?" Katharine freed herself from her lover's grasp. "You must have known, guessed; we thought you would . . . "

"I didn't. Not until now."

"You would never *listen* to me, Clem. You're always in a dream. You never *listened*, never paid any attention to me at all. I could never *tell* you!"

"I see." That was true, she had never listened. Being an utterly self-absorbed person, she had never found the time. "I'm sorry not to have listened. So sorry." She ran to the door, turning her head for an instant. "I am happy for you. It's not to do with you, I—I mean, I hope you are very happy!" She fled to the stairs and called out again. "I hope you are very happy! I'm glad, really glad!"

Chapter Twenty-seven

Winter was long and warm that year. The rain fell intermittently after February and many lambs were born in the spring. The shearing was a busy time for Clem and her father. He would help with the wool classing in the wool shed, while Clem and the cook arranged the meals.

The shearers were itinerant workers of every nationality and every age. Some of the more experienced men could shear a hundred sheep a day with their long blades—dangerously sharp shears which could rip the fleece from a sheep in a matter of seconds.

They would arrive at the cottages, their blue blankets about their shoulders, some on foot and others in carts or drays, wearing roughly woven cabbage tree hats and talking shearers' talk. Clem had been allowed to run in and out of the sheds as a child, but now, of course, she could not be seen near any of them, unless it was solely in her capacity of mistress of Querilderie.

She recognized faces from previous years, yet there were also many newcomers—younger, rougher men, with coarse country accents and a crude colonial language of their own.

She'd managed to survive the winter by helping with the horses and the kitchen work, organizing the shopping and the running of the household, and reading, often very late into the night.

The shearing brought her back to life. She liked all these rough men, envying them their freedom. She longed to talk to them as another man might, wanting to know all about their lives and histories.

Fanny noticed how she would look at them as they passed the kitchen on their way to the wool shed early in the morning. "They do fascinate you, Miss Clemency. Mebbe you'd like to be one of them; I always have." Fanny would look wistfully after them, as they swaggered down to the shed. "Better to be born a man in this country."

"Yes—we poor females lead such closed-in lives."

She remembered her words one evening as she sat at the long dining-room table, her father silently eating his plate of mutton ham and boiled potatoes at the other end. He was at least nine feet away from her, yet she could smell his strong tobacco breath even at that distance. "Father!"

He had not heard.

She didn't try to attract his attention again. How long, she wondered, would they sit here, night after night, with nothing to say to each other? Was this what "keeping to the land" meant? Land was *his* reason for being, not hers.

"Father!"

"Mmm?" He looked up briefly, returning to his newspaper and his mutton as he listened to her.

"Angus and Katharine will have children to inherit all your *land*. I do not think I want it." She got up to stand by her chair, her arms straight down at her sides. "No, I have lost my interest in the *land*."

"Rubbish! What else have you got?"

"Nothing. But I *want* something else. I'm not staying here forever." She would have preferred to broach the subject more tactfully, but the only conversation possible with her father was brief and to the point.

"No—you won't stay here forever. Some young fellow will come and sweep you off your feet and away you'll go." He felt for his wine glass and finished his claret. "Want more of this?"

Clem shook her head. "I've had too much already; otherwise I wouldn't be talking to you like this. I'm going, Father. I'm going tomorrow."

"For God's sake—where?"

"North." Matt had gone up north. "Yes, I'll go up north." She went around to her father's chair, her footsteps light for the first time in many months. "I'll say good-bye now, as I'll leave at dawn." She bent down and planted a firm kiss on his hard cheek. "Good-bye, Father."

"I know there's nothing I can say to stop you. You've been a great help to me over the past year—in many ways—and I'm grateful." There was a catch in his voice. "You will have some money, of course."

"Just a little, thank you."

"But—"

"I won't need much at all."

"Are you going to your aunt's?"

"No. Well, perhaps after a time. I'll write." She walked out of the room, leaving him staring blankly after her.

Her father let Fanny accompany her, relieved his daughter was not quite insane enough to think of traveling alone.

"He said," said Fanny, as they were packing the old buggy on the following morning, "to take good care of you, you being a bit like your poor mama and all."

Clem nodded, wondering how in the world she could possibly be like her mother, and the two women harnessed Mulga and a sturdy stock horse to the buggy and drove out into the home paddock. Fanny stared back at the house, but Clem only looked back once as she was opening the gate into the horse paddock.

Even now it looked strange. It would be a hard house to return to. She closed the gate behind her, imagining her father and Edith all alone in the wide dark rooms. Everything would have been so different if Marianne had stayed. Perhaps he wished she would come back. But Clem knew she never would. A man like her father did not inspire enough love in anyone for that.

The horses drank at the water hole beneath the emu bushes, a bright olive green in the early morning. The Burrundi road passed the edge of the Brennan land, so she'd decided to join it from there.

She watched for the Brennan house, but as the Christmas tree was not in bloom she could not see it until she was almost on top of it. It still stood at the edge of the iron barks, even after the strong winds of winter. She thought of riding as far as the moon tree, but she dared not go, even to the Brennans' house. There were too many ghosts . . . and the white parrot.

She knew she would never return. Querilderie had lured her back under false pretenses. She had chosen it instead of Matt from a ridiculous sense of duty. It was an old and trusted friend that had cruelly deceived her. She breathed a deep sigh of freedom as she gained the hard surface of the Burrundi Road.

The long straight road stretched to the flat horizon. The paspalum grass shivered in the warm breeze, and the horses walked slowly into the middle of the day.